# A Bottle of Storm Clouds

## STORIES

## ELIZA VICTORIA

avenida

<h1 style="text-align:center">A Foreword,<br>12 Years Later</h1>

A Bottle of Storm Clouds, my first book and first collection of short stories, was originally published by Visprint in 2012.

When the book turned eight, in 2020, the world was thrown into chaos, and Visprint announced that it was closing its doors for good.

Every now and then I would get a message from a curious reader wondering where they could get a copy of this book. A very small part of me was relieved it was out of print – it had a good run, I don't write like that anymore, I have outgrown it. Time to move on.

But now, at age 12, the book has come back to life.

It was a strange experience, re-reading this book. In many ways, it read like a journal. I could see myself riding the MRT with the characters in "Earthset" and "The Man on the Train", living on university campus in "Sand, Crushed Shells, Chicken Feathers", feeling the same frustration brought by HR paperwork and the pain of regret in "An Abduction by Mermaids".

In later years, as I grew older, I would fight against specificity in my stories, aiming for some kind of timelessness, but I liked how specific these stories were, how they clearly belonged to a particular time and place. The references to current events (these stories saw first publication circa 2008 to 2011), how the characters referred to "cell phones" and DVDs and checks sent in the mail, how there was so much newspaper jargon in "Mermaids" that was once a big part of my life (I used to work in a newspaper, a long long time ago).

What I'm saying is, reading the stories more than a decade later, some parts made me cringe (I mean, we were all young once), and some parts made me admire the woman in her 20s who wrote these stories and just went for it.

What I'm trying to say is, it was fun to revisit this book.

What I'm trying to say is, I'm glad this book is back in print.

If you've read these stories before, thank you so much and welcome back.

If you're new here, where have you been?

Hello. We've been waiting for you.

Eliza Victoria

2024

TABLE OF CONTENTS

## SALOT

Isabella had been hearing the strangest of stories lately.

But then, there had always been strange stories. Isabella, now seventeen, would begin college by next June. She had been to the city several times now—passing requirements to the University, checking out the classrooms, inquiring about dorm spaces—and every time she returned home, it would become clear to her how small her town was, how backward, how infuriating in its paranoia. In the University, while waiting in line, she had met people who grew up and lived in the city their whole life, who called her Issa or Izzie ("'Isabella' has *way* too many syllables"), who had no use for rituals.

In their town, before anything was built, a chicken had to be killed, its throat slit, its blood spilt on the ground before the cement was laid. Every time there was a gathering, a plate of food must be set aside for the spirits dwelling in the house with the family—there would always be spirits—and placed on the ground at the back of the house. (Interestingly, if there were dogs roaming about, the mongrels never, *never*, came near the offering. Isabella, growing increasingly skeptical, attributed this more to the quality of the food than to the existence of whatever entity.)

Isabella's mother said that when they first moved into their home, her father suffered from constant stomachaches. The doctors couldn't find anything wrong with him—not ulcer, not stomach spasms, not appendicitis, not cancer. Her mother, at the bidding of their older neighbors, marched over to Ka Ambo (now long-dead), a healer of some sort (that was how Isabella described him when she felt the inclination to tell these stories, *a healer of some sort*), who glanced at her mother and said one word. *Children.* There were ghosts of children in their house: lost children, passing children, confused children, "who found Father amusing".

"Then *Ka* Ambo came over, did his thing, and Father's stomachaches went away," Isabella would finish, now bored of her own story. "Anyway, he's dead now."

"Oh my God, your *father's* dead?"

"No, Christ, I meant *Ka* Ambo. My father's doing okay. He'll come with me tomorrow to look at dorms again, bleh."

"I see. Have you been to the library? They tell me it's *huge*."

That was how conversations like these always ended for Isabella: a trip to a huge library, or lunch, or another line in the name of university red tape. The people she talked to never asked follow-up questions about her town and her strange stories. They felt uncomfortable, Isabella thought, not unkindly. If they asked questions, she would have told them about *Ka* Lina, whose house was also infested with ghost children, who got up from bed one night and smashed her head against her bedroom wall.

Or about Noemi. Everyone in town knew what happened to Noemi. Ten years ago Noemi came home to her grandfather's own house and couldn't find the book she was trying to finish. She remembered, clearly remembered, putting the book on her study table before leaving for work (she taught at the high school). Later that afternoon, when she came back, it was gone. She couldn't find it anywhere. The story went that Noemi sat on the narra chair in the living room and asked for help. *Help me find the book. I know it's here somewhere.* A request like that should never be whispered in such an old house, said the people who told Isabella this story. Who knew who would answer? An hour later, Noemi went back to her room and found the book on the study table, on the very spot where she had originally left it. She prepared dinner when the hour came and realized she wasn't hungry.

She wasn't hungry the next morning. She didn't eat the entire day. And the day after that. And the day after that. She felt weak and couldn't figure out why. She lost ten pounds in four days and collapsed during her class. Her mother, who worked in another province, was summoned, and Noemi was taken to the hospital and fed intravenously. But even at night she would try to pull out the needles. Both Noemi's and Isabella's mothers kept vigil to prevent this from happening. One night, Noemi's mother left to get food, leaving one of Noemi's little nieces with Isabella's mother. Isabella's mother dozed off. When she woke up, Noemi's niece was staring at her and studying her face. What? Isabella's mother said, and looked up. Noemi was still on the bed, but the machines attached to her were beeping furiously.

"*Manang,*" Noemi's niece said as the nurses and the doctor rushed in, "the children took *Tita* away."

Uncomfortable, oh yes, Isabella thought to herself.

But then she would also very promptly amend herself: *Oh, who am I kidding? Uncomfortable, my foot. Bored stiff, is what they are.*

Isabella always wondered how people in the city managed to exorcise magic from their homes. Or was it all just about distractions? Put enough video game consoles in a house, and even the most stubborn poltergeist would cry from lack of attention.

The people in her town certainly needed some distraction. Toward the end of the year (it was December now, and cold: the night came earlier, the day scurrying away like a person late for a meeting), Isabella had heard several stories of townmates hearing someone call their names in the voice of a person they knew.

Isabella rolled her eyes the first time she heard this. "All right. So you were called by someone using the voice of your mother. Well, could it *be* that it *was* your mother calling you? I don't know, Marie, I mean, I'm just guessing here."

"Now, don't be obnoxious," Marie said, and Isabella laughed.

"And it's not funny," Marie said.

Marie's mother often volunteered at the church, so she often came home late. Most nights, too, she would forget her key, so Marie would be awakened by a sharp knock on her bedroom window and her mother's clear voice calling, *Marie, Marie, Marie.*

One night, Marie was in bed half-asleep when she heard the familiar knock, the familiar voice, calling, *Marie, Marie, Marie.* "I should have known there was something wrong," Marie told Isabella in their kitchen, while eating bread, and cocooned in the heat of noon. The bright kitchen offered no shadows and no reason to be frightened. Isabella was feeling sleepy by then, but she tried to keep her eyes open because she didn't want to annoy Marie further. "I sat up and peered out the window, and there was no shadow. I know my bedroom window has thick glass, but even then I'd see my mother's silhouette, a shadow of her hand. I sat up and I could hear a knock and I could hear her say *Marie, Marie, Marie,* but there was no shadow."

"And *still* you opened the door," Isabella said. *Just like the stupid, sexy blonde in a summer horror flick. The one who dies first.*

"I was half-asleep," Marie said quietly.

"Go on."

"I said, *Sandali lang, 'Nay.* I went to the front door and opened it. Nobody was there. Then my mother came out of the kitchen and said, 'Now where are you going? *Gabi na.*' Apparently she's been home since eight p.m."

"What time did this happen?"

"Around midnight?"

"Hm."

There were other stories, other voices, other knocks in the middle of the night, all of them asking to be let in. Isabella's boyfriend, Nick, had by far the freakiest experience. (Isabella liked using that word with her new-found city friends. *Freaky.*) In the living room, Nick was watching TV with his seven-year-old nephew, Cris, when his seven-year-old nephew's voice called from the other side of the front door: *Tito Nick, Tito Nick, papasok na 'ko.*

"And the boy was sitting in front of me!" Nick said.

"Shit," Isabella said, but she was thinking of the fact that Nick didn't pass the university exam, that he would go to community college, that he would be stuck here in this town, that she was smarter and deserved better, that she'd have to break up with him, and soon.

"I would have gone on ignoring it, but the knocking moved to the windows, and Cris was getting ready to cry, so I shouted, '*Bobo*, my nephew's right here! I won't let you in!' Then the knocking stopped."

"And how's Cris?"

"*Hay, ayun.* Now he can't go anywhere on his own, even to the bathroom. Poor kid."

"Hm."

"You mentioned that Marie opened the door, right? She shouldn't have done that." Nick breathed deeply, and sighed. Isabella found this all too theatrical, and raised an eyebrow. "My *lola* says whatever it was—well, she called it a *demonyo*, but I don't know—my *Lola* says whatever's knocking is testing which house will let it in. Did you know that it had the names wrong before? Albert said someone knocked on his brother's door, months before what happened to Marie, and the voice said some random name. Pedro, or something like that. Albert's brother said, '*Wala hong Pedro dito.*'"

Isabella didn't comment. A short silence, and Nick said, "Maybe Al shouldn't have said that. Now, whatever's knocking has learned to do its homework first."

"Well, the voice still made that mistake with you."

"Right. Oh, maybe I shouldn't have said anything, too. *Putangina.*"

"Can I see you Sunday night? After church?" Isabella said. "My parents will be out visiting my mother's cousin, so I can stay out late." *I need to tell you something,* she wanted to add, but it might scare him more than the knocking *demonyo*, or whatever it was.

"Oh, of course," Nick said. Isabella, who was looking elsewhere, only heard the smile in his voice. "That should be nice."

Before the meet-up with Nick, Isabella heard that the knocking did indeed continue at Marie's house. Marie had opened the door, and the gesture made whatever was knocking feel that it was welcome there.

"But it's different now," Marie said, when they met at the marketplace the next morning. "Now when I look out the window, I can see a shadow."

"It's getting better," *Ka* Cora, the storeowner, suddenly piped up, before handing a plastic bag of potatoes to the visibly worried Marie.

That night, Isabella came over with her father to help Marie and her mother sprinkle salt around their house. If it happened again, Marie's mother said, they'd buy a chicken and slit its throat and offer it, appease whatever had to be appeased.

And Isabella's first thought was, *Well, what a waste of chicken.* You couldn't possibly make *tinola* out of an offering to a demon.

"Or can you?" Isabella asked her father when they got home.

"Of course not." Her father looked horrified with the very idea. "And you wouldn't want to. You'll get sick."

"I see."

"Demons can take on a human form, you know," her father continued. "But not completely—there will always be something wrong with their disguise. Cloven feet, a discolored eye, too-large hands. You know about the *salot* they saw in the town up north?"

Isabella had heard the story from her mother's friends. "Yes. After the storm? After the landslide?"

Now, that was truly horrifying to Isabella. One man was working in the city and when he came home for the weekend, not only could he not find his house, he couldn't find *his entire barangay*. Streets completely wiped out, houses erased by mud. Isabella imagined herself coming home from university with homework and dirty laundry to find nothing but a flat landscape where their house used to be. How could you survive such a sight? How could you carry on?

"Not after, *before*," her father said. "They saw the *salot* before the storm came."

"Did he have cloven feet?"

"He had the legs of a chicken."

*Now that's new,* Isabella thought, and felt an unexpected chill. "So maybe he came to them to warn them."

"Or to bring the storm to them." Her father shrugged. "It's a demon. Demons are tricksters. They can appear pitiful when they're looking for a way in."

*A way in to what?* "Mother said they drove the *salot* away. Threw stuff at him and so on."

"Oh yes, I heard that story. He was standing in an empty basketball court the night before the landslide. He was about to open his mouth, but someone saw his feet, and they came after him."

"Did he bleed?"

"Well, of course. He took on a human form. That always makes them vulnerable, becoming human."

"They should have at least listened to what he had to say."

"Who'd want to listen to a demon?" her father said.

Isabella dreamt that night. She dreamt she was in the storm-swept *barangay*. In the distance she saw the man in the city climb up the small hill created by the landslide, the hill that used to be his home. *Nanay*, he called, his voice breaking. *Nanay*. He was so far from her Isabella could have raised a hand and erased him from the landscape with her palm, but his voice sounded so clear, so close, as though he were standing right beside her. *Nanay*. Isabella heard him sob and felt like crying. *Nanay*, he said, and she wanted to tell him to stop, stop it, stop calling, it hurts too much.

She was awakened by the sound of knocking. Isabella sat up in bed, groggy, heavy-lidded, and waited for someone to call her name, but nobody did. Eventually the knocking stopped. It must have been a branch, Isabella thought. Just a branch. Dregs of her dream lingered within her, and before she fell asleep again she thought, *Stop calling, they are all dead.*

Isabella's parents left at eight the next night. At around ten, she led Nick into the living room to watch TV. During a lachrymose scene (Isabella didn't know what show it was) he leaned toward her, like he was dipping his mouth for a drink, so of course she had to tilt her head and respond. Let him down gently, all that. She wouldn't want Nick to go berserk so early in the night; her decision couldn't be overturned, but she still wanted to take the time to explain everything. After a few minutes, he wanted them to go to her room so they could lie down, but she felt that was too much, so she led him out of the house to stop him from thinking of such things.

From the front door, they passed by the flower garden on their left. Her parents went Christmas lights-crazy this year, so there were strings of them strewn around the *gumamela* and *sampaguita* bushes. Her mother had individual pink roses growing in several pots, all in full bloom. They all looked pretty in the moonlight. On the right side of the pathway the tree with her childhood swing sat dark and unadorned.

She didn't want to sit on the swing, so she swung the bamboo gate open and sat on the wooden bench outside. Her father made that bench himself. Nick sat beside her, the wood creaking beneath his weight. Right in front of them, a lamppost buzzed with moths.

"I need to tell you something," she said, but she never was able to tell him anything that night.

The tree with the swing was right behind them, behind the bamboo fence. The swing began to move. There was no wind. "*Putangina,*" Nick said, glancing back, wide-eyed.

Isabella saw the man first. Because it was so dark where he came from (the direction of the *barangay* hall, the high school, and Nick's house), it seemed as if he had simply emerged from thin air. He was wearing a black jacket over a white shirt, and a pair of black slacks. The jacket was made of cotton and actually looked stylish. *It fits him well*, was what Isabella thought. His white shirt had blood on it. Just a few droplets, like what one would have if one had a nosebleed.

The man was wounded. He had a gash on one side of his forehead and the blood was trickling down so thickly he had to close one eye. He was moaning a bit, whimpering almost, perhaps from the pain. He was walking so, so slowly, so it was impossible not to notice what he had instead of feet.

Behind them, the swing continued to move.

"I have to go," Nick said suddenly. He had turned around just in time to see the man walking under the glare of the lamppost. Isabella noticed an interesting thing: the moths hovering near the light stopped moving when the man stood beneath them. She thought they would fall, but they didn't. They just stopped moving, even their wings. As though time itself had stopped.

"My nephew," Nick said, then stood up and ran.

The man must have heard Nick run away, because he stopped and glanced back, frowning at him. Then, he remembered his pain and lifted a hand up to touch his face. "Ah, *damn it*," he whispered, grimacing, when his fingers came away coated with blood.

The wound on the man's forehead looked even more horrible in the light. He swayed a little on his (*feet?* Isabella thought) feet, and looked as though he would collapse.

Perhaps it was reflex. At that moment, Isabella stood up and said, "Oh dear."

The man straightened up, startled. "Okay," he said, sounding breathless. "Okay. Look. I'm bleeding already. No more."

"We have gauze inside the house," Isabella said, then tried to remember where her mother last put it. "I think."

The man tried to look at her face, and then closed his eyes. Tight. "I'm feeling really dizzy right now," he said.

"Come in," Isabella said.

The man opened his eyes, raised his eyebrows. *What?*

"Come in," Isabella said. She walked to the gate and opened it. The swing by the tree stopped moving. "Come in."

The man moved toward her. He looked sheepish, wary, and worried. He looked scared of her. Isabella was oddly touched.

When he moved away from the light the moths began moving again.

The man was good-looking and young, possibly in his early twenties. She led him to the house. "Wait," he said, before entering. "I'll mess up your floor."

*Well clearly we don't have slippers that would fit you,* Isabella thought, but realized quickly that he meant the blood dripping from his head.

"Oh, don't worry," she said. "I can just wipe up later." The man's (*claws,* Isabella thought, trying hard not to stare) feet scraped against the floor as he walked, the sound teeth-grindingly loud.

Isabella turned on the television and sat him down on the sofa. When she came back with the first-aid kit (more like a collection of gauze and alcohol and Band-Aids and cotton inside her mother's old purse), the man was staring at the TV with a gloomy expression on his face.

The lachrymose TV episode was still on. "Sorry," Isabella said. "There's really nothing good on TV at this hour. Do you want to change the channel?"

"It doesn't matter," the man said without looking at her.

Isabella briefly wondered if she was going insane.

She walked to the kitchen, poured hot water into a basin, doused it with a wallop of cold water from the faucet, and submerged a hand towel. The man thanked her when she came back with the water and a bar of soap in a plastic container the shape of a flower. The man regarded the flower-shaped container for a few quiet moments, and Isabella felt unexpectedly tender toward him.

He wrung the towel in the basin and wiped his face clean, then rubbed the towel against the soap and cleaned his gash. He sharply sucked in his breath whenever the towel touched his wound. The water turning pinker each time the towel was wrung. "I'll get some more cold water," Isabella said. In the kitchen, she stared at the blood in the basin for almost a minute, wondering, wondering, before pouring the water down the sink.

The man rinsed his face and his hands, then took out the gauze and the tape. "Do you think this is enough?" he asked, pulling a length of gauze and holding it up to her.

"I suppose," Isabella said. As he struggled with the tape, Isabella realized, with a sudden jolt, that she didn't want to touch him.

From the doorway, a heavy pounding.

Isabella, who almost fell off her chair in surprise, felt her heart skip a beat and race.

"Don't mind it," the man said. The pounding on the door was so hard and so loud Isabella was sure the wood would cave inward and break.

From outside, a man's voice, also young: "I saw you enter this house." Not taunting. Flat, just stating a fact.

The man sitting with Isabella looked worried again. "I was invited!" he said. "All right?"

The pounding stopped. Isabella remembered a dream she had frequently as a child, of faces forming outside her bedroom window, peering in. The fear she felt in those dreams—the faint skin-crawl— she could feel it now.

"So you were, eh," the man outside said. "May I come in, Isabella?"

He knew her name.

"The swing outside," the man continued. "It had your name carved in it."

Of course. And suddenly she lived again in a world of logic. "Is that your friend?" she whispered to the (*salot?* Isabella thought) man sitting with her. "You don't think he has a weapon, right? I mean, he wouldn't stab me, or anything like that?"

"He won't." The answer was so quick and so sincere that Isabella nodded to herself, convinced.

The man standing outside the door looked older than the man Isabella had invited inside the house. Dressed completely in white, he wore no shoes. His bare feet were smooth and clean.

The man in white smiled at Isabella. "Hello. Sorry to bother you. And sorry about the crazy knocking earlier." The man paused and cocked his head toward the direction where the other man sat, "He tends to do this a lot."

"Do what?" Isabella said.

The man in white considered her for a moment. "Run away."

For a brief instant, Isabella wondered if it were an order.

"He's in there," she said, and allowed the man in white to enter.

He walked around, staring at the ceiling, and appraising the room. "Do you know that you're not alone in this house, Isabella?"

"Children," Isabella said, unable to help herself.

The man in white stopped walking and looked at Isabella, surprised. "*Children,*" he echoed, and emitted a short laugh. "Children. Interesting. I suppose they can take the shape of children, yes."

"You really need to shut up now," the other man said.

The man in white turned to him and reared back slightly. "Is that *gauze?*" he said. Isabella saw him reach a hand to touch the dressed wound, but the other man jerked his head back. "Seriously? *Gauze?*"

"Really," the other man said, "just shut up. I *beg* you."

"What are you *doing?*" The man in white looked annoyed and disappointed. "You could have waved away this hurt *in an instant.*"

"You are really, *really* giving me a headache right now," the other man said. They looked so much like brothers bickering that Isabella almost laughed, amused. "*Please.* Stop talking."

"What happened?"

They all fell silent. She was so surprised by her own question that she almost reached a hand up to cover her mouth.

(But, really, shouldn't that have been the first thing she said upon seeing the young man outside their gate? *What happened?* She should have asked before inviting him in. She should have asked. She should have asked first.)

Before the two could answer, however, she heard someone calling from outside. *"Ineng,"* a man said. *"Ineng. Ineng."*

"Excuse me," Isabella told her guests, and opened the door and walked out. There were five or so men outside the gate. *Barangay tanod.* They were carrying flashlights and sticks. One seemed to even have an unsheathed *bolo* knife.

*"Ineng,"* said one of the men. She recognized him as one of her father's regular drinking buddies. "Stay inside the house all right? Lock all your doors and close your windows. There is—" The man paused and glanced at his companions. All the other men looked away. "There is a man walking about. A man from out of town, mad, and possibly violent. Are you all alone? I heard your parents left town tonight."

"I am alone, *Manong,*" Isabella said. "But it's all right. I always lock the doors."

"I would have left a *tanod* with you here, but we're short—"

"Really," Isabella said. "It's all right. What did the man do?"

"Attacked the *kapitan,*" another tanod said. He was shushed by the others.

"Oh," Isabella said. "I see."

The men said goodbye. Each murmured a half-hearted "Merry Christmas". Isabella smiled until they were gone.

The front door was locked when she went back to the house.

Isabella couldn't believe it. *They've locked me out,* she thought, and turned the knob. She slammed an open palm on the wood. *I invited them in, and now they've locked me out. They're going to live in our house now.*

"One moment," the man in white said from the other side. The door swung open. The man in white looked as if he were just trying to keep himself from laughing. The other man was standing behind him, his arms crossed. "There must be something wrong with your door knob."

"We're leaving," the other man said, suddenly. He stepped forward and bowed. (Isabella stepped away from him a little, thinking *What if he took my hand? I don't want to take his hand. I don't want to take his hand.*) "Thank you for all your help. We'll be on our way now."

"Oh, we're leaving?" said the man in white. Then he started whispering to the other man, his whisper low and urgent. Isabella only heard the words *invited* and *claim* and *why not* and *claim now* and *you idiot.* The other man whispered back (Isabella heard nothing) and walked out the door, pushing the man in white ahead of him.

"What did you tell the *kapitan?*" Isabella said. Again, the men fell silent. They glanced at her, the man in white smiling, the other man looking worried. "What did you say to him?"

But they wouldn't answer. They walked away from the front porch and headed, slowly, toward the gate. Isabella would have followed them, and asked and asked and asked, but she remembered that the swing did not bear her name, not anymore, not since the last storm. The wind destroyed her swing, and her father replaced it with new wood. How did that man know her name?

Isabella stood for several minutes on the front porch, watching them walk away. After the men were gone, she thought of how she wasn't able to tell Nick what she wanted to say. Maybe she would text or call. She would do it when she was already in the university, far away and foreign. She wondered if Nick would cry, and realized she didn't care. After the Christmas break, it would be the new year and just three more months of high school, just three more months, and then graduation (she would have a white dress sewn by her mother's friend, and a pair of black pumps), then she would fold all her clothes, board the bus with her parents, and then she would meet her roommates. They could go out for a drink and later on agree on a color for the curtains (she'd vote for peach) and she would finally be able to put posters on her wall, because her mother wouldn't allow her to put anything on her wall, she said it made the walls look messy and ruined the paint.

She thought of the landslide in the town up north, and that man in her dream calling, *Nanay, Nanay.*

*So maybe he came to them to warn them,* Isabella had said to her father, and her father had said, *Or to bring the storm to them.*

The lights in her mother's flower garden twinkled like so many stars. How beautiful, how beautiful, Isabella thought to herself, and felt her heart fill with ice.

## Ana's Little Pawnshop
## on Makiling St.

Tala used to own this pair," Ana said, holding up a pair of spectacles for me to see. The oval lenses were framed in glass filled with nebulae, turning a rich mauve-blue at one moment, a bright golden-green the next. Every now and then, stars formed, twinkling, and floating around the lenses and toward the temple arms.

"Lisa would love that," I said. Lisa was my girlfriend. She got her first pair of prescription glasses two weeks ago, just a simple pair, framed in black, square and serious. She said the glasses made her look like a dork. I wondered if lenses framed by star-forming clouds would make her look less of a dork. Probably not.

"I'll give this pair to you in exchange for your most treasured memory of the night sky," Ana said.

I had several. My top choices? There was a meteor shower last February with Lisa beside me, sitting open-mouthed and speechless. I had a clear view of the night sky in Bohol as we lay in the sand, momentarily forgetting the impending end of summer vacation.

"No thanks," I said, smiling as I remembered.

"Good for you," Ana said.

I almost asked what Tala's eye grade was, but then realized that for an entity that oversaw all the stars of the universe, Tala most probably had perfect vision.

"Tala gave this to me in exchange for *this*."

*This* came out as a grunt as Ana leaned sideways to pick up another item. "The mask of Alunsina," Ana said. "She said she'll have someone pick it up for her today." It was a golden half-mask with a handle, and covered in garnet, sapphire, and amethyst. Ana held it up to her face, and the mask turned the soft pink and yellow of dawn.

My jaw dropped. "Wow."

"Wow, indeed," Ana said, cradling the mask in her hands. "I think Tala had underpaid me in this deal." She laughed.

"What did Alunsina get for it?"

"A good night's sleep," Ana said. "She just wanted to get rid of the thing. It bores her, she said. Alunsina gets bored a lot, ever since she relinquished the realm of the golden dawn and became a mortal. She said it's hard to become too aware of the passage of time. The minutes now weigh on her, when before she could watch a century pass in the blink of an eye."

"She should have internet connection at her house," I said.

Ana found that hilarious. "I'd tell her that when she drops by. Can you hand me that box, please, Eric?"


I came upon Ana's little pawnshop by accident a month ago, when I found myself cycling through this street looking for a pen I dropped. It was hours after school. I came from the bookstore with this expensive fountain pen that my father wanted for his birthday. I had it wrapped and all, but I was so busy speeding through the road to reach home in time for dinner that I didn't realize I had lost my gift until I touched my breast pocket. I had to get off my bike and walk back to retrace my path. Thank goodness it was a residential street, quiet and cozy, the houses all elegant and expensive and bordered by flower gardens, not a dark alley where I could lose things other than that blasted pen. I passed by a group of boys playing basketball, but I had my eyes trained on the ground, so I only heard their voices and the thump and clink of the ball as it hit the pavement and, occasionally, the ring.

All of a sudden all sound disappeared. I looked up in surprise and found myself on a stretch of road lined with quaint little shops. One sold secondhand books, another dresses and jewelry, and still another, lamps and chandeliers. All of them were closed, however, except for this one store lit by a yellow light from inside.

"Lost something?" a woman said. That was the first time I saw Ana. She was in her thirties and looked breathtakingly beautiful, her lines as defined as the stars in those forties films that Lisa liked so much: dark lids, red lips, wavy hair. There was something very warm about her presence.

I found myself saying, "I lost a pen."

"Ah," Ana said. She was in the process of moving a large flowerpot closer to the door. The flowerpot contained the biggest sunflowers I had ever seen. She straightened up and wiped her palms on the side of her jeans before going inside. Her shop had a display window, behind which a hand-painted sign rested on a stand and read, *Ana's Pawnshop*. Taped right on the glass was an announcement written with a black Sharpie: (1) ASSISTANT NEEDED. PART-TIME OR FULL-TIME.

I moved closer and settled my bike right beside the flowerpot. The pawnshop was cluttered but looked snug and warm, with its gleaming hardwood floors and a certain syrupy smell in the air. Ana was behind the glass counter. At her elbow was a wicker basket filled with letters. All of the letters were unopened, which I later learned were sealed with moss-green wax bearing two intertwined M's. On the other side of the counter was a bare table with two chairs.

"Is this it?" In her hands was a rectangular box with a silver bow.

"Yes," I said in wonder. "How did that get here?"

"Lost things arrive here to be found," she said.

"Oh," I said. "Do I have to pay for this?"

"No," she said with a laugh. "I only sell the unclaimed items."

I looked at the shelves. "That's a lot of unclaimed items."

Ana looked wistful. "People lose things every day. Most just give up looking and forget."

I was curious about the shop and the sudden sadness in Ana's voice, but I was pressed for time, so I thanked her and said goodbye.

(It must be mentioned, though, that despite the time I spent looking for the pen on that street, and the time I spent inside Ana's shop, I arrived home in time for dinner.)

I visited again the next day, staying at least an hour, having tea, eating bread, and looking over her inventory. She said her tea was made from the boiled petals of *rosas, gumamela* and *sampaguita*, and was incredibly sweet and refreshing. I was sure she had ingredients besides the flowers; if I were to boil the exact same petals I would just end up with something foul and slimy.

Ana said the lost objects appeared in the storeroom behind the shop, located beside Ana's kitchen and her bathroom (she slept in a bedroom upstairs), and would remain there until claimed. If the items remained unclaimed for 30 days, they would be moved to the shop to be appraised and sold.

The shop had all sorts of things. Wineglasses and mugs, magnifying glasses and spectacles and sunglasses of all shapes and sizes and colors, tables and chairs from various eras, curtains and clothes and bags and purses, typewriters, cameras, shoes and boots and pumps, chests of jewelry, musical boxes, dolls and other toys, lace and silk, bronze candelabras, combs inlaid with pearls, hats adorned with hand-sewn designs and rhinestones, large vintage buttons, books and notes and letters.

"My human clientele look through the shelves for items they could use as décor," Ana said. "Some of these things were too old and broken to be worn or used. They pay me with human currency, and that's what I use to pay the humans who come in to pawn their products. My non-human clientele, on the other hand, usually just end up bartering each other's items. They have no use for human objects, and humans more often than not refuse to pay the price I ask for the items of magic."

"Is this an orientation?" I asked, and Ana looked at me in surprise, and burst out laughing.

I knew before we finished our tea that I would ask about the sign taped on the display window, that she would (perhaps jokingly) ask me to apply, and I would pretend to consider and say yes. I would say yes; she was a nice, sincere lady and I liked her and I could taste her loneliness in the very bread she served.

And this was exactly what happened.

I didn't need a part-time job, but working with Ana was a pleasure. I only worked after school because I spent the weekend with Lisa (and Ana understood that).

Ana didn't really need a helper. Clients didn't come in droves. But she only had her books and she couldn't understand the appeal of TV or radio. She was hungry for constant company.

My schedule was like this: school, have lunch with Lisa, extra-curricular shit (through Lisa's clever maneuverings I found myself signing up for the school paper, and now I couldn't find a way out *anywhere*), say goodbye to Lisa, change out of my uniform, go to Ana's shop. That would be around four, so I'd arrive in time for tea and bread, then I would clean up, check the storeroom for new items, and help Ana move the heavier objects around the shop.

Ana opened her shop late, because clients usually came in at night, like nocturnal customers prowling a convenience store for their chocolate fix. There was always the usual pawnshop business of this-wristwatch-for-cash, but I had also seen my share of interesting trades. A blind girl exchanging her singing voice for sight (Ana stored the girl's voice in a jar and placed it on the topmost shelf), a basketball player exchanging a week's worth of laughter for the quick mending of a broken bone. There was one night when a man came in and bought a bottle of storm clouds. He claimed to be a poet.

"I needed the rain," he said. "I couldn't write in this goddamn heat."

"What did he pay for that?" I asked once the man had left.

"That's just a week's supply of storm clouds," Ana said, "so I only asked for six months of his life. I'm going to use that for my sunflowers. That way, they wouldn't wilt for a long time—isn't that fantastic?"

I hoped the man wrote good poems.

Ana also had a lot of visitors, mortals and immortals alike. I was there when Alunsina banged in, wearing a short black dress and dark sunglasses, and smelling of acrylic. "A human!" she said when she saw me. "How interesting."

I wondered about the sunglasses. It was six in the evening.

Ana embraced her and arranged their teacups on the small table. Alunsina was asking about the mask. "So who finally bought the damn thing?"

"Tala did."

"*Tala?*" Alunsina burst out laughing. "Where will she use it?"

"It's a good accessory for an evening gown," Ana said.

"What, she'll throw a party? Good grief." She turned to me, and I realized that it wasn't acrylic wafting off of her—it was cheap gin. "Hey, if Tala ever invites you to her party, don't go. She's as dull as a dying galaxy."

I didn't have first-hand experience, obviously, but I was pretty sure a dying galaxy would be anything but dull. I believed it would be fantastic, breathtaking, heartbreaking. Not dull. But ex-immortal or no, Alunsina was drunk and seemed unstable, so I just nodded my head.

Alunsina's gaze strayed toward Ana's wicker basket of unopened letters. "Ohhh," she said. "Is the queen giving you a hard time?"

Ana sighed. "I bet they're strongly worded missives regarding my refusal to become a stockholder," Ana said. "I'm happy with my small shop. I don't need dividends."

"You shouldn't have trusted her," Alunsina said. "She's corporate now. She'll screw you over one of these days."

"Sorry about that," Ana said, after having seen Alunsina out the door.

"Who's the queen?" I asked.

Ana looked at me a moment, then smiled and shook her head.

"Sorry," I said, my face reddening. "I couldn't help overhearing—"

"Alunsina and her big mouth," Ana said, laughing. "It's all right, Eric. Who *is* the queen? I own this shop, but the rest of the block is owned by Mariang Makiling."

"I see," I said. "But doesn't she live in a forest?"

"This is the forest!" Ana said, gleeful, as though she had caught me in a trap. "Was. We're sitting right in it. A corporation bought the land from the government, tore down the trees, burned the grass, and filled it with concrete and buildings. Instead of hurling curses all around, however, Mariang Makiling simply dusted herself off and struck a deal with the mortals. So now she's a stockholder and a businesswoman. I believe she now responds to 'Marie'." Ana shrugged. "I don't blame the poor girl. She's suffered through a string of heartbreaks. If she believes she could heal by jumping into finance, then good for her. I just hate how the business has affected her, how she now treasures the impersonal. She's been sending me letters instead of coming here to have tea with me." She shrugged and waved a hand toward the wicker basket, as though she wanted to banish it away from her sight. "Did you think what Tala gave me in exchange for her mask was useless?"

Alunsina had been berating her about it. "No," I said. "I think it's a really cool pair of glasses."

"Yes, but I've broken the frame." Ana took out a jar sealed with a black rubber cover. The contents of the jar sparkled. "I've poured the nebulae here. They've been busy. Look how many stars they've made!"

I peered at them and smiled and nodded my approval.

I wanted to ask her why she bought the shop in the first place, but it seemed that every time I planned to ask her, Ana would talk about something else, deftly changing the subject.

Until that night I began yammering on about this little girl who went missing. Like I said, Ana didn't own a TV, and she didn't seem particularly interested in the newspapers, but it was all over the news and one moment I just found myself talking to her about it. The girl was last seen leaving her kindergarten class with her *yaya*.

While watching it, my mother mentioned that girl who disappeared years ago. It was the same scenario: last seen with the *yaya* leaving school. A day later, they found the girl's shoes in the playground. Little pink shoes with straps and silver buckles. The girl had been missing for close to a week now. They couldn't find the *yaya*, too. No calls, no ransom demands. Just those pink shoes.

"She was found dead inside a Samsonite bag three months after," I said. "The bag was fished from a river."

"How horrible," Ana said. "I hope the missing girl won't end up the same way."

"Yes."

Silence.

"Have you had a person suddenly appear in the storeroom?" I asked.

"A person?"

"Humans get lost, too," I said. I imagined the little girl suddenly appearing in the storeroom, bewildered but safe.

"I deal with lost things," said Ana. "Lost humans are beyond my realm."

I thought that was the end of it, so I just nodded and busied myself with the inventory list.

"I've lost a little girl, too," Ana said, all of a sudden.

I was so surprised I didn't manage to say anything.

"But no. She's not really lost." Ana wiped her palms on her jeans, watching her hands as she did so. "My, I'm an awful storyteller. Let me start again," she said. "I fell in love."

Ana was still Anagolay then, she said. She visited the world, fell in love with a mortal, gave birth to a girl, and lived as a married woman and a mother for years. But the man fell out of love, and Anagolay found herself abandoned.

"We met in this town, but he has moved away," Ana said. "I decided to stay here because I have fallen in love with the place, and there is still that faint hope that he'll come back. Maybe then he'll explain why he did what he did." Ana gave me a sad, resigned smile. "He took our daughter with him."

"That's awful," I said. I almost asked for the man's name. I thought maybe I could Google him.

As though reading my mind, Ana said, "I tried looking for them. But then I thought, if I find them, *what then?* What use is it, to find people that don't want to be found? They're not lost: one decided to remove himself from my world, one was taken away. Better if I wait for them to come to me.

"So when I heard about Mariang Makiling's business endeavors, I visited her and asked if I could be given a piece of land in this realm. I paid a portion of my influence for a small shop and her protection. With her glamour protecting this property, this is definitely the safest spot in town. In here, you need not worry about fire, or floods, or the sort of evil that forces men to throw a dead child into a river. I can sleep soundly with the front door unlocked. It's a good deal. I run my shop, and I sit here and wait."

If the missing girl's mother knew this, she would have bought protection for her child in a heartbeat. I would. I would buy protection for my family. For Lisa.

But Mariang Makiling asked a big price in return, and I didn't have powers to barter.

Meanwhile, the letters bearing Mariang Makiling's seal kept ending up inside the wicker basket. More than once I was tempted to open one of them, but I kept my hands to myself and did my work without saying anything.

One day, a man in a suit dropped by the pawnshop. I had just arrived and wasn't even done putting butter on my bread when the little bell on top of the door tinkled. I thought we had an early customer.

"Greetings, Anagolay," the man said.

"Greetings, Michael," Ana said, rising. "But please, call me Ana. Eric," she said, turning to me, "would you mind it so much if you moved to the counter?"

We were sitting at the table. "No prob," I said, and took my tea with me.

I saw Michael glance at the wicker basket and sigh. "I see you haven't read any of Marie's letters."

Ana sat down again. "I don't want to become a stockholder," she said, a bit grumpily. "And I came to Mariang Makiling when I bought this shop. Would it be too much if she showed courtesy and came to me?"

"Don't take it that way," Michael said. "She's really, really busy. And the letters aren't about the stock control issue."

"Then what does she want?"

"They're tearing down the building, Ana," Michael said. "Marie's human partners want to build a mall."

I almost choked on my tea.

"And she's allowing this?" Ana said. This was the first time I saw her look so distraught. "But I own this shop."

"Yes, we'll provide you with another venue. But you'll have to pack up and leave by tomorrow. We had given you several months, but you never opened the letters and you never replied."

Ana chewed on this. Then: "Let me speak with Mariang Makiling."

Michael placed his briefcase on his lap and said, "I really just came here to present you with the documents—"

"Tell her to come."

Michael sighed. "Very well," he said, and dialed a number on his cell phone.

I didn't hear Michael talk to anyone on the other line, but he suddenly told us, "She's here," and the glass door banged open and in strode a woman in a white business suit and red pumps followed by two female assistants and another man in a suit. The woman, who had long ebony hair and light-brown skin, looked stern and no-nonsense, her arms crossed as though she would rather be elsewhere. Her assistants looked bored, as though unimpressed with the pawnshop's display. The other man in a suit, probably her bodyguard, was wearing sunglasses and looked like he couldn't care less.

Mariang Makiling flipped her hair over a shoulder, and the shop was suddenly filled with the heady scent of *sampaguita*.

"Greetings, Maria," Ana said, and Mariang Makiling slumped her shoulders, smiled, and drew Ana closer for an embrace. I thought even this sudden friendliness was artificial.

"Greetings Anagolay," she said. "I assume Michael had told you the news."

"Is there no way I could keep my shop?"

"You *will* keep your shop, Anagolay. We'll just relocate you."

"Where? Somewhere near?"

Mariang Makiling didn't reply.

"I am sure," Ana said, "that you could let your mortals build this mall or whatever-it-is around me. I paid for this space dearly, Mariang Makiling. I paid for protection."

That got to her. Mariang Makiling placed her hands on her hips and took a deep breath. Her female assistants typed on their Blackberrys, Michael sighed and fidgeted, and the bodyguard stood as still as a sentinel.

"All the memories of your life's greatest love," Mariang Makiling said after that long pause, "and you can keep your shop."

Ana received the blow as gracefully as she could. "That would include memories of my daughter, Maria."

"So be it," Mariang Makiling said. "Consider my terms, Anagolay. I have a business to run."

And so they left. Only Michael looked apologetic. Ana only said, "Well", and nothing else, and I left her with her silence.

Then it was time to leave. As I was picking up my backpack Ana tapped me on the shoulder. I turned, and I felt a jar shoved into my hands.

"It's a gift," she said. "I believe Lisa will like it."

It was the nebulae from Tala's spectacles, the star-forming clouds that I admired but for which I refused to give my night sky memories. Ana had tied a red bow around the lid, and attached a card that said, *To Eric and Lisa, from a dear friend.*

"Don't do it," I said.

Ana looked surprised. "Don't do what, Eric?"

"Don't give her what she asks for. Just relocate. If it's protection that worries you, buy locks, buy a stun gun or a bat, buy a proper cash register. I'll help you! Don't give her what she wants."

But that was all in my head. All I really said was: "Are you going to move?"

Ana smiled. "I haven't decided yet," she said. "I wonder, though: if somebody asked you to part with your unpleasant memories, wouldn't you say yes?"

"But your memories with your husband and daughter couldn't be all bad," I said.

"I know," Ana said. "That's the tricky part."

There was silence as I put the jar carefully in my backpack.

"Will I see you tomorrow?" I asked.

But it was as though Ana didn't hear me. "Good night, Eric," she said. "Take care."

What else could I say? "Good night, Ana."

I walked out the door and heard the familiar tinkle of the bell. I looked back as I moved my bike. Ana, nestled in that yellow glow, smiled and waved goodbye from behind the glass door. I smiled back, gave her a salute, and pedaled away, the jar inside my bag quickly filling with stars.

## Intersections

There was no storm but when Jacob woke up it was raining again. It had been raining for five days now. Every now and then the skies would take a break, but the clouds were too thick to let the sun shine through. These rainless episodes did nothing else but surprise him with the sudden silence. He would be checking papers or re-reading the story he would be discussing with his sophomore class later in the day, and he would look up, suddenly filled with dread. *Isaac?* he would begin to call, before he'd realize it was just the rain, the absence of it, and he'd catch himself just in time, before the name could leave his mouth. Once he almost fell asleep re-reading *The Pied Piper of Hamelin* for what felt like the hundredth time (Just how many years had he been teaching this class?) when the rain stopped, and he sat up and shouted, "Isaac?" Jacob was in the kitchen eating pandesal, surrounded by photocopied pages and notes, and somewhere inside the apartment unit a blanket was thrown back, followed by an irate growl. "Fuck it, Jacob," Isaac's voice called. "It's six in the morning. What is your problem?"

Jacob remembered feeling embarrassed, feeling like a small child.

Jacob looked out of the window in the living room, then down, dismayed at the sight of the flood in front of the building. Travel was going to be a bitch. The wind was making the droplets of water fall at a slant, and Jacob was reminded of how Isaac hated the rain. He said weather disturbances interfered with his calculations.

Jacob wasn't like Isaac. If he felt a project was hopeless he'd admit failure. After the collapse of the August portal, for example, he bought gin, got absurdly drunk, and agreed to accept this life that he had embraced because he thought it was just a temporary arrangement. He was trying to humor the universe. *Okay, I'm here, might as well wing it.* Isaac took it hard, but being Isaac he refused to talk about it.

But really, he was alive. Isaac was alive. Must they still care about where they were? Must they still care about going home? But when the disappearances began, he found he couldn't wing it any longer. Isaac, hunched once again over his formulae, became more irritable as the days passed. Especially after Adalina disappeared. When she broke the news, the girl's aunt thought Isaac's reaction stemmed from despair. Isaac, who often stayed home, allowed Addie to watch television inside their unit, and seemed to be quite fond of her, the aunt said, smiling that sad smile of hers. Jacob knew better. Isaac despaired, sure, but only because he was envious. Jacob knew that Isaac wanted what he believed Addie had found: a way out of this place.

Jacob ate breakfast in the living room, in front of the television. He ate slowly, savoring a second cup of coffee as the newscasters talked about the "slow-moving storm" causing the days and days of rain.

"We do believe it's connected to the portal," a voice said, and Jacob looked up. Onscreen was some expert, some guy in glasses and a crisp suit. The news shows had a segment about what happened in August almost every other day. At first the experts were all frightened and excited, but now only the fear remained. What if the portal wasn't an entryway, but a vortex? What if it was now eating the world, piece by piece?

They flashed the names onscreen. Twenty-four people living in the surrounding areas, more than half of them children.

"An affinity? Based on age, you mean?" said the expert, echoing the question. "We really cannot say."

A quick shower. Laptop picked up, books swiped into a bag. He was just about to close the door behind him when Jacob turned back and decided to check on Isaac. Isaac's room was unlocked, the curtains drawn. The computer monitor threw a square of light on the sheets. The bed was empty. Jacob found that he couldn't breathe, his mind clutching at the first thought that arrived. *He found it. He found it, and he left me here alone.*

"Jacob?"

Jacob jumped. Isaac was coming from the kitchen, carrying a bowl. "You're still here?" Isaac said, and brought the spoon to his lips. A crunch of cereal. "You're already late."

Jacob by then had calmed down enough to say, "You're still working on it?"

"Now? No." Isaac sighed. "I'm working on an ad copy. But maybe later." He entered his room and drew back the curtains. "It's still raining," Isaac said, mostly to himself. He sounded weary. He sounded as though he had been betrayed.

Jacob wasn't in a hurry to get to the school because he knew; with the weather, only a handful of students would come to his class. So he was surprised when he found more than ten students waiting for him, bundled in jackets and sweaters and looking either stupefied or sleepy. Ten, nearly half the number of his total students. They must continue with the session then. "You losers!" he said when he banged in, startling the kids out of their stupor. "What in the world are you doing here?"

They laughed. He was the Literature professor, the teacher with the subject genuinely loved by at most five people in any class, but he was young, he was everybody's buddy.

Jacob leaned against his table and crossed his arms. "Do you really want to have class today?"

The students just smiled at him.

"I'll do you a favor," Jacob said. "Let's turn this into a review session for the next big exam then we'll call it a day. Also: an automatic five points for every one of you."

The kids cheered. Out in the hall, in an area that Jacob had earlier avoided, tiny spotlights were trained on the pictures on the corkboard. Addie smiled in one of them. HAVE YOU SEEN THEM? the board asked, the words pasted above the illuminated faces.

According to the legend, the Pied Piper of Hamelin lured the rats away from the wretched town with his music. When he didn't get his payment for his services, he lured the children away.

The numbers vary, but usually the stories say the Pied Piper left the town of Hamelin with 130 children. The stories say he sealed the children in a cave.

"He made them enter a doorway in a cave?"

"He made them enter a *portal* in a cave," Jacob said. "That's how I see it." He was so in love with this theory he actually used this in an introduction to the first paper they presented to the Institute.

The stories say at most two children survived: a blind child, who tripped and was not able to follow, and a deaf child who didn't hear the music and was simply dragged along and later was left behind.

If only he were blind and Isaac deaf.

"Where do you think he took them?" Jacob asked.

"He drowned them," Isaac said. "He drowned them in the Weser River, like what he did with the rats."

Jacob still remembered the list:

One. The prisoner in Moscow, known only as C. Gress, who disappeared into thin air in front of his own captors.

Two. A young couple in Vigan, a Mr. and Mrs. Adlawan, who ordered take-out from a restaurant, but wasn't there when the delivery guy came. There were two mugs of hot coffee on the dinner table but the house was empty. Nothing was missing and there was no sign of a break-in. The call to the restaurant was made just twenty-eight minutes earlier. Twenty-eight minutes later, the man and the woman simply ceased to exist.

Three. An unnamed boy in Albany who left the house to fetch water and was never heard from again. The boy's sister and father looked for him, and they saw the boy's footprints in the snow. Except that the tracks stopped halfway through their yard.

There were more.

The portals were phenomena that could not be predicted, until Isaac and Jacob came up with an equation and a program that could pinpoint the location and the date of appearance of a doorway. Just like the weather forecasts, the program predictions were never perfect, but it was a start.

The first item that was thrown through the first portal they found—the Institute had to fly them all the way to the United Kingdom just to test if the coordinates their program had coughed up were correct—was a copy of Rizal's *Noli Me Tangere*, in the original Spanish. The portals were invisible. That was what got to Jacob. They had the coordinates, they could throw the book and watch it disappear, but they couldn't see the door at all.

The coordinates led them to a small town thirteen miles outside of London. Jacob remembered freezing in the cold and goofing around with Isaac, saying that the people on the other side might just throw the book back at them. "We should have given them the Filipino translation," Isaac said.

"Or Derbyshire's," Jacob said.

"Heck, we should have given them food," Isaac said.

But they wondered: they found the portals, there were records of people and objects disappearing, but nothing ever came out of the doorways into their world. Nothing was thrown back. As though the doors were one-way, swinging shut and locking themselves; and you were never given the key.

The ultimate goal was to *create* their own portals to carve out their own doorways whenever and wherever they wished. For what? Exploration? Invasion? Who knew.

If this did happen, Isaac and Jacob were no longer around to see this.

They disappeared on Institute grounds.

Their third discovered portal had became quite an Institute event (there were at most only eight people who knew about the project, but it was an event nonetheless) because it was the first portal predicted to appear on Philippine soil.

The coordinates pointed to the tennis court. All eight of them—Jacob and Isaac the only ones in their twenties—crowded around the invisible door predicted to appear between 11:30 to 11:45 p.m. for at most fourteen seconds.

They must have stood right next to the portal and went through by accident. On the other side, they landed not on pavement, but on grass, and it was still the Institute but the buildings looked wrong. The night janitor thought they were college brats high on some drug and took pity on them. "I'm pretty sure that department doesn't exist, son," he told Jacob, and led them out.

They sat under a waiting shed outside the campus and couldn't move. "Shit," they said almost every half hour, looking around, touching the stone bench, looking up at the sky. "Shit."

It was Isaac who finally took charge, dragging Jacob, who could only say "This cannot be happening" over and over.

But it was happening. They had cash on them, plenty, but of course their credit cards were useless. They checked into a cheap hotel, with papery sheets and unyielding pillows, and Jacob remembered feeling too shocked to cry that first night. He remembered even falling asleep.

"If we got back, we could write a paper about this," Jacob pronounced the next morning over a breakfast of coffee, fast-food eggs, and *longganisa*. The television blared news, all the while sounding both alien and familiar. It was the word *if* that got to Isaac, the word *if* that swung him toward desperation and the dusty phonebook on the bedside table. Jacob watched Isaac whip through the pages, searching for a name. The equation was in their heads. They knew. They could do the calculations again. What they needed was money, time, basic hardware, and a roof over their heads. The security of an identity. How long would it take? A month, a year? Several years? What Isaac needed was hope, an answer that would turn that *if* into a *when*.

Isaac pushed the page toward his face. Isaac's name was in the phonebook. Jacob's name was not.

When Jacob said it was ringing Isaac stood up and began walking in a tight circle between their beds. Jacob watched Isaac, the movement of his feet, his worried expression.

"Hello?"

Jacob tried hard not to scream. "Uh, hi," he said into the receiver. "Can I speak with Isaac Buena, please?"

"Yep, speaking."

All the endless permutations and another young man ended up with the same name. There had been cases of twins separated at birth who found, thirty years later, that they had given the same name to their first daughters. Could the same connection span worlds, jump through the holes between universes?

"Hi, Isaac," Jacob said. In front of him, Isaac paced and paced and paced. "This is Jacob."

Silence, then a short laugh. "Now you'll think I'm an ass, but I'm very bad with names," Isaac said. "Have we met somewhere before? Were you at that seminar?"

Isaac Buena's address was in the phonebook, anyway, and Jacob was too shaken to lie. He hung up. Isaac stopped pacing and sat on his bed. "Well?" he said.

"He doesn't know who I am," Jacob said in a small voice.

A simple online search yielded several networking accounts for Isaac Buena, his status messages, unrestricted, now and then betraying his location. *Here at SM looking for a Wi-Fi router.* Because the Institute did not exist, Isaac Buena did not belong to the Institute. He worked for a small ad company, writing copy for digital projects, and oftentimes worked from home in an apartment unit in the city.

A search for Jacob's full name yielded nothing. No birth records, no obituaries. Nothing. While Isaac searched for a reliable city map online, Jacob sat on his bed, listening to the noise of the busy streets below. *I am not*, he thought, looking at the pale sky outside the window, at the traffic, at his face reflected on the TV screen. *I am not.* All the endless permutations, all the pathways that could have been taken, and yet he did not come to be.

They went to the apartment building at around nine the next night with a rental car and a plan so general and so vague it allowed room for improvisation. And failure, too. Jacob didn't want to think of that as he climbed up the stairs with Isaac. They were able to easily pick the door's lock. Inside, Isaac examined the furniture, the books and DVDs on display. "I cannot imagine living here," he said. Jacob didn't comment.

The Isaac of that time and place finally arrived. He had the habit of locking the door first before turning on the lights, so he practically flattened himself against the wall when the lights came on and Jacob was standing there with—

"What the hell?" said that Isaac of that universe. In his head, Jacob called him Isaac Two.

It was Jacob who did the talking. He talked as though he were running out of time.

"We just need to stay here," Jacob said, "until we can find another portal and leave."

All three of them were still standing as Jacob finished.

"No," Isaac Two said. "This can't be happening."

"Believe me, that's exactly what I said when we ended up here," Jacob said.

Isaac Two entered a room without a word. He came back carrying a baseball bat.

"Get out," Isaac Two said. The bat was still lowered but Jacob raised his arms and moved toward the door. Isaac stayed put. "I want the two of you to get out."

Jacob's face fell. "Don't tell me you don't believe me." He pointed at Isaac. "Look at him! Unless you have a twin you have *no way* of explaining his existence."

"Get out!" Isaac Two looked terrified. He raised the bat. His hands were shaking. Jacob silently thanked him for not having a gun. "Get out. Now!"

"We tried, Jacob," Isaac whispered, and Jacob could only nod.

Isaac turned and tackled Isaac Two to wrench the bat from his hand. It took a minute of struggle. It took three blows. Jacob was so repulsed by the sight of a second Isaac bleeding on the floor that he thought he would throw up.

They bundled him up using several bed sheets. Neither Jacob nor Isaac said anything. As they clambered down the staircase they both wondered (but didn't say) why they even bothered to disguise the body—there was no one else standing in the hallways. They put the body in the trunk along with the shovels and drove away.

They could also burn him, but they chose the other option. As far as they knew, no one else was with them so no one else saw them. They considered this lack of witnesses as the universe granting permission. Isaac was the designated driver, but his hands—covered with dirt and scrapes—were shaking too hard when they got back into the car, so Jacob took over. On the drive back to the apartment unit that now belonged to them, Isaac stared at his hands and burst into tears.

They spent the first week alternatively fighting and psyching each other up. *This is temporary, this is temporary, this is temporary.* Isaac hacked into Isaac Two's email account and sent a message to his boss saying that he was not feeling well and would like to go on vacation for at least a week, and could he be given an update on the projects that he should be working on? They worked on the equation again, coding the program from scratch. As Isaac fed calculations to the program, Jacob took a walk around the neighborhood, thinking of a job he could take. He ended up in a park and sat down, resting his legs. Beside him sat a girl watching his father buy fish balls from a stand.

"Hello," the girl said. Jacob turned to her, surprised, and then smiled.

"You live in the apartment." It was not a question.

"How did you know that?" Jacob said.

"I've seen you," the girl said. "You're friends with Isaac?"

Jacob felt slightly cold. This girl knew the Isaac they had—

"That's right."

"Isaac's nice."

Jacob wondered about that. The Isaac he knew didn't like children very much.

"I'm Adalina," the girl said. "Addie for short."

"I'm Jacob," Jacob said. Then he added, "I like being called 'Jacob' just fine."

Addie laughed. Later on Jacob was introduced to Addie's father, who tipped him off about the faculty vacancy in the nearby high school.

And so Jacob sprang into existence as the high school Literature professor. He was an English major before he joined the Institute in his other life, so it wasn't too much of a stretch. At first he was worried about the (fake) documents he passed to the school, but after nearly half a year with no incident, he began to relax. He wouldn't say he loved this new life, but he thought it wasn't so bad.

Only when Isaac received calls from his parents (the same parents, it turned out, as the ones he had in the world on the other side of the portal) did Jacob feel desolate. He didn't exist here; he had no one to call and no one to call him. Back home, both his parents were alive and well. He had a sister and a brother. He wanted to see them again. *This is temporary,* Isaac would say, and he would nod and try to believe him.

However, there was nothing temporary in the way the streets twisted and turned in what was supposed to be his hometown and nothing temporary in the way the garments factory stood on the lot where his house was supposed to be. He asked around, the first and last time he decided to explore, but not a single face looked familiar to him. He tried to track down his parents, using the phonebook and the internet, but he couldn't find them anywhere. Were they simply not born? Were they given different names? He found names of friends, but every time he called, he would remember the other Isaac, how clueless he was and how open *(Were you at that seminar?)*, and he would hang up before he could hear a voice respond.

What else could he do? An entire universe stood in his way.

Isaac told him about a positive reading around late July, seven months after they went through, and Jacob felt a rush of joy, strong enough to make him keel over. *Around August*, Isaac said, and pointed out the intersection on the map. Jacob checked the variables himself and could hardly believe his eyes. The portal would appear around August. They didn't care if it appeared in a marketplace or a mall. They would go through, even in front of several hundred people. They would go home.

It turned out that the intersection was a street. When they got there, Jacob knew at once that this portal was different because when it appeared in the midst of midday traffic that August it had a distinct shimmer to it. Jacob shouted at Isaac to *run, now, run* but the jeepney driver saw the shimmer too and was so surprised he drove off the road, toward the sidewalk. Jacob yanked Isaac away and hit his head and lost consciousness. Somewhere in the pile-up, Addie's parents were injured upon impact. They later died.

The portal remained open for twenty minutes—a record in itself. Police tape was rolled out. Guards with shields came, shooing away children who threw rocks at the shimmering wall, whooping as the rocks magically disappeared. The media set up their cameras, interviewing the experts who came over. *What is this?*

Isaac could have run to the portal alone if he had wanted to. Jacob asked him at the hospital. "I'd feel too guilty if I left you here," Isaac said. That's true, Jacob thought, but there was also the pile-up and the screaming victims, there were the guards and their guns. Too many obstacles. If they were not there, could Isaac have—

But Jacob did not want to ask that question.

"That's it, then," Jacob said. "We're stuck here for all of eternity."

"Of course not," Isaac said. "There'll be another portal, soon enough."

The first person who disappeared after the August portal collapsed was a male college student renting a room in a house along that street. His landlady said the boy came down to apologize for the late payment and said he would go get his money now. The college student went up the stairs and into his room. The landlady said she waited for "almost an hour", watching the TV, and when she couldn't wait anymore she went up to look for him, and couldn't find him.

"There was no other way for him to get out of the house other than the front door, or the windows in his room," the landlady said, "but the windows were locked from the inside when I checked on his room, and all his clothes were there, his bag, his money."

After the third disappearance Jacob knew that somewhere, in an office, the Institute was being formed. Not the exact Institute that he and Isaac knew, but an Institute nonetheless.

It was possible that the portals were now appearing at such a frequency and in so short a time that Isaac couldn't keep up, couldn't pin down their locations.

Maybe one day Isaac would walk into his room or the kitchen, and there would be silence, and Jacob wouldn't be at all surprised.

This was what he was thinking when he got home and found that the apartment unit was empty.

Jacob tried calling Isaac's phone, but it wouldn't even ring.

He set down his books and his bag and made his own dinner, drank his coffee. He turned on the TV and watched whatever was on. He waited for three hours.

*This is it, then,* he thought to himself. If the collapse of the August portal would indeed lead to the creation of the Institute in this particular universe, then he had better find a way to contact its members and present his case. *Help me,* he imagined himself saying to them. *Please help me.*

And if there was no Institute, if the portals had disappeared forever—what then? What's next?

When Isaac finally burst through the door, arms full of stuff from the grocery, his keys between his teeth, Jacob couldn't quite explain his sudden tears, his feelings of mingled relief and remorse. Isaac set down his bags and sat in front of him, open-mouthed and confused, and tried to find the words to console him.

# THE MAN ON THE TRAIN

In the city was a man who rode the train every day. There was nothing remarkable in this; everyone rode the train. Maybe not every day, but at least five days a week on workdays, office employees congesting the air-conditioned coaches with their wet hair and unlined eyes, shirts untucked, ties hidden somewhere in the linings of their laptop bags, stockinged feet cushioned by flip-flops because heels could kill you. And the man wasn't even thinking about that joke they always say about stilettos. (Could one really use them as murder weapons? Are they sharp enough?). He was thinking of the woman he saw last month. She was wearing pumps; she tripped on her way into the train. It wasn't her fault: the women behind her were jostling her. It was perhaps a week after the train administration approved segregation: women, children, and the handicapped in the first car of the train; everybody else in the other cars. The train administration thought they were doing something smart, throwing the young, the expecting and the vulnerable into a crowd of women. They thought the women would take care of them, they thought the women would be gentle. But the women were employees, too, beating the clock, dealing with colleagues they wouldn't even consider as friends, running late for an appointment, waking up cranky. The man wondered if he were being sexist. No, he was thinking not only of the women. He was thinking also of the men, maybe even the drivers, the guards, the people sitting behind the glass, breaking bills and handing out the cards with the punched-out hole and the President's face. It's true, he thought. The train turned everyone feral.

No. No. Not the train. The train was a resting place, a sanctuary unless there were too many passengers and you had no choice but to stand, pinned to the doors, someone's pelvis cutting the circulation in your leg. But if you were sitting beneath the air-con the train ride could be glorious. It wasn't the train, no. No. It was work. Schedules. The night shift. Not ever arriving at home to find your children awake. Stupid, irrational bosses. The city. She broke her leg, the woman who mistakenly wore heels to the train and tripped. There was a sharp crack and the other passengers drew away, wincing, horrified. The woman didn't die, the man supposed, it was just one leg, one bone; she didn't die but she screamed as though she was going to. Everyone in the station was late for an hour, and they didn't feel at all sorry for the woman who broke her leg.

He was old enough to remember the city before the trains came. The horrible traffic jams, the smoke. They were still there, he knew; sometimes he had to stay late at the office. Before the train administration extended the train schedules he was forced to take the bus. It could be as comforting as the train but the ride wasn't as swift, or as silent. In the bus, the noise of other vehicles came in unfiltered, every honk like a signal for an impending death. (Once, the man was awakened by a sudden noise. He saw a pile-up ahead. One car veered into the wrong lane. It's those stupid pink fences, people said. You can't see the pink fences in the dark. A family died, he learned later. Two children. This was the reason he didn't drive anymore, he remembered. Also, the gas prices were incredible.)

The rudeness also was more pronounced. The man would think that since most of the passengers were on their way home they'd be too exhausted to scream at each other. It must be the long travel time, cruel in its extension. In the congested streets, the ride home seemed like a second shift at work. It must be worse in the mornings, with the heat and the evangelists clambering up the steps to deliver their speeches and their Bible verses in the aisle, telling the listless, suffering passengers that they loved them and that they were damned.

He was old enough to remember these days, the lack of alternatives to maneuver the streets. But he was also young enough to be considered "young". Gen X, he believed. Alex Garland and *The Beach*, Bret Easton Ellis and—practically all his books. Especially the one that got turned into a film, the successful one, the one with the handsome young man and an axe. Chuck Palahniuk, that movie with Brad Pitt, all that anger. The man tried to think of a Filipino novel that could serve as counterpart, but with Marcos to hate even years after his death, who had the time to be jaded and cynical? He thought of Gen Y. What is Gen Y? He read there was now a Gen Y but he couldn't see the difference. Weren't all "young" people the same? Disillusioned, world-weary, bored out of their minds? That constant need for an adventure, that constant need to ridicule suburban life and jobs that keep you deskbound and microwavable food and comfort. Everything was fake, and every day had to be a day closer to finding the genuine, or else just stop bothering and jump off a bridge. They were always single, these "young" people, childless, unattached, and maybe rich. Selfish. Maybe Gen X grew up and gave birth to Gen Y. Soon, Gen Y will get tired of backpacking across Southeast Asia and settle somewhere, have children, and tie themselves to a single place.

He remembered being "young", and being horribly, horribly selfish. How infinite he felt. Now, he found comfort in the predictability of the train. But he didn't miss his young self. Even then he knew he was lost.

He was still lost, even inside the train, despite the certainty of its destination, the one direction in which it proceeded. He found a constant for a little while, but there were so many people in the train station and their surge made even the constant slippery. When was the last time the train arrived on schedule? Never. The trains didn't even have a schedule. The only certain thing was when the station opened, and when it closed. Whatever happened in between was indefinable. For example: he thought the train ride last month was just any other train ride, but there was a sharp crack and a crowd drew away and all of a sudden there was a woman howling on the floor.

For example:

What?

*There were other examples,* the man thought.
He was sure of this.

Another thing he was sure of: A man could be allowed in the first car of the train, if he had a child, or a pregnant companion.

The train administration saw this exemption as a privilege.

Wait, the man thought. What happened in between—from the time the station opened to the time it closed—could also be defined. Ride the train often enough and you would find a pattern in its apparent randomness. Sundays. Holidays. Weekdays between twelve noon and three in the afternoon. These were the times when the train could breathe, when passenger volume fell. According to the latest surveys, more than half a million people rode the train every day. Half a million. Every single day. Half a million walking across the platform, riding the cars, changing the landscape like a steady raindrop inside a cave. It was a wonder the train had not yet buckled beneath all that weight, had not yet fallen like a decaying raft to the concrete sea below.

Sundays. Holidays. Weekdays between twelve noon and three in the afternoon.

After the train administration extended its office hours, the man added *midnight to two a.m.* to the list. At half-past one every day the cashiers pulled down the blinds in their stalls; at exactly two a.m. the trains stopped running and the station closed. Few people came to the station between the hours of midnight and two a.m. The man was sure the train was losing money. The man was sure in a few weeks the train station would go back to its old office hours. If it insisted on being open longer it would go bankrupt.

One Monday night he went to his office building, but not to work because he was on leave. He had been on leave for almost two weeks now. He went to the office to eat dinner with a friend. *How are you doing,* his friend asked. *It's so nice to see you up and about.* They were in a coffee shop where all the lights were yellow and almost everybody's face was obscured by an open laptop. It was a sight to see, the faces awash in blue-white light, hanging suspended in yellow. Earlier, he had given the coffee orders to a young barista, who smiled as brightly as the others behind the counter, but with half the spunk, her brightness dimmed by a flicker of worry. Doublemint Choco Ice Blended Tall, he heard her muttering to herself, Macchiato Over Ice Tall—

"You're new here?" he had said to her, trying to sound friendly and sympathetic, but he did not get the intended reaction. She looked even more worried and flustered, and did not bother to return his smile.

The man was concerned. He did not mean to hurt her. He imagined her sitting in the train, already in uniform, nervous about her first day. He did that sometimes, study the train's other passengers. Willing them to have a good day, to not worry too much. Wondering about their lives. Wondering if they were happy.

"Who's staying at home with you?" his friend asked when they sat down.

The man frowned. "Just me." Who else would be staying at home with him?

His friend's face dropped. "You're alone," he said. This seemed unacceptable to him. "I thought you went to your brother's house."

"I didn't want to impose."

"He invited you. You should stay with him."

"I'll think about it," he said, just so his friend would shut up.

After dinner he walked with his friend to the parking lot. He watched his friend throw his car keys in the air and catch them. The man ached for that, a moment with no worries, the confidence of the gesture. His friend said, "Come on. I'll give you a ride."

But it was close to midnight, so of course the man said, "That's all right, I'm taking the train."

This was what the man was trying to do: He was trying to find a way *into* the city. He was trying to pierce through its surface. Its grime, its buildings, its dirty water. He was not trying to find a way *out* of it, as most of his friends had assumed. He had tried that before but didn't find satisfaction in it. He wanted to ask it a question. How could it answer if he chose to run away?

On the face of the clock in the train station, the minute hand swept past 12. It was now Tuesday. There were at most eight people in the station. The man was at the first station, the origin. The train route had thirteen stations. The man bought a southbound ticket. Being at the starting point he had a myriad of stops from which to choose, but only one direction to go. He really had no choice.

The guard didn't hassle him when he entered the first car—the car reserved for the women, the handicapped, the children, and the pregnant. With less than ten people in the station, it just wasn't worth it; the guard was standing at his little podium, comfortable, drinking coffee. The other passenger in the first car was a young female nurse wearing enormous headphones, who glanced at him when he entered and sat down at the far end, but she didn't seem to mind that he was in the car with her. The rest of the passengers were men and were law-abiding, and so entered the non-restricted cars. The man saw them through the glass, and felt a little ashamed.

Just five stations later, the train was already empty. It did not pick up any more passengers in the other stops. Bankruptcy, the man said to himself, and it sounded like a spell. He wondered what he would do if the driver suddenly decided to strike up a conversation. It must get really boring, driving a nearly deserted train that merely proceeded in a straight line. The train was colder now, and the man pulled his jacket tighter across his chest. He stared at his reflection. He soon got tired of this, and he just stared at his hands.

The thirteenth station was fast approaching. "Last station," the train driver informed him, using the microphone just for the heck of it. Before the train fully stopped, the driver advised him to check his belongings, not lean on the doors as the other passengers alighted, and have a good day. "Last station," the train driver said again, and stepped out.

The air-con died and the lights went out. The man sat in the darkness and waited for a janitor to come in and clean the car, waited for a security guard to bark at him to get up and leave the station, we're closing. The train doors remained open, but the man didn't move. Nobody came. The last station appeared to be empty.

The train doors closed. The man remained where he was, waiting. Seconds later, the air-con came back to life with a whir, and the lights crackled to life. The train doors opened. At the far end of the car, near the driver's nook, a young boy of fourteen or fifteen entered and sat down. The boy was wearing jeans, a dark-green shirt, a black jacket, a pair of dirty Chucks that could have been gray once. The boy looked tired, like a worker ready to turn in after a long day. Why wasn't the man surprised the boy looked so much like his son?

Only when the train began moving again (it was the last station, no driver came in, but the train began moving again) did the boy look up and notice him.

The man wondered who would say the first words. But the boy just looked at him, so it had to be him.

"Hello," the man said.

The boy blinked.

"Hello," said the boy. "You're not supposed to be in this car."

The man glanced out the window. He couldn't see anything. It was too dark.

"This car's for women and children," the boy said. "And the handicapped."

The man looked at the boy.

"I used to ride in this particular car," the man said. "I used to have an excuse."

"I see," the boy said. The boy stood up and held onto the back of the bench and the hanging hand straps to support himself as the train swayed. Eventually the boy reached him and sat across from him.

"What's your name?" the boy asked.

The man told him.

The boy seemed to commit this to memory. Or perhaps he was sifting through a pile of information he already had, and was just trying to connect some details to the name. "I am the city," the boy said after a moment.

The train whined to a halt, creating a sound like that of a large, very old animal in pain, and stopped at a station that looked identical to the last station.

The man reached into his jacket and took out a foldable knife. He flipped it open, and the boy jumped slightly.

The lights of the train flickered. Only the man looked up.

"Wait," the boy said, holding out his hands.

"Get up," the man said.

"Wait," the boy said. "This isn't neces—"

"Get up."

They were frozen in their respective poses for several seconds, the boy's arms outstretched, the man's knife glinting in the light of the train.

"You don't have to—" the boy began to say. He eyed the man's knife, checked himself for sudden movements.

The man and the boy stood up at the same time, by degrees.

"We're getting out of here," the man said.


The platform was well-lit but empty. They did not meet another person as they made their way down the stairs and out of the station.

The man and the boy stood on the sidewalk. No cars or buses or taxis passed on the street in front of them. A soft breeze blew, and it was cold.

The man still had his knife out, pointed at the boy's back, but the street was as wide and as deserted as an airport runway. The boy could have escaped him easily yet he didn't move. He stood in front of the man, surveying his surroundings.

"Walk," the man said, but didn't tell the direction because he didn't know where they were.

The boy turned to his right, and the man followed. They passed by a building renting spaces to several establishments. The shops' accordion doors were closed and locked, their signage curiously blank.

More buildings.

All of the buildings looked abandoned.

They came upon the entrance of what seemed to be a residential subdivision. The man and the boy moved to the center of the road.

On either side of them were houses with lawns and flower gardens. The houses were all lit from within, but all of them were empty.

"I come here often," the boy said, and the man nearly jumped out of his skin, still unaccustomed to the eerie silence. "For the quiet."

The man tried to calm his heart, and said nothing.

"Where are we going?" the boy asked.

"Just walk," the man said. "I used to have a son."

The boy nodded. "What happened to him?"

"The city took him," the man said.

They came to a park. Beneath them the soil was soft and wet. The man and the boy passed the surrounding trees in silent awe, as though the trees were sacred.

They came to a bridge, its existence announced by a lamppost. The boy walked on the bridge. After a few steps he gasped and stopped.

Either the bridge had been destroyed, or was unfinished. The man didn't care. From the edge of the almost-bridge was a steep drop to a river.

The man raised the knife, pointing at the boy's nape. The boy hunched his shoulders, feeling the blade.

"Where is my son?" the man asked.

In the silence following the question, the man heard the boy say, "Gone," before collapsing into sobs.

"He was eight years old," the man said. *Is,* he corrected frantically in his head. *Is is is.* "I was with him, on the platform. We were going to the mall." *I was going to buy him this toy helmet that could change his voice because he dropped the last one and we couldn't fix it, but he didn't know that because it was going to be Daddy's surprise. It was going to be Daddy's surprise. I woke up that morning waiting to see the look on his face the moment he got the toy, and I never got to see it.*

Last month, on the train. His son stood beside him on the platform with the women. The loud crack. The woman was howling on the floor. The crowd pushed back and away. His son was gone.

The boy had stopped crying.

"That's not how it happened," the boy said, facing him now, his arms still raised, the victim of a stick-up. As the boy turned, his shoes scraped off pieces of broken concrete from the bridge. These fell into the river. The river was so far down they didn't hear the sound the concrete made when it reached the water.

The man backed up a step, the blade of his knife now pointed at the boy's neck.

"That's not how it happened," the boy repeated. "You didn't lose him when he was eight. You weren't there on the platform when he was eight. He was with his mother. It was your wife who bought the toy because you were away on a business trip. But you did see his face when he received the gift, your wife took a picture and you had it printed and framed on a desk in your office—"

"Shut up!"

"You didn't lose him last month," the boy said. "You lost him two years ago, when he was fifteen. He was in high school. He took the train to get to school. Last month, your wife left you and you couldn't handle it. At work you were always in pain—"

"He was eight," the man said. "My son was eight. I should have held his hand but he was a big boy, he didn't want his hand to be held all the time—"

"No, that's not how it happened."

"I lost him in the crowd. The security guards couldn't find him. The police couldn't find him—"

"He was fifteen," the boy said. "He took the train to go to school. There was a box in one of the cars and in the box was a bomb."

The man's hand—the one holding his weapon—had started to tremble. He lowered his arm and fell to his knees.

The boy looked at him with pity. "He was among the dead."

The man remembered taking the bus, the evangelists, the pile-ups. There were bombs inside the buses, kept in boxes in the bus stations. When the trains came, the bombs found their way into them as well, hidden beneath the seats, and strapped to warm bodies. There were bombs outside the trains. Hidden within homes, safe inside the schools. He remembered the soldiers taking control of a hotel in the city, rigging the city's landmarks with bombs. His wife saying, "I understand their frustrations, but nothing they say can excuse the bombs." But maybe they found that the placards were useless. You see, everything is better with bombs. When a bomb says *Say yes,* you say Yes. He recalled those moments when the air was tense and the city was at a standstill. There was talk of a second Martial Law Era. Distrust and fear. He lay at night imagining his wife pregnant, giving birth, his child growing, his child holding a placard in a protest march, burning in the sun, minutes later losing a shoe in a chase, minutes later bleeding to death on an unfamiliar sidewalk. Or else walking along a sidewalk, carrying no hatred toward anyone else, and being stabbed to death. Or else riding a train, nervous, fearing to enter a car and hear a bomb say, *Say yes*. Fearing that he would never be given the time to respond.

Why have a child at all, why let a child live with all this fear?

"I lost my son before my wife could even carry him to term," the man said, and felt a happiness wash over him, felt relief. Yes, this feels right. This must be it. "My wife fell down the stairs and—"

"No," the boy said, lowering himself to the man's level. They were now both kneeling on the ground, the boy's back to the precipice. "No, that is not your life."

Tears rolled down the man's cheeks. "I am a backpacker in Malaysia—"

"No," the boy said.

The man cried.

"I have a son," the man said, slowly. "I have a son and he was fifteen and I lost him."

"Yes," the boy said.

"The explosion peeled the skin off his face. We still couldn't find his right arm. We buried him with just one arm."

"Yes."

"You should have just given yourself to them," the man said, sobbing, "to those people who left the bombs. They wanted you; you should have just given yourself to them."

"It's not that simple," the boy said.

What was stopping the man now to believe that the woman who last month (and was it last month?) fell howling didn't just break her leg? He heard a crack, it could have been a gunshot. There were people who carried firearms in crowded places. There were those who hurled themselves in front of speeding trains.

"Everything is so impossible to clean," the man said. "You have no hope at all."

The man waited for the boy to contradict him, but the boy just looked at his knees.

Eventually the boy helped him stand up. The man thought of wars, of cities burned to the ground, of preemptive strikes, of salt scattered on the soil to prevent the plants from growing.

"You have no hope at all," the man said.

The man aimed for the vein in the boy's neck, but the boy deflected the blow. "No, no, please," the boy said, wide-eyed and scared, and the knife shot out of the man's hand and over his shoulder, down to the water below. The boy's hand was bleeding. A portion of the remaining half of the bridge cracked beneath them and in reflex the man moved back quickly, pulling the boy with him. The concrete collapsed and fell into the river. The man tried to push the boy off the broken bridge. The boy clung to him, to what's left of the bridge, his grip hurting the man's arms.

"Let me go!" the man shouted, and pushed the boy sideways. The boy landed hard on his right shoulder and screamed.

Somewhere in that unfamiliar landscape, lampposts lining a street flickered and died, and a house crumpled unto itself and turned into rubble.

The man stood up, watching the boy writhe on the ground. Just one kick and the boy would fall off the bridge, like the knife, like the portion of the bridge, like the loose pieces of concrete. The boy was lying on his side and was trying to sit up, but he couldn't move. He could only scream and cry, the tears washing his face. The man stayed where he was. After a few moments the boy stopped trying to get up and just lay there, sobbing, his face turned to the ground.

The man knelt, moved closer, and the boy flinched as he raised his arms. "I'm sorry," the man said. "I'm sorry." Gently he placed his arms around the boy's waist (the boy whimpered as the man brushed against his broken right arm) and helped him up.

The man took off his jacket and made a sling for the boy. He tried to stop the boy's bleeding. They walked back to the train station. The train was still there, empty and waiting. They sat in the first car for what felt like hours, then the air-con came to life and the doors closed, and the train moved toward the sunrise.

"I lost my son last month on the platform," the man said. The boy was leaning against him, almost asleep. The boy stirred when he spoke. "He's only eight. I hope he's all right."

"He's all right," the boy said in a soft voice.

"You think so?" The man placed a hand on the top of the boy's head, brushed back the hair from his damp face. The boy did not reply.

"I hope he doesn't get too cold," the man said, his voice trailing away, the rocking motion of the train lulling him. "It gets too cold at night here, sometimes."

# Night Out

They are sitting on the front steps of the Puso Theater. He wears a black jacket, a blue tee, pants. Nalla is in a sleeveless pink top, a red sarong, a pair of flip-flops. He has to be my age, Nalla thinks, studying him closely. She sees him often enough on the same sidewalks, waiting the night out in the same places with her fellow Fleshies. He works alone, without a Caller, a trick that is hard to pull even if you're extremely likeable. She dumped her own Caller recently after catching him cheating on the commissions. Now, she is having a hard time; customers ignore her like she has WD. Too damn many Fleshies, Nalla thinks.

But this one appears to be doing well, she thinks, moving a step lower, sitting next to him. A Zoner Player is clipped on his ear, his black eyes now blue, flickering every now and then with vidlink static.

Two cars streak across the sky: one red and one yellow, like colored balls, air traffic starting to get as congested as land traffic. Maybe thirteen, fourteen, Nalla thinks. Fourteen, tops.

"Oh, for crying out—" The boy reaches up and unclips the gadget from his ear. His eyes turn black immediately. "Unbelievable," he mutters.

"Lost Net connection?" Nalla fires up a cigarette and smokes slowly, savoring the taste. She'll never be able to buy another packet, with the way things are going. "Sucks, huh? Net's congested around this Area, especially at night."

He doesn't reply. Nalla turns her head slightly and sees him staring intently at her.

"You're smoking," he says with wonder.

"Yes. Want a stick?"

"That's bad for the environment."

Nalla frowns and holds up the packet to the light thrown by the air cars. "The packet says these sticks are treated."

The boy pauses, then smiles. "Treated cigs," he says. "Those things cost a fortune."

She laughs. "That Zoner costs more."

"Darn thing doesn't work anyway."

Silence. The boy holds the Zoner loosely in his fist. Now robbed of entertainment he simply stares at the traffic over their heads.

"So," Nalla says as she exhales the smoke. "Are you waiting for a customer?"

"No," he replies.

"I am. He's late. I think he's already dumped me."

"I'm waiting for my boyfriend."

Nalla takes another drag and nods. A lady in front of them raises her hand and an air autocab lands in front of her.

"Are you going to marry him?" she asks.

The boy's expression is bleak. "I don't know," he whispers. "Maybe. If he'd like to."

"Why not? The government will pay for everything once you agree to raise a tube kid."

He clears his throat. "He's an Area Lord."

The Area Lords are the estate owners, the rich entrepreneurs, the bosses.

"Oh." Nalla laughs. "Excuse *me*."

They fall silent again, waiting. A blue air car pulls away from the air traffic and lands on the sidewalk.

"Here's the customer," Nalla says.

"And here's the boyfriend," says the boy.

Nalla lowers her cigarette. "Are we," she said "looking at the same person?"

They are. The boy turns to Nalla, and his eyes widen.


The boy stares at Dave for a very long time before screaming, "You idiot. You heartless, sick idiot."

They are standing behind her, the boy screaming loud enough to attract glances from the pedestrians but not loud enough to actually engage Nalla's attention.

"You're smoking." Nalla glances over her left shoulder and sees Dave looking at her. "That's bad for the environment."

"They're treated."

"Aren't you even listening to me?" the boy shouts, looking very distressed. Nalla finds his expression both touching and oddly amusing.

Dave turns to him and sighs. "I have nothing to say to you, Cy."

Cy. She smokes. Cy. So that's his name.

"The fuck you don't!" Cy retorts. "You've hurt me and now you want to hurt her, too?"

"Whoa." Nalla raises her hands. "Whoa, whoa, *whoa*."

Dave says, "This isn't helping."

"Oh really?" Cy starts to cry. "Then what will, Dave? Tell me what will."

"You know what," Nalla says. "If you just chose to fuck girls over guys, you wouldn't have this problem."

Dave looks away.

Cy pitches forward and yanks Nalla by the wrist. "You're not sleeping with her," he says.

"Then who will?" Nalla asks dryly. Cy looks at her. She couldn't read his expression. "I'm not joking. I need the money."

"Die alone," Cy tells Dave, and pulls Nalla away.

Cyan met Jonah weeks before Dave happened. He was inside the Puso, sitting in the center row, shoveling popcorn into his mouth. An old Tagalog film was playing.

Jonah was sitting behind him. Another man was sitting two seats to Cy's right. It was this other man that Cy had been studying from the corner of his eye. The man was not paying attention to the movie.

Cy continued to watch with growing boredom. One of the leads had just exchanged her virginity for a hamburger. He snorted. The man sitting two seats away leaned a little bit closer and said, "Do you have the time?"

"Fifteen minutes to one," he replied. The man nodded and thanked him as though the information had saved his life.

A few moments later he leaned again and said, "Is this seat taken?"

"No," Cy said. He was starting to get annoyed. *Maybe I should just jump on the guy and get it over with,* he thought.

The man stood up and moved a seat closer to Cy. Onscreen, the actress flapped her skirt and shouted, "Hamburger! Hamburger!"

Cy laughed.

"*Hoy.*" The man had unzipped his fly, his plump manhood standing erect. "You want to touch it, kid? Come on. Touch it."

"You should be ashamed of yourself."

Cy and the man glanced over their shoulders. Jonah was glaring at the man.

"Mind your own business," the man said.

"That's a good idea," said Cy, and turned to his customer. "Look," he said exasperatedly. "I don't have a Caller, so I can do you at nine-five. Where do you want to go?"

Cy heard a sudden intake of breath, like someone had just been punched.

"You're a Fleshie?" Jonah said.

Cy rolled his eyes.

"This is unbelievable," the man said. He shook his head in disbelief and zipped up his fly.

"What?" Cy said. "Wait!" But the man had already stood up and left.

"What is wrong with you?" Cy told Jonah, who wouldn't look at him. Then realization hit. "You thought I was just an ordinary kid?"

"Oh, God," Jonah said.

Cy laughed. "You actually thought that?"

"I think I better leave."

"No, sit down. It's okay."

He sat down obediently and covered his face with his hands. "God, this is embarrassing," he whispered.

Cy smiled. "What's your name?"

"Jonah. Look, I am really, really——"

"It's okay. I'm Cyan."

Jonah seemed to calm down a bit. "Cyan. Hi."

"Hello."

"How old are you, Cyan?"

"Thirteen."

"You're young," Jonah said. "You've been a Fleshie long?"

"Ever since I got emancipated," Cy answered. "So, Jonah, you want to do this? I can lower my fee to eight."

Jonah looked at him.

"I'm in a bad situation here, you know? I have to pay my rent."

"I'll pay you," Jonah said, "but not for that sort of thing. Just talk, I guess. I live within the Area."

"You know," Cy said. "I had a customer once who made me dress up like a tiger. And I thought *that* was weird." He paused. "Okay."

Cyan knew at once that Jonah was an Area Lord the moment they boarded his car and pulled up over the city. One so rich he could afford not to work. He owned a penthouse apartment with its own parking pad. They zoomed right into it, fifty floors above the ground, saving them the trouble of riding packed elevator cars.

A Hover Guard with Jonah's monogram pointed its camera eye at Cyan. "Identify yourself," it said.

"It's all right, he's a guest," Jonah told it. "Guard the pad."

The Hover Guard soared away.

"Wow," Cyan said. "I wish I could afford one of those."

Jonah's home was neat and bare. "You want something to drink?" he asked as he shrugged off his jacket. Cy smirked.

"What, you don't have a robot to do that for you?"

Jonah groaned. "I hate those things. The last one I bought broke down so often I just end up doing what it's supposed to do." He folded the jacket in half and slung it on one arm of the couch. "So? Drink?"

"No thanks." Cyan sank on the couch. Jonah had disappeared into the kitchen. "Jonah? How old are you?"

"How old do you think?"

Cy shrugged. "Nineteen?"

Jonah came back with a cup of coffee. He was smiling. "I'm twenty-five."

"Really?" Cy sat up. "So you're a War Orphan."

The smile faded a little. "Yes." He sat on a recliner. "My father fought in it."

"Do you remember how it was like," Cy said, "before the war?"

"Kids acted like kids," Jonah said.

Cyan's eyebrows rose. "Are you married?"

"Was." He waved a hand. Cyan followed the gesture and saw a row of framed photographs sitting atop a narrow table pushed against the wall behind him. There was a woman in most of the pictures, smiling heartily.

"Did she die?" Cyan asked, standing up to approach the table.

"She sued me for divorce three years ago."

"So you have a kid." Cyan picked up a picture showing Jonah and his ex-wife together. They were on a beach, the sea and the sky shining the same radiant blue. It was probably taken in Australia, which did not participate in the war. The remaining seas in the country did not look that blue anymore. "I mean, the courts won't grant a divorce unless you have at least one."

Then Cyan found him, a little boy in green shorts standing on the same beach.

"His name's Justin," Jonah said, watching Cyan as he picked up the photograph. "He chose to be with his mom." Cy heard him gulp. "Well, I don't blame him. Maui lets him do anything, maybe even download porn feeds. I'm the strict one, the bad cop. I want him to stay inside the house. But I'm not doing that just to make him miserable. I want Justin to be a kid, for once. I want him to treat me as a parent. I want him to be innocent."

"So you want your son to be baffled when a guy sits next to him in the theater and asks him to touch his dick."

Jonah lowered his eyes, looked away. Cy glanced at him.

*I'm sorry,* Cyan wanted to say, but then thought, why bother?

"When you're innocent, you feel safe," Jonah suddenly said. "Like the world makes sense. When you learn something too early it becomes hard for you to be happy."

Cy wondered if Jonah was high on something. Then he thought, when was the last time I felt safe?

Cyan turned back to the pictures. In one of them, a younger Jonah held the newborn Justin in his arms. Justin's eyes were closed and his skin was very pink.

Cy has dragged Nalla into a tiny diner. The sky is brighter now, lit up by the air traffic jam.

"I don't think I understand what is going on," Nalla says cautiously. The diner is not very clean. The tables are rusty and the cups are chipped; the floor is sticky with spilt coffee. One of the waitresses is a robot, but she's not very efficient. Everything looks old.

"What's your name?" The boy is now looking at her. Finally. He's been staring outside the window through bloodshot eyes for the most of the twenty minutes they've been sitting in that booth. He has made a call through his Zoner a while ago, but he didn't look at her then, either.

"Nalla," she says. "Cy, right?"

"Cyan," he says. "Sorry I had to—"

"Look," Nalla leans forward. "I don't want to be rude, but I'm sure sooner or later you're going to cheat on Dave, too, because everybody cheats in this day and age. *I* think—"

Nalla hears a sharp zing and a whoosh—the sound of a card being swiped, followed by the diner door opening. Cy straightens up as if the sound is a promise and smiles, his face brightening considerably.

A man in shirt and jeans emerges from the street and surveys the place for a second, his gaze sliding over the stools and the waitresses like fluid, dead-tired, like he's seen this scene too many times and is sick of it, his eyes lingering on the few faces like he knows what he is looking for and where it is but doesn't want to come to it, yet. *Or maybe it's just me,* Nalla thinks, fighting the urge to light another cigarette. Then the man approaches them, to her surprise, and slides into the booth, sitting next to her.

"Hello, Jonah," Cyan says.

"Cyan." The man looks at him, takes a deep breath as if to say something, reconsiders, looks at her. "Hello."

Nalla stares at him, mouth agape. "Well," she says. She looks at Cyan. "Someone sure recovers fast."

"It's not like that," Cyan says.

Nalla raises an eyebrow. "Oh, please. You're rich enough to have a Zoner. Share a little! Are you into three-ways, sir?"

Jonah shrinks back, looks at Cyan, takes a deep breath.

"It's not like that," Cyan says again, but Nalla doesn't care anymore. She has been insulted.

"You drive away my only hope for pay tonight and now you bring me to the seediest diner you can find just to parade a customer I can't have," she says quickly and softly. "I have to applaud your creativity."

"Nalla, it's not—"

"Let me guess," Nalla says, jutting her chin at Jonah's direction. "You're an old customer."

Jonah shakes his head.

"A former Caller?"

"No."

"Um, a mentor? Benefactor?" Nalla makes circular gestures with her hands. "Brother?"

"Just a friend," Jonah says.

"Oh," she says. "I don't get it."

Nobody speaks for a moment. Jonah looks at Nalla as if she were a new species. Nalla hates him already.

Jonah says, "Is there a problem, Cyan? Your call sounded urgent."

Something in Jonah's voice sounds concerned but stern, as though he's annoyed but is just too polite, or too weary, to show it.

Nalla looks at Cyan and sees that he has picked it up, too; it is all over his face.

"Is it money, Cyan?" Jonah says. "Because if it is, I—hello?"

Nalla notices that Jonah also has a Zoner, only he has the smaller, more expensive kind, no larger than an ear plug, Version VX something-or-other, with holo-capabilities and wider range. Jonah's eyes shine blue, and he starts grinning like a fool. "Of course," he says. "Of course." A moment later his eyes turn black again and the grin disappears. "Sorry about that. Justin needs a ride home. Would you like to hop in? We can talk in the Skyscraper."

"You have a Skyscraper?" Nalla exclaims, unable to contain herself. She slaps Cyan's hand playfully. "Why do you get all the Area Lords?"

"Justin?" Cyan says almost at the same time.

"Yes." The grin comes back, and Jonah fights it, unsuccessfully. "I fought for custody."

"Huh," Cyan says.

"He saw Maui with a Fleshie and—"

Cyan stares at him. Nalla still cannot make heads nor tails of the conversation. She itches for a cigarette.

Jonah scratches his forehead, refusing to meet Cyan's eyes. "I didn't mean it to sound like—"

Cyan lowers his gaze and stares at his folded hands on the tabletop.

"I mean, if you're going to come with me to Justin's school, you can't tell him that you're—"

"Who is Justin?" says Nalla. But nobody answers.

"Is it money?" Jonah asks again, almost eagerly, like he wanted to redeem himself.

"No, it's okay," Cyan says, to Nalla's disbelief. "I'll call again."

"Here it is anyway," Jonah says, laying a card on the table. "I have to go get Justin."

Jonah stands up and walks to the door. He pauses long enough for a person to change his mind but Cyan waves his hand, waving goodbye, shooing him away. Nalla looks out the window, watching Jonah walk from light to dark to light, his jacket cut into pieces by the glare.

When she turns back to face the table Cyan is already eyeing the card like he wants to burn it.

"Let's get out of here," he says. They stand up and the robot waitress comes to life, startling the customers sitting on the stools by the counter. "Thank you for coming to—" she starts to say, but something twangs and she slumps over. Something that happens all the time, thinks Nalla, because the human waitresses walk around her, saying, "Coffee? More coffee?"

They've gone back to the Puso Theater, to the steps. Cyan wants Nalla to choose where to go—a bar, a resort, anywhere, he's sure Jonah's card can handle anything—but Nalla suddenly feels too exhausted and can't decide.

A neat-looking man with a briefcase approaches them and says, "Uh—"

"Sorry, sir," says Nalla. "It's our day-off."

Oh, the man says voicelessly, and walks away like he has a flight to catch.

"I'm sick, Nalla," Cyan says.

She sits up. "What?"

"I'm sick," Cy repeats. "I have Walker's Disease."

Walker's Disease. The deadly WD. In Japan, where it started, they call it AIDS-II.

"You got it from Dave?"

Cy nods.

"Where'd he get it?"

"Oh, I don't know. He travels. Maybe he went to Tokyo or Taiwan." Cy smirks. "Danced with somebody."

Nalla fiddles with the cigarette packet. "Are you doing okay?"

"He knew," Cy says, not hearing her. "He knew he had it but he still wants to spread it around. What kind of monster would do such a thing?"

Nalla pries the packet open and pulls out a stick.

"I'm just glad I caught him in time," Cy says, looking at her. "Before—before he—"

Nalla lights up the cigarette and pulls a long, deep drag. She spews the smoke and smiles at him.

"Please," Cyan says. "Please tell me you didn't sleep with him."

Nalla's smile trembles at the edges. She shakes her head.

Fresh tears roll down Cyan's face.

"I'm sorry." Cy takes her free hand in both of his. "Nalla, I'm so sorry."

"It's okay, you know," she tells him. "I knew this would happen sooner or later." She pulls her hand away. "Didn't you?"

A softdrink commercial comes on the Net, and all the windows of the buildings and the passing cars turn blue, washing the ground with blue. It's like the city is taking a call on a Zoner Clip, ignoring them.

"So," Cyan says, sniffling, "have you decided where you want to go?" He brandishes the card in front of her eyes. "This is a gold mine."

Nalla laughs.

"Come on," Cyan says, pulling her up and down to the sidewalk.

"Where are we going?"

"Oh, I don't know. Anywhere." Cyan looks up at the air cars, his hand poised. He laughs as though the cars have said something funny. "Australia."

Nalla stands close to him. The commercial ends, and the city regains color so abruptly that Nalla has to shut her eyes for a second.

"Australia sounds good," Nalla says, opening her eyes, and Cyan smiles at her and raises his hand.

# An Abduction By
## Mermaids

The day the mermaids appeared on the surface of the river in his hometown, David was too busy figuring out how to get a copy of an NBI clearance as soon as possible. The one in Carriedo required an NSO-authenticated birth certificate. To get *that*, David thought bitterly and wearily, entailed shelling out Php125 thrice. HR wouldn't accept photocopies *so that means I have to pay around four hundred* and half a day of sitting in that sad East Ave. office with the wooden benches and the dark and the people who assume automatically that you want to leave the country. David *did* have a copy of his birth certificate, only it was frayed and torn and looked like a flat sheet of butter, being as old as he was. It was sitting at the bottom of his sock drawer in his family's house in Bulacan, a tricycle ride away from the river full of mermaids.

*Or,* David thought, he could go home to Bulacan, get his birth certificate, and bring *that* to the NBI office in Plaridel. NBI branches were less stringent than the main office. *But the thing is,* David thought again, backtracking mentally but feeling the fatigue settle on his shoulders, *if I had a namesake in the records I'd have to wait for a week.* A week, and David Cruz wasn't an extraordinary name. Surely a David Cruz somewhere, sometime, has murdered or raped someone.

David felt exhausted thinking about it all. When his mother's call came, he was writing TO FOLLOW opposite NBI CLEARANCE on his requirements checklist, fighting the urge to add IN A HUNDRED YEARS OR SO.

"There were what," David said, softly, into his cell phone, not because he wanted to be polite; everyone in the office was barking orders into telephone receivers, at fax machines, or at computers that were too slow, so it didn't matter whether he screamed at his mother or threw his phone at the floor-to-ceiling windows surrounding the cubicles, which was what he was aching to do. When he heard the steady drone of his mother's voice, he knew everything was hopeless. Again he wondered how it had come to this. Again he wondered why he didn't just change his SIM card, why he even gave her his number.

"Mermaids, David," his mother said. She said she saw one when she went out with Agnes to the market yesterday. The boats were pulling in, it was very early, and there was a mermaid in the shallower parts of the river. "The *ilados* and that noisy *tindig* didn't see her because they were too busy counting the *kalakal* and hauling off the coolers."

Her mother said Agnes went out again yesterday night. "She saw five," David's mother said. "She told me. The moon was full, and she saw five of them.

"And now Agnes is gone," his mother said, sobbing now.

"David," an editor called. "David!" David turned away from his computer monitor, head canted at an angle to keep his cell phone from falling off his shoulder. "David!" A press release was stuck in one of the fax machines. "Storify this one once you figure out how to remove the damn thing," the editor said. "I need this ASAP. Inside pages, okay?"

"I woke up this morning and she's gone," his mother said in his ear. "Your sister's *gone.*"

David knew he was supposed to feel guilty, but he had been feeling guilty for many years now, and he believed he'd had enough. "I don't need this right now, Mother," David said, and stood up to get the damn press release out of the stupid machine.

"So how's your first month?" Monica said when they met up at lunch break. Sam was already there, staring at the TV. ANC's on. ANC's always on. CNN, sometimes. *Eat Bulaga!*, on rare occasions. There was a cafeteria on the ground floor, but Monica and Sam—they did layouts—ate at the round table in the middle of all the cubicles and the computers and the wires, surrounded by stacks of first edition newspapers. Their food came from the free lunch at the editorial meeting, which, according to Sam, did not taste bad but was not spectacular either. Monica told David to get some from the buffet, but David had already ordered take-out from McDonald's.

David was employed as an editorial assistant. His tasks included writing the kind of stuff that the reporters couldn't be bothered with, like that press release, or the occasional obituary, and basically being ordered around by any of the seven editors present on that floor. The skills required in his job included, but were not limited to, pressing F5 on his keyboard to refresh the company email, which was where the reporters sent their stories, looking at the wall clock immediately above his workstation so as to know what time to put when logging in the articles as they came, and waiting, waiting, waiting, until all the articles were sent and all the editors/reporters/researchers/outsiders sufficiently pampered. He believed he had the longest time-out range in the entire building: between 7 p.m. and 2 a.m.

On his first week on the job he had already downloaded several gigabytes of free online games and the most inane sitcom episodes from YouTube to keep him company during the empty hours.

"*Uy*," Sam said, nodding at David when he sat down. He and Sam started working on the same day, but Sam had already given HR all of the requirements. David thought of Bulacan, birth certificates, NBI, his mother. Agnes. David suddenly wanted to sleep.

"All right, so far," David told Monica, who smiled approvingly. "Still alive." David wondered why Monica even bothered to ask him this every single day. He always said the same thing.

They ate. "Can somebody tell me why the 'Inside' box is on the *second page?*" a female editor said to no one in particular. She clutched today's edition of the newspaper in one hand. "Why tell me what's 'inside' when I'm already *inside?*"

David saw Sam heave a deep sigh, but said nothing.

"Honest mistake," Monica whispered, now also staring intently at ANC. The news said it rained hailstones in Quezon City just that morning.

"Damn it," Sam said.

"Oh come on, Sam."

*"Damn it."*

"Hailstones, huh," David said.

Monica glanced briefly at him. "Maybe it's the end of the world."

My sister saw five mermaids last night, David thought, but didn't say. He offered some fries, but nobody wanted them.

"I've heard of weirder stuff," Sam said, who had apparently already recovered from the lashing. The female editor thumped the newspaper on her desk and sat down, fixing her makeup. "I have a cousin who takes up Socio. They do immersions, ethnography, that sort of stuff. Once they went to this town, which was cursed—"

"Cursed," Monica said, still looking at the TV. One of the editors fired up a cigarette and changed the channel, switching to a soccer game.

"Cursed," Sam said, nodding. "My cousin and his classmates stayed there the whole day. They mingled with the townsfolk, ate their food, went to the local chapel. Everything appears normal. The town looked like just any old town—"

"Where is this?" asked Monica.

Sam shrugged. "So by sunset they said good bye. The town mayor went with them to the town exit, you know, that place with the arc marking the boundary—"

"Yes, yes, yes, yes." Monica said, her eyes on Sam. Either she was excited about the story's climax or she wanted to say something. David glanced at the TV screen, watched the ball weave around feet and legs, so much green surprising his eyes. The editor smoked.

"When the sun set," said Sam, "the town captain walked back into the town *on his hands.*" Sam smiled. "Apparently, that's their curse: everyone in that town, come sunset, will walk on their hands. Isn't that fucked?"

"And they don't get bothered by it?" Monica asked. She made a face. "This *sinampalukang manok* is horrendous."

"No," said Sam. "My cousin said the people there walked on their hands like it's the most normal thing in the world. They just watched from the arc, of course. They were too scared. I can have the chicken if you don't want it. You can have my *daing*."

David watched Monica and Sam fish into each other's plates. "Man, their palms must've hurt like hell every morning."

"Yes. You know, we should pitch this story at the editorial meeting."

"Oh. Yes. For colors."

"Why were they cursed?" David asked.

Monica and Sam looked at him as though surprised he was still sitting there.

"I don't know," Sam said. "It's like a long time ago they killed a witch's kid. Something like that."

"I know another fucked up story," Monica said. "Although this is truly fucked up, because yours is at least based on some real curse. Unless your cousin was high on rugby when he went on immersion."

"That sounds plausible," Sam said. They went on to make jokes out of the words "drugs" and "immerse" and "rugby", until they ran out of wit. David looked at his fries, took one, chewed on it without tasting it.

"I know it happened in Bulacan," Monica said, automatically looking at David. No, David wanted to say, don't look at me. I don't know the province like the back of my hand. No, I haven't heard of it, whatever it is. No, I've been there only once in the past four years so it is impossible that I—

No, I don't want to go back there ever again.

"San Miguel?" said Monica. David shrugged.

"Anyhow, a barangay there," Monica continued. "There's this river, all right. Every year, people drown in that river. Townspeople believe it's cursed. The people it takes are sacrifices for some past atrocity their ancestors committed. One day, they found that there were people under the river who pull those who swim there to their deaths—"

"Mermaids?" Sam chirped. David flinched.

"No," Monica said. "*People*. Employees of the local funeral parlor. They were killing people for profit."

*"No."*

"Yes," Monica said. "Google it. I think GMA made a report about it a week or so ago."

Silence. "That *is* fucked," said Sam.

"I know, right?" Monica said. "I wonder how they can sleep at night."

"That must have made the superstitious want to hide their faces."

Monica laughed.

"I know there's a place in Batangas, or, I don't know, somewhere in Central Luzon. You know, like an open field." Sam gestured 'an open field' with his arms, "where you can hear your own voice speaking to you at midnight."

"Brrrrr," Monica said, shivering. "Now *that's* scary. What will it tell you?"

"Stuff about the other side."

"In your own voice?"

"Yep."

Monica shivered again, without the vocal equivalent.

David wondered what his voice would say if he had stood on that field.

*Hello,* David imagined himself saying in the darkness. *Hello there. Speak up.* If I had known this place existed I would have saved myself an awful lot of time.

Back in his hometown, he and three of his good friends—Sarah, Marco, and Marco's younger brother Allen—were Red Cross volunteers. The chapter in their barangay held seminars every other Saturday. They decided to sign up high school senior year (Allen's freshman year) for the free lunch and the chance to blow air into the old Red Cross CPR dummy, whose mouth tasted unsurprisingly like a thick wad of rubber bands. Their concern for extracurricular points came later. When their adviser did the tallies for high school graduation one of them was as good as dead and so they hardly cared anymore.

What started it all was that early morning in December when they were hanging out by the river after the mass, when one of the fishermen's children fell off the boats while the coolers were being hauled off. Marco dove in and carried the boy back, then "breathed life into him", as Sarah phrased it.

It wasn't the fact that Marco just saved a life that stuck to them, the way the December chill stuck to their bodies. What they carried home was the fact that the boy, when he came to, said he saw a small white dot on the top of Allen's head. The white dot was actually on Allen's scalp, white against his thick black hair, a scar from a fall when he was young.

What the boy Marco just saved was saying was that he floated above everybody, that he left his body when he drowned and flew.

They've heard of near-death experiences before, of course. Who hasn't? But the boy's confession innocent, firsthand.

Marco and Allen were orphans. It always bothered them that they couldn't know for sure whether their parents were still around in spirit, whether they could hear them whenever they spoke to them. Their maternal grandparents believed in the afterlife with fervor, but Marco and Allen didn't care much for their grandparents.

David couldn't now remember who initiated that first suicide. His best guess was Marco, but it could have also been Allen, or Sarah, with all the books she'd read about how many minutes the body could safely stay dead before revival and so on.

David remembered it wasn't him, but now he wasn't sure.

David remembered that it led to another chilly December stay by the river, this time at the dead of night, and this time not by the marketplace where all the boats docked, but farther, past three barangays into the next town. They rode in Sarah's father's tricycle, driven by Marco, the cold wind rushing at them, every whoosh like a laceration. Sarah told his father that they were just going to finish a project in Marco's house, and Sarah's father trusted Marco enough not to phone his and Allen's grandparents to check.

They brought flashlights, spare batteries, towels, spare clothes. For the 'project', Sarah told her father.

Marco parked the tricycle by the river in that other town and asked his brother, "Are you sure you want to do this?"

"Can you carry David?" Allen said, grinning. "With Sarah I don't think you'd dare."

Sarah would have hit him with a fist, but that night she simply tested the flashlights and took out the towels.

David tried to read Marco's expression, but it was too dark.

"Yes," Allen said then, and before they knew it they were pouring out of the tricycle and Marco and Allen were wading into the river—"I can't feel my balls!" Allen shouted gleefully—with David following a few feet behind.

He looked back once: Sarah stayed by the tricycle, spreading one of the towels on the ground with the flashlight lit and held in place with her chin, her face shining like a ghost from a movie.

Marco stopped when he thought it was deep enough and held Allen underwater until he stopped floundering, which seemed to David like a long, long time.

Then they were running back, Marco holding Allen's head and shoulders and David carrying his feet. They lay him on the towel, and Marco administered CPR. There was a moment when David thought all three of them would crack: Sarah was already crying and Marco screaming like someone deranged—*Allen, Allen, Allen, come on*—but then Allen gasped and coughed and everything was fine.

The first thing Allen did after he got over the coughing fit was cry his lungs out.

"What?" Marco said, shaking him gently. "What is it?"

Allen said he saw their parents.

They obsessed over it for weeks and weeks. They didn't want to do it in the river again—they caught colds and Allen ran a slight fever—and naturally they couldn't hang themselves or cut themselves because that would leave marks. So David smothered Marco with a pillow one day and Sarah the next.

Marco said he saw his father sitting beside him, with that grin he remembered, that grin that seemed to ask: what are you boys up to *now?*

Sarah said she saw a light, which comforted her.

(It comforted her so much that she sought it years after that, until she jumped from the twenty-first floor of a hotel, junior year college. She and David attended the same university; he heard of the jump from the TV and covered the event himself for the college paper. In the article, he talked of her like he didn't know her.)

Allen wanted to do it again, so Marco straddled him in his bedroom and covered his face with a pillow. It took a very long time to revive him, and it affected his brain. Something about oxygen deprivation; David didn't listen to the doctor closely. Allen lost the ability to speak, and Marco was shattered. Naturally, the 'project' had to stop.

It was Marco who smothered him, David remembered well.

David saw nothing.

There was that struggle, then darkness, then he was breathing hard, staring at the ceiling, gasping for air on the bed with Marco holding his face saying, Easy, easy.

David didn't lie to them. He said he saw nothing.

David said, *I feel cheated.*

On that field, will his voice answer him? David wondered.

There is nothing here, it might say.

It might say, This is all there is.

David knew Agnes wasn't abducted by mermaids not only because he didn't believe in mermaids but because Agnes had been dead for nearly three months now.

Agnes killed herself. She hung herself with one of her black stockings in her bedroom one afternoon when no one was home.

Their father saw her first, coming home fresh from a K of C meeting.

Their father wasn't a Red Cross volunteer, so he didn't know how to do CPR. In any case, CPR wouldn't work because Agnes had already broken her trachea the moment she kicked the chair from under her.

So it didn't matter that David wasn't there to help cut her down or 'breathe life' into her.

David blamed himself anyway.

David guessed it was the grades. Their mother was a control freak. David saw, when the mail from the university finally arrived, that Agnes had to retake three electives because she failed to pass the finals. Agnes was two years younger and taking up Computer Science, a far cry from Journalism. David didn't care much about her. Even during their high school days they were never close. David had Red Cross and his three friends; Agnes had Physics tutorials and books and the TV.

Their last interaction was on David's first day as an official unemployed college graduate, and Agnes's sophomore year, a week before her suicide. They met outside SM North EDSA because Agnes wanted to borrow David's laptop, which annoyed David no end because he needed the computer to fix his resume and portfolio.

"So when can I have it back?" David snapped when they met. Agnes said something about having to rush three papers, which made David's blood boil even more. Agnes sounded like it's his fault she couldn't write her papers on schedule.

"And *kuya*," she said, "can I borrow money? I have this project that's *so* costly I—"

"Are you crazy?" David said. "I'm job-hunting. Why don't you ask Mother for money? Why do you always have to come to me?"

David was indignant, but he knew, deep down, that he was also ashamed he couldn't even spare his sister a few hundreds when she needed it.

"Okay," Agnes said, and shuffled away with his laptop. *Okay* was Agnes' last word to him, her last word to him on the planet. Okay. She said it with a sigh, with a tone that said, *At least I tried.*


Marco was present at the burial, and he cried harder than David's parents when the casket was shut and lowered. David didn't cry at all.

"I didn't really see him," Marco told him, sobbing. "I didn't really see my father when you—I just said it because Allen was so happy and I didn't want—"

Marco looked at Agnes's casket being covered with dirt, looked at the hole like it was the most horrifying thing in the world.

"You said you didn't see anything," Marco said. "David—"

Marco looked at the casket fast disappearing beneath the dirt, and touched his shoulder. "David, I am so—"

*"What?"* David said sharply, jerking his body away from Marco's touch. "What else do you want from me?"

"Let's bring these back," Monica said, collecting her plate. They stood up. David looked at the leftover fries and the mound of ketchup, rolled them all up with both hands.

"Yes. I still have two pages to finish."

"Yes. And maybe *this* time you can put the 'Inside' box on the front page."

"Fuck you."

"Who wrote this article?" an editor asked.

David cursed under his breath.

"You," the editor said. "Were you present at the orientation?"

Monica and Sam scurried away.

"Yes, sir," David said.

"And what's our policy about direct lifting?"

I didn't lift from the press release, David protested in his head. I wrote my own lead, I looked at previous articles, I—

"Sir, I didn't—"

Or did he?

"You've wasted enough of my time already," the editor said.

This is the part where I'm supposed to blow up, David thought, but he was too tired. He threw the rest of his lunch into the trash and urged his finger to work. F5, F5, F5.

No new news blew up after 7 pm, so the banner stayed, and David got home early. It didn't matter; he rented a bed in a boarding house filled with college boys. The house was empty when he got home, being a Friday. All of a sudden, he missed his roommate, a law student named Carlos. David normally hated him because Carlos couldn't stop talking about himself—throw him a question, any question, like, "How many units are you taking this sem?" and off he would go, as though he were arguing passionately before a judge, tackling not only his 'toxic semester' but his favorite professors and his abilities and the awards he took home while in undergrad and on and on, making David avoid asking him *anything* at all costs. Now, there was only the sound of cars passing outside and David wanted to hear a voice other than his own.

He got his wish after taking a shower. He was about to go to bed when he found his cell phone flopping around on his bed like a fish.

"Yes, Mother," David said.

"Oh, Bert, he's awake!" his mother said to someone else. "David? David?"

David didn't reply.

"David," his mother said, tearing up again. "About Agnes—"

"She's dead, Mother," David said.

"No, no," his mother said. "The mermaids—"

"She's *dead*."

A brief silence before she began sobbing. David heard the phone change hands. For a long while his father didn't say anything.

"You could have tried to be nice to her," his father said.

David wanted to scream. She's losing her mind, you dumb fuck, don't you get that? *Why don't you do something?*

But David so wanted to sleep, and the house was so oppressively mute, so he ended the call. He thought of the line, lines, he had to wait in after tonight, thought of his stupid job, his measly salary, his mother, the brokenness he was going to inherit after his father passed on. The nothing that comes after, the nothing that Agnes was in now, because there are no mermaids, there is no comforting light.

David cried, clutching his cell phone with both hands, sobbing so hard his chest ached.

David dreamt that night. In the dream, he was standing waist-deep in the river of his hometown. He believed, without a doubt, as men are wont to believe without a doubt in dreams, that he would find his sister if he looked down into the water. He knew he would see her face, if he looked close enough.

# Sand, Crushed Shells, Chicken Feathers

The streets were still wet from the heavy downpour of an hour ago, and already it was starting to drizzle again, the sky getting ready. Zachary looked up. No stars, no moon, nothing but black. In the distance, darker spots passed for clouds. It was midnight, the cigarette in his mouth was starting to die, and he was pissed because today was his third overtime of the week and he didn't have an umbrella and he had to wade through ankle-deep Ortigas flood just to get on a bus. He put the hood of his drenched jacket over his eyes, spat out the stick between his lips, and lit himself another cigarette. The feel of the flame against his cupped palm reminded him of how cold he was. This is what you get, he thought, for living in a different city, for still living on campus, for being too lazy to go house-hunting.

The apartment building where they lived stood a block from the university bookstore. The bookstore was the only well-lit building on the street, and from the light coming from it Zachary could see a shadow standing by the gate to the apartment. Zachary walked on, taking a drag from his cigarette as he did, and coughed in surprise when he saw that it was John.

"Zac!" John said when he heard the sound. His eyes were red-rimmed. He had been crying. And from the looks of his hair and his jacket, it appeared that John had also been standing in the rain for some time.

"What's the matter?" Zachary said. "What are you doing out here?" He wondered if something had happened to John's parents. His father. That heart attack John had been worrying about ever since Emma died.

"They took my cell phone," John said.

"What?" Zachary said, and stepped closer. He looked over his shoulder, scanning the area: waving trees and puddles on the ground glinting in the dark like teeth. He took a deep breath and felt his lungs fill with ice. He looked his friend over. "Are you hurt?"

John had been talking but he wasn't able to hear. "John," Zac said.

"I said, it's not like they snatched it," John said, shaking now. "I was trying to dress one of them, and it was in the pocket of my shorts, I hope—"

John was crying.

Zachary clutched his arm. "John."

"I just hope they figure out how to use it."

"John," Zachary said, nudging him. "John, you're not making sense. Who are we talking about here?"

"*Them!*" John shouted. "Aren't you listening? There were two of them. They panicked when they saw themselves. I don't know where they went, I've been trying to look for them for hours—"

Zachary liked John. They had known each other and had shared an apartment ever since they were college freshmen, but he was getting tired of playing nurse. "John," he said, trying to keep his voice calm, "why don't we get inside. We're both drenched, and it's going to be pouring soon. Let's figure it out in the morning." Zachary glanced at his watch and saw that it *was* morning, just ten minutes past twelve.

John wouldn't budge. "I have to find them," he said. "This is my fault."

"For goodness' sake, John," Zachary said, and let his arm go. John's arm plopped against his side, and he staggered back. "I don't know what this is about. Is it a girl? Is this what you're trying to say? Did she take something from you?"

His phone rang. John looked wide-eyed with hope. Zachary pulled his phone from his jeans pocket, flipped it open. John's name was on the screen.

"Well, will you look at that," Zachary said. He pushed a button and put the phone to his ear. John was quietly saying Please, please, please. "Hello?"

A rush of wind. Someone was breathing hard on the other end of the line.

"Hello?"

"There's a wall here."

It was a girl's voice. Her voice came to him hollow and tiny. She must have been shouting, but was holding the cell phone away from her mouth. Zachary wanted to punch John in the face.

"Who is this, please?" Zachary said, glancing at his friend and shaking his head.

*What?*, John mouthed, and said, "Are they saying anything?"

"There's a wall here. We can't get through it." Zachary almost dropped his phone. The girl had suddenly placed the phone next to her mouth, the tail-end of her sentence reaching his ear as a frightened scream. "I don't understand why this place won't let us go."


John said he heard voices in the apartment. All sorts of voices. He confided in Zachary when Zachary wouldn't quit urging him to go to the doctor about his headaches. "It's just these voices," John said. "They're too loud." Zachary must have looked at him a second too long. "I'm not *nuts*," John insisted.

"All right, then," Zachary said. "What are they saying?"

"I don't know," John said. It was junior year, finals week. John was lying on his side on the bed, facing the wall. Zachary was sitting on the floor, surrounded by bags of chips, soda cans, photocopied readings, all of these illuminated by John's gooseneck lamp.

"I don't understand them," John went on. "It's like they're speaking a foreign language."

Zachary pulled a sheaf of papers toward him and studied them. "Aren't you taking French 1 this semester?"

John lifted his head a little and glanced at him. "I knew I shouldn't have said anything."

Zachary laughed, then stopped. "Look, I'm sorry," he said. "John…"

A beat. "What."

"Do they scare you?"

John thought for a moment. "No."

"No?"

John sat up, joined Zachary on the floor, and began sorting through his readings, stacking them in neat piles. From time to time he would pause and cock his head, as though listening to something, waiting for advice. "No," he said again, too strongly, as though someone was contradicting him.

John was fascinated by the supernatural. He would gravitate toward the films, watch the documentaries, read the books, even talk to people about it—a habit which, depending on the setting, proved both beneficial and disastrous to his relationships. He played bass for a University-based goth band till their sophomore year, and seemed to be the only member in the band who actually believed in the lyrics of their songs.

Zachary, on the other hand, didn't buy any of it. The supernatural wasn't completely foreign to him; his grandmother came from Cagayan Valley and whenever she came for a visit she would tell him of the many times she had fallen victim to *kulam*. That time her back itched, and whenever she scratched her skin her fingernails would come away filled with sand, crushed shells, chicken feathers. In that story it was a scorned lover's revenge, the problem of her itchy back solved by an *albularyo*'s counterspell. In the other stories she'd tell him of boils, limbs temporarily frozen and worthless, the handiwork of jealous neighbors, disinherited relatives.

The stories were interesting, all of them, but Zachary wasn't there when sand (and shells and feathers) seeped through the pores of his grandmother's inflamed skin, so Zachary didn't buy any of it. He found John's enthusiasm hilarious and immature, the goth band's music horrendous. "But at least," he told John once, "I'll always have someone at hand whenever my date needs to re-apply her eyeliner."

John didn't find that funny at all.

One weekend during their senior year, John failed to come home to the apartment. Zachary didn't even realize he wasn't home until John showed up at the door on Monday at two in the morning, slightly bleeding from a gash on his forehead, his arms dirty and filled with cuts. John looked as if he had just pulled himself out of a deep hole in the ground. Zachary sat him down on the couch and went into the kitchen to get some paper towels. From the corner of his eye he saw John reach up—

This was the part where his memory broke down, every time he told himself this story. At this point he would remember that he saw John reach up and pull a piece of white cloth from thin air. That was impossible of course, so he would try recalling that moment a second time, and this time he would see John opening his bag, taking out a towel to hold against the wound on his face. This version was more logical, and therefore more acceptable.

"Is that clean?" he had asked John that Monday morning, and John had said, "As clean as it can ever be." John came back somewhat changed after that lost weekend: quieter, more pensive, more susceptible to panic. After graduation they applied as copywriters to the same ad agency and got accepted, and Zachary saw that John got along well enough with the other people at the office. He was okay, same old John, just more silent. So Zachary never stopped to ask, Where did you go during that weekend? Why did you come back with cuts on your arms?

Emma was John's sister, four years old. Zachary met her only once, two weeks into the new job, when John's folks came over for a visit. She zipped across the room like a tornado and hung onto his leg, saying, "Hello, *Kuya*!" *Kuya* Zac, she called him, after John told her his name. One school day she sat on a defective swing at the playground, pushed herself up, and fell, tangled up in rusting chains that broke off the swing's frame. She hit her head upon impact and died instantly.

Emma's death silenced the other voices in the apartment. Now all John could hear was Emma. One afternoon after the burial Zachary found him sitting in the living room. The TV was on, the volume turned up high enough to be heard in the other apartments, and yet John continued pushing the button, watching the green bar fill the bottom of the screen. Zachary took the remote from him and switched off the TV.

"You want to talk about it?" he told John.

"Emma's crying," John said. "She misses Mother."

"Why won't she just come visit your mother, then."

"She said they couldn't hear."

Zachary didn't know what to make of him. Sometimes, when he felt generous, he'd coax John out of the building, and they would play ball, watch a movie, waste time playing online games inside a coffee shop. People have different ways of dealing with grief, but he was starting to think that maybe what John was going through was something clinical, more serious, something that needed a prescription and a lot of pills, quick. And yet he couldn't bring himself to say it. Whenever John's parents called to ask how their son was doing, Zachary could only say, "He talks about Emma a lot."


"What is this about, John?" Zachary said. The girl was still on the line; sooner or later the battery would run out, the cell phone would die in her hand, and perhaps tomorrow after the storm the guards would find her half-naked on the soccer field, wasted and deranged, but Zachary was losing his patience. He thought he deserved to waste a few more seconds.

They were indeed wasted. John just stared at him. He seemed deranged—from panic or lack of sleep or unnecessary medication, Zachary could only guess.

"Just stay where you are, miss," Zachary said into the phone, staring hard at John's face. "What's your name?"

He was answered by a sob.

"Just stay," Zachary said, enunciating the words carefully, "where you are. We'll go get you. Did you see where she ran?"

This question directed at John. "No," John said.

Zachary clucked his tongue and looked about. "She said something about a wall." The street they were standing on ended at a cul-de-sac. "Come on."

They started walking, away from the light of the bookstore and past the apartment building where dry clothes and a cup of coffee waited. He didn't hang up. He had placed the phone inside his jacket pocket. He could hear the girl crying. Zachary took a deep breath to steady himself. The last time this happened they were still in college, John still wore eyeliner, and it was only pot.

"This isn't just pot, is it?" Zachary said. The rain was coming down harder now. Zachary swore and threw away his cigarette. To their left, an empty lot, trees, grass. To their right, a professor's house. The professor must have been on vacation because the house was completely unlit—normally they'd leave at least the porch lights on—and the orchids and flowers on his front yard appeared to be dying. The rain hammered against them, pushing them deeper into their pots.

More empty lots. A lonely lamppost, which too quickly disappeared from their view as they moved forward. More trees. To their right, an old one-story building, an abandoned kindergarten, the doors and windows shuttered. Zachary was on the side of the street closer to it and he bristled at the sight of decaying wood, the broken glass. *Kuya* Zac, he imagined hearing Emma. He imagined Emma standing beside that closed door, luminous in her school uniform, waving her hand.

It was too dark and Zachary was starting to get frightened and he didn't like it. "You said there were two of them?" he said to John. "Two girls?"

"The other one's a guy," said John.

Zachary had to stop walking for a moment. "What?"

"It looked like a guy." John had stopped walking as well. Zachary took his upper arm and pushed him forward, and they fell in step with each other once again. The kindergarten fell behind. Zachary fought the urge to look back.

"My God," he said. "What in the world did you guys take?"

"Zac, it isn't like that."

"Talk to me when you're not high anymore, okay? *Jesus.*"

They had run out of pavement. In front of them was a wall, but there was nobody there.

"Great." Zachary took the phone out of his pocket. "Hello? Are you still there?"

"They won't let us go," the girl said.

"Can you describe your surroundings to me? Can you see a—can you see a building? Some sort of landmark?" Zachary started thinking, What if they're not on-campus? What if they're not even in the damn city?

"There are people here."

"What?"

"They're surrounding us. They won't let us through." She sounded out of breath. "They're just staring at us."

Zachary held his head. "What did you take?" he wanted to ask John, but John had disappeared. He swung around and found him sitting on the ground, his back to the cement wall, crying into his bent knee.

"John," Zachary said, screaming down at him. "Come on—what did you take?" Zachary was thinking acid, some party pill, but where would John get that? He wondered if they had a pusher at the office.

John wouldn't answer. "Miss?" Zachary said. "These people. Can you describe them to me?"

"They're just staring at us. They're surrounding us. They won't let us through."

"What do they look like?"

"They change," the girl said. "The shadows fall on them, and they change."

"Have you tried speaking to them?"

"I don't want to."

"Just try, all right?"

There was a silence, then: "Hello? *Hello?*" The girl's voice came through so clearly that even John looked up. "Hello? Please, let us go. We don't understand anything." Pause. "They're not answering."

"Well, that's because they're not real," Zachary said, unable to help himself. "John, I swear—"

The girl said: "Why are they staring at us?" It must be a slight change in the tone of her voice; somehow Zachary could tell that she wasn't talking to him this time.

The voice that answered her was male. Zac could hear him faintly from the other line. "Because they can see us."

"We need to get away from here," the girl said to him.

"No!" Zachary shouted. "No! Just stay where you are!"

Either John's phone had finally died, or the girl had hung up.

"John," Zachary said. He was so tired he felt as if his legs would give in. "John, get up. We need to go to the police. Do you know their names? *First* names, at least?"

"I don't know who they are," John said. "I don't know *what* they are."

John was crying like a child: loudly, shamelessly. His jacket didn't have a hood, so the rain fell directly on his head, plastering his hair to his skull, the water rolling down his face. Zachary felt sorry for him. He helped him to his feet and kept his arm around his waist, guiding him gently away from the wall, the dark cul-de-sac, the abandoned kindergarten.

They were nearing the lamppost when John said, "I was trying to materialize Emma, just Emma. I was trying to make her appear in flesh out of thin air. But instead, those two appeared. I don't know who they are."

Zachary moved away from him with a jolt, as if John were live wire. "What are you talking about, John," he said, but the moment he said it he saw John pulling cloth from thin air, telling him, *It's as clean as it can ever be.*

"They've got to be people," John said. "Right? They've got to be people before. Zac, I don't know who they are."

"Where'd you get the drugs, John?" Zachary said, and John turned away from him in distress. "John, just tell me. I won't say anything to your parents."

A girl was coming from the trees behind the lamppost, running toward them, toward light. She was wearing one of John's old shirts, and a pair of shorts that sagged because they were too big for her.

She was barefoot. There was blood on the front of the shirt, her bare arms. They couldn't tell for sure, but the blood didn't seem to be coming from her own skin.

The rain was washing off some of the blood, and Zachary could see that she was holding John's cell phone in one of her hands. There's something wrong with her skin, Zachary thought. That faint glow. He decided that it was just the lamppost, his eyes playing tricks on him, this crazy night.

"Where's the other one?" John asked her. Her eyes and mouth were open and she was pushing her arms to their faces, as though showing off the blood, daring them to touch her. She cried. She said a name with a sound they would remember, but would never be able to pronounce.

Zachary snatched the phone from her hand. "Let's go, John," he said, pushing John back.

"We can't leave her here."

The girl was looking at her arms. She touched her skin, pulled at it, and let out a frightened shriek, as though horrified it wouldn't come off, that she was inside it, that it was too much a part of her. She fell to her knees. The shriek turned into a scream, and even John moved back.

She was looking at John as she tugged at her arms. Please, she said. But what does she want? Zachary thought. She was still speaking even as he grabbed John by both arms and dragged him away. The apartment building was silent. Zachary frantically looked for the keys in his bag when they reached their floor, only to find out that John had left their door unlocked. When Zachary flicked on the lights John rushed past him, almost tripped on a chair, but reached the bathroom just in time. Zachary peeled off his jacket and sat outside the bathroom door, listening to John retch, cough, and throw up something liquid. John heaved air and fell silent. "John?" he said.

"I'm fine," John said, and appeared by the bathroom door. "I need to lie down."

Zachary walked into the room with him and took off his shoes, the now-soggy socks, threw him a blanket. Zachary sat in the living room and turned on the TV. He told himself he was just waiting for the sun to arrive.

The rain poured in heavy curtains the moment John fell on his bed. It continued for three hours, then stopped, that silence after a bath, the faucet switched off. The sudden hush unnerved Zachary, and he increased the volume of the TV set. The morning news started at five a.m.; at a quarter to six the footage started rolling in one of the networks. A young man was found dead on a lot behind the abandoned kindergarten on the University campus. He must have tripped on something, fell on a broken beer bottle. Someone probably stumbled upon the body, the newscaster said, because when the young man was found he seemed to have been turned over, maybe even touched. They pointed at the blood stains on his clothes. Everything was shown in black and white.

On the other end of campus, a dead girl was found in front of the Social Sciences building, a thirty-minute walk from where the boy lay. She didn't have any wounds, except for the cuts on her legs and the soles of her feet, but those cuts weren't fatal. It's possible that she died from the cold, walking in the rain from God knew where, without an umbrella, without a jacket.

Zachary remembered how strong the rain fell that early morning, and shivered. Why didn't she stop? Why did she keep walking?

And he thought, I was able to take John's cell phone, thank goodness. But the boy was wearing his black shirt, the one with the print he liked. He might even be wearing his jeans, too.

When John finally got up the shows were already showing fluff: film reviews, interviews with celebrities, the morning workout. Zachary was in the kitchen, convincing himself that the police couldn't possibly trace those clothes back to them. They weren't special, or expensive; they could've belonged to anybody.

Zachary took bread from the cupboards, a block of cheese from the refrigerator. "They've shown anything about them yet?" John asked when he sat at the kitchen table.

The news footage wouldn't be replayed for another hour. "No," Zachary said. "Maybe they got to a shed?"

"I hope so," John said. "Zac?"

Zachary sat down and cut up the cheese.

"It made them crazy, didn't it."

"What did, John?"

"Suddenly being alive. Having flesh."

"What do you mean?"

John didn't reply.

"I'm making coffee," Zachary said. "You want some?"

"It was supposed to be Emma."

"Emma's dead, John."

"I know." John placed his hands over his face and cried. Zachary placed the bread on a plate and sat staring at the table. He waited for John to stop crying.


John said that he dreamt of his sister. Emma was older in the dream, fourteen years old, fifteen, the high school student that she would never become. Pick me up here, she said, calling him through her cell phone, telling him the number of the building where she was waiting, the name of the street. In the dream, John reached the building, but his sister was not there. Where are you? Right *here*, Emma said. The building number was staring John right in the face. Well, I'm here, and I don't see you. He walked away from the building. Can you see me? If I can, then I would have called out, right? Emma getting annoyed, then amused. *Hay, Kuya,* she said, laughing into his ear. Emma, John called, walking from one end of the street to the other. The street was deserted. He could not find his sister.

## Sugar Pi

I was woken up at four in the morning by a phone call from my friend Vincent, who—breathlessly, hysterically—said that he just had a dream, and in the dream he was able to catch a glimpse of the final few digits of pie.

*"Pie?"* I said, incredulous, twisting the cord around my shoulder, making the phone hang precariously from the edge of my bedside table. Vincent liked numbers; it was his domain, his nymph, his piece of the universe that he could manage and manipulate, his fenced property that I could never share in spite of his many attempts to make me jump over. In school he was allowed to take college-level Calculus, and was also not prohibited from showing up in the regular class, perhaps just to make us look like insects. "No," Vincent said gently. "To make you look like starfish." I actually took pride in Vincent's analogy for weeks; starfish looked like strong creatures, and they could regenerate. Then I learned that starfish didn't have brains.

Once, when Vincent was discussing with me the Constant Multiple Law (the reason behind which now I couldn't remember) I found myself almost nodding off to sleep, and in hopes of halting the conversation, I blurted out, "What's the square root of fifty-six thousand three hundred twenty-five?"

"Two hundred thirty-seven point thirty-two," Vincent replied, just as abruptly, which made my seatmate turn several shades paler. Then Vincent narrowed his eyes, looking suspicious and annoyed, and said, "But that's not the *point*."

So, of course, to hear Vincent talking about dreams with numbers was just as natural as hearing me talk about the plot of Final Fantasy VII. But to hear him talk about *food* with numbers. *That* was getting too far, I thought. The final digits of *pie*, indeed. I wondered if *tilapya* had a square root in his world.

"Yes, *pie*!" Vincent shouted. I told him I still didn't get it. I heard him sigh at my stupidity, could almost picture him rubbing his eyes beneath his glasses. "*Pi*, Ivan. *Pi*. The ratio of a circle's circumference to its diameter?"

I could vaguely remember a Greek letter on one side of an equal sign. "Ah," I said, just to humor him. I was too sleepy even to scream at his insensitivity. Who in their proper mind would call at four in the morning just to share such a stupid find? It was just a number. But then I wouldn't have the courage to say that to Vincent, even over the phone. He'd think it was blasphemy.

"So," I said, wrapping the word in a yawn. "What *are* the final digits?"

Silence.

"Well?"

"Well, uh," Vincent said. I'd never heard him falter before. "Frankly, Ivan, I can't remember."

The phone crashed to the floor, as if on cue, dragging the receiver with it. Vincent, you jackass. I went back to sleep, ignoring the phone. I wouldn't be able to reach that far anyway.


I met Vincent in my second year. He was a transferee from some public school in the United States, and we were seatmates, so unfortunately we were condemned to talk to each other. Math, as it turned out, flowed in his blood: both his parents are engineers, and his mother even worked as a lecturer in MIT. I did not understand the significance of this fact until I talked to my sister, who was a Math major in the University. I can't fully remember her initial reaction. I think she screamed. I think she slid across the dining table and shook me like a rag doll. "Befriend him! Befriend him!" she said. I did not befriend him because his mom was a lecturer in that far-off ("MIT, my *God!*" I can still hear my sister shouting) place. I befriended him because that was all there was to do.

And so he became a familiar sight in the family room, coming to our house whenever we were let out early, along with the other boys in our class who also liked Final Fantasy VII and more than enjoyed spiking up our electricity bill. My sister hated them, naturally; she said they barged into the house in violent red and purple light, like moving bruises, and dented her calm. But she liked it when Vincent's around. He's covered in light blue, she would say, like the sea, like the sky, like the color of a cat's pupil in the dark. Somehow the other boys began to like him, too, but not because of his aura. Vincent could watch a single sequence of FF7 and immediately figure out a workable strategy out of any given dilemma. I still don't know how he does it. It's part of his genius, I suppose. This afforded him a small place in our circle and an opening in a conversation every morning, but anyone could tell (even Vincent) that he was not completely accepted. I was the only one who *did* accept him, I think. I was the only one who talked to him about things other than video games. I don't know why. I liked him, I suppose. He was okay, he was nice, he wasn't annoying (except when he talks too much about Math), and sometimes he says interesting things.

The other boys didn't think much of him. He was just there.

Vincent's father died in a construction accident. He couldn't remember all of the details, and so he just made them up. Sometimes, his father got hit on the head by a mallet. Sometimes, he fell from rickety scaffolding. It depended on the day of the week. I didn't believe Vincent felt any amount of loss, especially over a memory so flexible. But he did remember the day his mother abandoned him. He was ten and he had been in his room. He saw his mother leave with a man in a big car. From the window, Vincent could clearly see her face. She was smiling.

"Smiling?" I said, because I couldn't reconcile the image with that of a Math lecturer.

"Yeah," Vincent said, "like she's not leaving anything behind."

But apparently his mother knew. When he flew to the Philippines, Vincent began receiving letters, packages, too-early or too-late gifts, which he promptly threw away. He told me that his mother, despite her mathematical genius, despite her much-coveted position, despite her many papers and equations and awards, could not perform the simple deduction that her son would never forgive her for the rest of his life.

Or perhaps she simply didn't care, I thought, but kept it to myself.

He now lived with his paternal relatives, who I think, with their shelves overflowing with Tagalog pocketbooks and their stereo with April Boy Regino presets, were slowly driving Vincent insane. I don't know how a person like Vincent could survive in a house like that. They were not into Math. They were not even into the Humanities. (Vincent liked reading books; he once said that the one thing he'd look for in a girl's home was a copy of William Goldings' *Lord of the Flies*. I told him that unless he imprisoned himself inside the College of Arts and Letters, he'd be a happy ninety-year-old virgin.) Whenever I passed by that house to pick him up, he'd zoom out of the front door and drag me down to the sidewalk, clutching my arm. "Get me out of here, Sir Ivan," he'd stage whisper, in a surprisingly passable British accent. "Ride me out of here, out to a tower, a fortress, where we could lock out the world."

Vincent did not mention his abruptly truncated phone call when I got to school the next day. He didn't even apologize. I found him sitting on a tree in the main grounds, leafing through several pieces of bond paper.

"Here," he said, and dropped the missive, which promptly landed on my upturned face. He didn't apologize that time either. I picked it up, scanned the first page. *The Mountains of Pi*, the title read, *by Richard Preston*. The copy was heavily highlighted, with notes on the margins, in Vincent's small, neat letters.

"In 1949," he said, "George Reitweisner of the Ballistic Research Lab in Maryland derived *pi* to 2,037 decimal places. In 1959, Daniel Shanks and John Wrench derived it to a hundred thousand decimal places. In 1981, Yasumasa Kanada derived it to two million digits. Three years later, he was able to extract fourteen million more. Then in 1985, William Gosper derived seventeen and a half million digits of *pi*. The next year, Jonathan and Peter Borwein got twenty-nine million decimal places of *pi*. In 1988, Kanada tried again and got 200 million. In 1989, the Chudnovsky brothers were able to derive 480 million digits of *pi*. Kanada continued deriving until he reached the 536-million mark. Then the Chudnovskys derived a billion digits of *pi*. Their last count is one billion, one hundred thirty million, one hundred sixty thousand, six hundred seventy-four decimal places of a number that denotes the ratio of a circle's circumference to its diameter."

He smiled suddenly. "Amazing, isn't it? A billion digits, a billion numbers. If you print all of those decimals, the paper would stretch from New York City to the middle of Kansas. And to think that computers nowadays had *pi* figured to more than two hundred billion decimal places."

I was ashamed to find out that I was flabbergasted. "How come *pi* has so many numbers?"

Vincent stared at me. "*Pi* is *infinite*," he said. "Its numbers won't end. It would go on *forever*."

I raised an eyebrow. "If it would go on forever," I began cautiously, "then why did these people bother to compute *pi*? It's—"

I wanted to say *pointless*, but was afraid he had something heavier than this article he just dropped on my face.

"They want to find out what it means," Vincent said, speaking of it solemnly, as if it were a deity. "These guys want to figure it out. Read the article. The Chudnovsky brothers think *pi* is a message from the Almighty, but unfortunately, because they can't find *pi*, they can't decipher the message."

I realized that I didn't like where this dialogue was heading.

"Well," I said, "have *you* tried deriving *pi*?"

"Are you crazy?" Vincent laughed. "An injured soldier once tried to derive *pi* by tossing wire on a wooden board with parallel lines and computing the statistics. He threw it 1,100 times, and you know how many digits he got? *Two*. You need a supercomputer to derive *pi*, Ivan."

Vincent was now looking into the distance. "Imagine if you derived a trillion digits of *pi*, Ivan. The Chudnovsky brothers said they could have managed that if they had a better computer, and if they didn't get bored. A trillion digits printed will travel from the Earth to the moon, and back, *twice*. Just imagine that. *Pi* can circle the sun; *pi* can suffocate the solar system! Do you know that the brothers mapped *pi* as a fractal landscape? Do you know what it formed?"

"What?"

"Mountains," Vincent said, awestruck. "Mountains, Ivan. And that's just the first billion digits. What else would have been formed if they were able to derive a few million digits more? A few *billion* digits more? Who knows, right? For all we know, *pi* could be the blueprint of the universe. Wouldn't that be exciting? The earth's plan written in mathematical language inside a circle."

While Vincent was talking, I saw Camille pass by with her group of friends. Camille, with her long hair and deep dimples like clear craters.

"Uh, Vince," I said, not even sure if I had just interrupted him or if he'd just finished talking. "Don't you think we have something more important to do?"

"*Pi is* important," Vincent said. I heard the finality in his voice, and realized with apprehension that I had crossed the line. Then his face collapsed into a grin, and he turned away, mumbling to himself.

"What's that?" I asked.

Vincent turned to me, still smiling. "I said, 'So what's that important thing?'" he replied.

I glanced at Camille. "The prom," I told him. "It's just a few weeks away, and we still don't have dates."

Vincent looked about from his perch. "What do you mean?" he said, probably seeing the girls spilling into the main grounds with their dark-blue skirts. "We're *surrounded* by dates."

I could not believe this Math geek was not worried about prom night. I felt slightly offended.

I didn't think I would read the Preston article. But I flipped through the pages anyway, during Filipino, just to make Vincent happy, and one highlighted passage jumped right at my face: *Ferdinand Lindemann, a German mathematician, proved the transcendence of pi in 1882; he proved, in effect, that pi can't be written on a piece of paper, not even on a piece of paper as big as the universe.*

I imagined God using *pi* to scoop up the universe, like dung; wrapping it, crumbling it, throwing it away.


"Why is *pi* a transcendental number?"

I posed this question to my sister, who jumped out of her bed with her beads and bangles and scarf, leaving her Enigma record blaring from her player.

"Do you know that *pi* can be solved by an equation?" she said. I heard her mood rings hitting each other.

"Yes," I said. I was holding the article on my lap. I turned a page. "The Leibniz series, right?"

My sister appraised me for a while. "Right. Then you know why *pi* is transcendental."

"No, I don't. I don't get it."

She sighed pleasantly and pulled my Science notebook toward her. "The equation looks like this," she said, and wrote:

$$\pi/4 = 1/1 - 1/3 + 1/5 - 1/7 + 1/9 - 1/11\ldots$$

"See?" she said. "*Pi*'s equation goes on forever. You'll have to exhaust all of the odd numbers. Then, when you reach the *end* of forever, the *end* of eternity, and have added *all* of the numbers—you'll get *pi*. But of course," she said, before I could open my mouth, "you *can't* reach the end of forever. So you can't get *pi*."

"So," I said, "it's impossible to see the end of *pi*."

"*Pi* has no end," my sister said, matter-of-factly.

I looked at her. "Vincent said he saw the end of it. In a dream."

"Real-*ly*," my sister said, lifting her legs. "Well, to have significance, he'd have to see and remember *all* of the digits of *pi*." She considered. "But then he'd be Rip Van Winkle."

We laughed, staring at the Leibniz series.

"It's nice that you brought it up, you know," my sister said. "I really like the notion of transcendental numbers, of infinity. It makes me think of the soul. A lot of people don't believe that a part of them can last forever, because they can't imagine it. But Math *believes* in it."

Two hundred billion digits. What if I wrote it? How long would it take? I imagined it covering all the walls of my bedroom, the ceiling, the floor, *pi* greeting me when I wake up in the morning, *pi* supporting my weight, *pi* staring back when I stare at the ceiling, at night, when I can't sleep. This might be Vincent's idea of Paradise, but I thought it was absolutely disgusting. The numbers would cover my Tifa poster, for one.

Two hundred billion digits. The longest book I've ever read was Harlan Coben's *Tell No One*. Three hundred-odd pages, roughly six hundred thousand characters. Two hundred billion divided by six hundred thousand. In the dark, I groped for my calculator. Three hundred thirty-three thousand three hundred and thirty-three. Three hundred thirty-three thousand three hundred and thirty-three volumes filling the foot of my bed, my room, my *house*, all of their spines facing me, all identical, all with the same two-letter title: *Pi*. I'll pick up Volume 1 and turn to the first page, and see 3 followed by a decimal point followed by 1, and 4, and *so on*. Yet Volume 333, 333 will not have THE END typed on its last page. There won't be an end.

Vincent loved ciphers. He created one on the day we met, and he gave me a copy of the crib sheet. It looked like this.

| 0 | 1 | 2 | 3 | 4 | 5 | 6 | 7 | 8 | 9 |
|---|---|---|---|---|---|---|---|---|---|
| A | B | C | D | E | F | G | H | I | J |
| K | L | M | N | O | P | Q | R | S | T |
| U | V | W | X | Y | Z |   |   |   |   |

The numbers replaced the letters, and in order to use the second and third-level letters, you had to add an x and a y, respectively. The first message he sent me was 81(y)03(x) 74(x)2(y) 07(x)4 4(y)4(x)0(y) which translated to IVAN HOW ARE YOU.

All of his messages started with this particular line. I knew it by heart and could sometimes see it dancing in front of my face whenever I took a long exam in Math: my name twirling across equations I couldn't finish, that friendly greeting cutting through already canceled integers.

"This is *pi*," Vincent said, and took a piece of chalk and wrote the digits on the board. It was long after class, and we were alone in the room. Vincent believed *pi* was simply a cipher, and he wanted to start the noble task of breaking it.

"But how about your x's and y's?" I asked, but he was already writing the letters, using a mental crib sheet. (He'd asked me to bring mine—81(y)03(x)  74(x)2(y)  07(x)4  4(y)4(x)0(y)  5(x)1(x)8(x)  17(x)83(x)6  27(x)1  8(x)7449(x)—IVAN HOW ARE YOU PLS BRING CRIB SHEET—yesterday, but I deliberately left it at home.)

The digits 3.14159 became DBEBFJ.

I tried reading it. "It sounds like a fart," I said.

Vincent tried different strategies, but *pi* still came out as a meaningless jumble of letters.

"Maybe you have to unscramble it," I said hopefully.

"It will make sense toward the end," Vincent said.


Vincent and I spent several more *pi*-filled days, creating a new cipher and a new crib sheet (which still didn't make *pi* any more coherent), researching, talking with my sister while she smoked in the bathtub. I even read the Preston article, and it turned out okay, after all. But then I woke up from this dimension that Vincent had opened up for me, and all of a sudden it was just four days before prom night, and I still had not asked Camille.

I decided to do so, right after Math, while the lunch bell was still ringing. "Cams," I said, as she passed by our table, Vincent watching me closely, "would you like to go to the prom with me? As my date?"

"Not really," Camille said, and walked right past.

It took about five seconds before the message sunk in. *Not really?* Wow, I thought. That was fast. That was like a knife cutting a limb. That was painful.

"You know," Vincent said, as I sat back down, "if she were a number, she'd be the cube root of seven."

I happened to be staring at my Math textbook, and the page I was staring at was headlined, "Numbers". I looked at the text, then at

Vincent. "Good one," I said, smiling, visibly relieving him. The cube root of seven is an irrational number.

"How about me?" I asked, after the pain had dissipated. I saw Camille leave the classroom, and wished she'd step into an open manhole and die. "What would I be, if I were a number?"

Vincent pursed his lips, thinking. I was secretly hoping he'd say *pi*, because I'd started to like the idea it represents. Infinity, impossibility, endlessness, cheat codes.

"You'd be the square root of negative one," he said. I had no idea what that meant, but was too lazy to open my book and find out. I just assumed it was something good.

When I got home and could properly flip through my Math book again, I found out that negative one *does not have a square root*. It's an imaginary number. It doesn't even exist. Whatever did Vincent mean by that? That I'm not real?

Just like the starfish, I thought. What a nasty mathematical joke.

I finally found a date for myself, just two days before prom night: Crystal, a short, bubbly girl from the graduating class, who gave me a hug before saying yes. Vincent was able to drag one seconds after Crystal ruined my rib cage. It pleased me; that meant he'd finally felt that distinct sense of panic, and was compelled to act.

On prom night we waited on the bench outside Crystal's house, where Vincent's date would also emerge. The two girls were friends, apparently. We sat in our hot, stiff suits, tugging at our neckties, wiping dust from our shoes every now and then. Vincent had been unnervingly quiet since that morning. He was staring at the house so intently I thought it would burn.

"I think I remember the last digits of *pi*," Vincent said, and I whipped my head around, almost falling off my seat.

"Really?" I said. No wonder he's so quiet! I suddenly imagined him publishing a paper, having a building in school named after him, making a speech for the Nobel, acknowledging me as partner in crime. We're going to be rich! Then the fact that he didn't look so happy about it zoomed me back to the present, to this cold bench, to the dust clinging to my shoes again. "Well," I said, wiping, "what are the digits?"

Vincent sighed. "Eight-one-zero-three."

I frowned, repeating the digits in my head. Eight-one-zero-three. Just like my sister said, it wouldn't mean anything unless Vincent knew the other numbers. I wondered how many numbers *pi really* had. I was just about to ask this when something else hit me. Eight-one-zero-three. I remembered Vincent's cipher, and the molding crib sheet stuck between my English compositions and my Games Master magazines. I remembered the dancing numbers, the first message he'd ever sent: IVAN HOW ARE YOU.

Eight-one-zero-three. If you removed all the pesky x's and y's, 8103 spells my name.

"Wha—" I began to say. But I thought I knew. I thought I understood. I remembered what he said, a long time ago, when I first contested his silly obsession with *pi*: *Pi is important.*

Oh, shit, I thought. OhshitOhshitOhshit.

"Oh, Vincent, for God's sake," I breathed, and he moved ever so slightly. I wished I could pull my necktie off. I felt so uncomfortable. Why would Vincent go through all the trouble of dropping all those little numerical hints just to tell me this? I should be angry. I should be stomping down the road, soiling my shoes, grinding Crystal's corsage into the ground.

But I wasn't, mysteriously. I was merely disappointed. Vincent spoke to me in the language he knew best, and I could only answer him Camille-style: Not really.

I wondered what I could do. I thought of his father's unknowable death, and his mother, leaving him, ten and alone, with a smile on her face. I didn't want to add to his heartaches.

But then perhaps he already knew the answer, I thought, as I watched Vincent stare Crystal's house into oblivion. It occurred to me that he didn't talk of his mother as if her leaving had saddened him, or broken him; he spoke of her with resignation, acceptance, quietly, without harshness, as if he had been aware of it for a very long time, and he had simply watched her leave just so he'd be able to see her face, and commit it to memory.

I found myself prying open the plastic box carrying Crystal's corsage, saw myself taking out the orchid, holding it out. "Hey," I said, and tried to tie the flower around his right wrist. Vincent looked shocked for a while as I fumbled with the ribbon, missing the knot twice, almost dropping the flower, a part of me thinking, *What are you doing what are you doing,* imagining my FF7-fanatic friends, imagining them watching us. What else could they be thinking? But a part of me was feeling serene, feeling *right*.

"Ivan," Vincent said, looking worried, and I said, "There", and finally tied the ribbon correctly. He smiled, I smiled. We sat in silence for a while, then he took the corsage off when the two girls appeared from the front door, and I placed it back into the box.

I could have said, "At least you wore it first", but decided not to, noting the evil ordinal number, noting the ordinal numbers that would follow, noting the numbers that might not stay but would definitely come, down to infinity, or into a void, like *pi*. I decided not to say that, because Vincent was a good person and a good friend, and I did not want to break his heart.

# Earthset

It must have been a feeling in the atmosphere. Like the world was dying. Like something was coming to an end. Did they see it in his eyes? Eric thought that was it, at first, then dismissed the idea. Not in this cramped train with the cramped passengers, their brains too tired to be paranoid.

If there is a bomb here somewhere then so be it, Eric thought. So be it.

It's the elevator syndrome, he imagined Maureen telling him. Maureen of the bookshelves and the lofty dreams of a doctorate; Maureen of the encyclopedic memory. It is okay for a person to stay with other people in a small space, even if he ends up facing them, so long as he doesn't look them in the eyes.

But if he were facing Maureen he would—

It happened when the train Eric was on was entering Buendia Station. The train's lighting was busted so the darkness was complete when they entered the tunnel, save for a couple of bright cell phone screens and the flashes of yellow light sluicing through the windows from the walls of the tunnel. That was when Eric felt the hand hold his. Eric's left hand was resting on his sling bag on his lap, and he was staring straight ahead, thinking of Maureen, thinking of bombs, thinking of nothing.

The hand was already covering his fingers before he realized that it was there.

Somebody was holding his hand. Even in his muddled state Eric thought that was strange. The hand was soft, not very big, could be a woman's, or a man's. Could be anyone's hand. Are you scared? he wanted to ask the hand's owner. Do I look scared to you?

Eric waited for the hand to move down, searching beneath his sling bag to his groin, but it didn't. For some reason Eric's eyes filled with tears, and he blinked them away fast. Without turning his head Eric turned his hand palm-side up and laced his fingers with the stranger's. They held on tight as the darkness of the tunnel seeped into the train. Don't worry, that hand seemed to tell him, and Eric was grateful. Everything will be all right.

Then they emerged into the station, into light, and the hand slinked away. The person sitting beside Eric stood up and got lost in the crowd pushing itself onto the platform.

Something weird happened to me today on the MRT, Eric imagined himself telling Maureen when he got back to the empty apartment. Somebody held my hand. He imagined Maureen rearing back, shocked. It's not dirty or anything like that, Eric would tell her. The person just held my hand because it was dark. It was comforting.

Then write a story about it, he imagined Maureen telling him with that smile of hers.

"I can't write anymore," Eric told the empty room.

Eric was sure the reporter was going to call again, but he didn't unplug the phone, or turn off his cell phone. He was thinking maybe he could drive home the point better if he simply didn't pick up.

Eric opened the refrigerator, wondered what he could possibly eat.

"It's for an anniversary piece," the reporter had told him. The obnoxious bastard. "An update of sorts. Everyone who attended the mass last year has agreed. If you're not comfortable in a group setting we can maybe set up a one-on-one?"

"I didn't even attend the mass," Eric said, and already he could hear the mental ballpoint pen click, a fresh page turned, the bastard ready to take notes. He should have just hung up.

"Why?" the reporter asked.

What for? Eric wanted to scream at him. So I can compare notes? Oh, yours lost a limb; mine was blown up to smithereens.

Maureen didn't cook so every night after he got home from work they would walk to the nearby fast-food joint and order.

"So what's the story about?" Maureen had asked the last night they were together. Eric worked at a bank, but he was features editor back in college and he wrote prose in his free time. That year he was planning to join a writing contest sponsored by a bookshop.

Eric liked talking to Maureen about his stories, even if they were not finished yet. Back in college he considered this practice a jinx, but not with Maureen.

"It's a sci-fi piece," Eric said. "The world at its end, blah-blah. Humans move into lunar colonies. I *know*," Eric said before Maureen could say anything, "it's cliché, it's been done before, but the story's still fuzzy. I'll think of something to make it new. Some extra," Eric rubbed his fingers together and wrinkled his nose, "*something.*"

"How do they move onto the moon?" Maureen asked.

Eric was stumped by the question. He thought about it for a moment, already hearing Maureen's giggle, and shrugged. "Kurt Vonnegut once said that science fiction writers know doodley-squat about science," he said.

"*Breakfast of Champions*, I believe."

Eric bobbed his head up and down. "Man," he said, laughing, "he was right."

Whenever Eric ate at that restaurant after that night he would choose a table with the trays and the leftover rice and the sucked on wishbones still on the tabletop. Eric would sit there and wish no one came by to clean them up. The mess made him less lonely, made the daydreams easier to conjure.

In the story that he started to write and couldn't finish, contestants of *Pinoy Big Brother* knew nothing about the planned mass migration to the moon. But they knew of the social unrest even before they entered the House; for some of the contestants, it was precisely the reason why they chose to enter the House. Inside the House they would be protected, and there would not be news of horrible things. But some of the contestants had had enough and decided to stage their own version of a revolt. In one episode, a man and a woman (which the producers wanted to present as a couple) sat in the living room talking about mundane stuff: nail polish, favorite Hollywood films, the latest eviction. Then suddenly the man nodded and the woman stared straight at the camera. "Why are you still watching this shit?" she shouted. "Why don't you look away and do something more productive? What, you haven't seen two people talking about Bronzed Platinum before?" After the woman's rant a hand reached from outside the frame and covered the camera with a towel. The producers switched cameras, but by then all the other cameras had been covered as well.

The rest of that episode became nothing but a series of sounds: people whispering, the clutter of utensils, chairs being pushed, a woman humming a song, laughter.

But the producers kept on airing the episodes, even without the visuals. And people kept on watching. It calmed them, the viewers told the sociologists who studied the phenomenon. Especially the older demographic. They said the show reminded them of their childhood.

Would the air smell different before the dawn of that final second, before the meteor struck, before the fire and the deaths? Eric had wondered if the customers of that mall sensed something different before the nothingness set in, if Maureen sensed something different. Experts went in, collected scraps of this and that, and found traces of what they at first believed to be RDX which turned out to be something else, something useless, telling them nothing. The police released their final report: gas explosion. Gas explosion. If it were gas they would have smelled something, Eric thought. He would have smelled something. But the day he dropped Maureen off at the mall entrance, the only odor he remembered was the scent of Maureen's hair as she brushed it back to give him a chaste kiss on the lips, that lush smell of lemons. Maureen walked toward the stairwell, disappearing into the throng of people and families milling about, and Eric walked back to the taxi bay to get to work. After the explosion Eric's ears rang for hours.

He ran back in along with the crowd, but by then police miraculously materialized and cordoned the area. Media men, photographers, and the *twack-twack-twack* of helicopters. The final report said the blast originated from the basement, beneath the stairwell. Maureen was heading toward the stairwell when Eric turned away.

Why did he have to turn away? He could have just walked backwards, like what he did during their college days, smiling that stupid smile of his. Tragic stories peppered the news. There was the taxi driver who dropped off two passengers. The passengers got off, the blast came, the passengers slammed against the vehicle. The driver survived, both passengers died. One was pregnant. They interviewed the pregnant woman's husband. If they could have been there a minute late, he said to the cameras, a minute late. She was seven months along. Just two months more.

Are you taunting me? Eric wanted to scream at him, at the television screen. If they could have been there a minute late, the husband said. I know what you are trying to say, Eric wanted to shout. I should mourn you, I should stop feeling sorry for myself. We're widowers both but my marriage to Maureen was too short to create a child. You deserve to feel shattered more than I do. Oh yeah? How dare you? How dare you taunt me?

The company allowed him to take an extended vacation. It took Eric three months to drag himself back into a mall, and when he did he immediately noticed the K9 stationed at the entrances. Now you're doing this? Eric wanted to shout at the young man holding the leash while the dog sniffed his backpack, but Eric knew the young man was just doing his job, it was not his fault.

Sometimes, Eric told Maureen's father during the funeral, I wish it were terrorists. Because then I'd have someone to blame. I cannot blame chemicals, can I? I cannot blame carbon atoms, I cannot blame combustions.

The phone rang again. Eric waited a beat, then picked it up.

"What?" he barked.

*"Kuya?"* a voice said tentatively.

"Edward," Eric said. His brother, still in college. Before the accident, Ed would call only if he was having money problems. "Is there something wrong?"

"That reporter called again."

"Don't talk to him."

"I told him not to call us again or I'd call the police."

Eric took a deep breath. "That should work, right."

They shared a laugh that ended too abruptly.

"So," Ed said. "What are you doing."

"I just got home." Eric had been sitting in his kitchen for more than an hour, staring at the wall.

"Oh." Ed paused. "Do you want me to come over?"

Ed hugged him tight when they met up in the hospital after the blast, which surprised Eric. They were close, but not like that. Apparently Ed thought he was inside the mall with Maureen. Since then, whenever Ed dropped by to visit him Ed would think of ways to put off leaving early. Eric remembered his brother standing at the door on the way out of his apartment and stopping to straighten his shirt, his jeans, over and over, as if the night were their mother and he wanted to look presentable.

"What for?" Eric said, and winced at the tone of his voice.

If Ed had picked it up, he didn't show it. "I don't know," his brother said. "To keep you company?"

"No," Eric said. "No. You don't have to do that. Thank you, though."

"Okay," Ed said.

"Okay."

Ed seemed to want to say more. Three seconds passed. Five. Eric felt a hopelessness settle in his chest. The feeling wasn't alien to him now, but he still felt it whenever it came.

On the other line, his younger brother took a deep breath and said, "Okay. 'Bye, then."

Eric hung up without replying.


In the story that he couldn't finish, all the peoples of the world rode away from the dying Earth, lush still with forests and deep seas but dead in its soul, rotten, drying up with its thinning atmosphere and many wars. They rode away in capsules with the Moon as their destination. In the capsules, they held hands, the dark of the chambers punctuated by the soft yellow glow of the sun. Don't worry, they told one another as their speed increased. Everything will be all right.


Maureen, I know doodley-squat about science but I think I know a bit about Einstein's theory of relativity. Time, space, and all that. One twin travels at the speed of light, the other stays put. The one who remains ages more quickly.

I imagine souls, if they exist, travel at the speed of light. Maureen, you are traveling so fast I can no longer see you. So I imagine you, now, on a swing, in a field somewhere, lost in space and time, traveling in your infinite speed and grace. Every arc of your swing, every leap and push and fall will be equivalent to a hundred years for me, the one who unfortunately has to stay put and age, without you. And when I come, when I become light enough to travel fast, I will appear behind you, Maureen, touching your lemon-scented hair, still fragrant after all these years, ready to push you up, and you'll say, like we've only been apart for a second, "Oh, there you are, Eric."


In the story that Eric couldn't finish, the peoples of the world arrived at the lunar colonies, at the end of the First Lunar Day. Together they stood on the strange sands of the new world, and watched the Earth set on the horizon, a blue and white globe, a child's marble, watched the Earth glow against the vast blackness of the sky, watched that glow diminish and disappear.

It was the kind of ending that Maureen would have liked, Eric thought.

Eric's apartment had only one window, but it was facing the wrong way. Even so, Eric knew the sun was just beginning to set. If only I can write again, Eric thought to himself. There was a bottle of brandy in his kitchen, plenty of ice, several more days like these in the future, and already Eric was sick of it, sick of the thought of it. The phone rang; he ignored it. He sat in his kitchen, waiting, not knowing what it was he was waiting for.

# PARALLEL

The sky was spotless, cloudless, except for that one merciless orb, the streets unusually bright, as though lit from underneath, the streets absorbing *and* reflecting. the heat. It was as if the pavement were glaring at him, staring him down, as if it knew who he was, knew he wasn't supposed to be there.

Ben arrived with a car Christopher didn't recognize.

"Now where the hell did you get this?" Christopher asked.

"My own garage."

Christopher did a double take. It felt as if his head were moving underwater, the air thick as mud. He could hardly breathe. He closed the door of the car and set the air conditioning to maximum.

"You're crazy," Christopher said.

"Don't worry, I left a note."

"You're *crazy*."

"He didn't see me."

"*You* didn't see you."

"*He* didn't see me," Ben insisted. "And besides, I left a note. *Wormholes do work! High five Einstein!*"

"You're—" Christopher began, then gave up.

"He'd love it, trust me."

"And if you called the police?"

"He wouldn't," Ben said, and clucked his tongue, annoyed. "Jesus, Chris. Why do you keep referring to them like that?"

Christopher didn't say anything.

Ben had picked him up on Krus na Ligas, in front of the girls' boarding house there, the best landmark to meet since the building was painted bright pink and it was the tallest establishment in the area. Ben changed gears and drove into Teacher's Village. Ben knew the turns and the streets; Christopher didn't have to tell him. It was 2 p.m., siesta time. The streets were silent, empty.

"Everything looks the same," Christopher said softly, watching the houses go by outside the car window.

"Maybe they have a different president."

Christopher stared outside the window.

"You want me to turn on the radio?"

"No." Christopher said.

They drove in silence for a while.

"Have you erased the message?"

"What?" Christopher said violently, turning on his seat, jolting Ben.

"The message," Ben said after a moment. "On your answering machine?"

Christopher sighed. The shrink had told him to erase it. Belinda wanted him to erase it, said it would help him "move on."

"I will never," Christopher replied, but found he couldn't finish the sentence.

"No, I mean, it's cool," Ben said. Damage control mode. "You know? If I were in your position, I thought I'd—"

Now Christopher looked at him curiously.

Ben refused to meet his gaze. "I thought I'd do the same thing."

"I haven't touched her room either," Christopher said. "It still looks the same, since that night."

Ben made a noncommittal sound.

"My therapist says it's not helping me any," Christopher continued. "I said, 'Right back at ya.'"

Ben didn't laugh.

"You know what really got Olive into Einstein and all these time theories?" Christopher asked. Ben barely reacted to the sound of Olive's name, but Christopher felt him shrink away, heard a sharp intake of breath, and Christopher felt sorry for Olive again, sorry for himself, his whole life. Suddenly the discussion didn't feel worth pursuing.

But Ben said, "What," and of course he had to answer.

"Christopher Pike," Christopher said.

"Fuck!" Ben said gleefully, disgustedly. "*Christopher Pike?*"

"We were in the Young Adult section of a bookstore and suddenly she says, 'Hey, he has the same name as you!'"

Ben smiled.

"I can't remember the book's title," Christopher said. "Anyway there's a character there who somehow was able to travel *beyond* the speed of light, and time slowed so much for her that she was able to watch the universe pass by, until the Second Big Bang. She saw the universe disappear and begin, right before her very eyes."

Ben snorted. "This is Christopher Pike."

"It is, it is," Christopher said, happy now. "Anyway, for her eleventh birthday I got her Hawking's *A Brief History of Time.*"

"Hawking," Ben said with awe, like they were talking about a basketball player.

"She wasn't able to finish it, though."

"Got bored?"

Christopher looked out at the windshield, watched the hood steam like a furnace.

"Oh," Ben said. "Sorry."

"You remember her jokes, Ben?" Christopher said.

"Welcome to Insult Comics: Brains Edition."

Christopher smiled. "I'm gonna hit your momma so hard, your momma in a parallel universe's gonna feel it."

"I'm gonna hit your momma so hard," said Ben, "the event horizon of the nearest black hole's gonna shrink."

They laughed, Christopher rapping his fingers against the car window.

"And that one time? That one time I asked her how old she was when your paper got published? She said, 'Oh, *Kuya* Ben, I would be…let's see…two and half figments of my parents' imaginations?' Apparently she wasn't born yet."

Christopher laughed.

"Oh, Olive."

A second later he was crying.

"Hey," Ben said.

"I'm sorry." Christopher tugged at his shirt sleeve and wiped his eyes.

"We're here, right? We're here."

"I know," Christopher said. "I know that."

They reached the end of the street and turned left and Christopher sat up and saw the same depressing pile of garbage on the empty lot two blocks down from their house, set atop yesterday's pile now reduced to ash, the same unused garbage cans buckling beneath an orange sheet of rust. It amazed him how everything looked the same, so normal, like he and Ben didn't just break several Institute laws just to drive on that very street.

Ben inched the car a little bit more forward and shifted to park. From their seats they had a clear view of Christopher's own front yard.

They waited. Christopher chewed on his lips and brought his hand up and chewed on his thumbnail.

Ben glanced at him and grimaced. "Will you stop it, Chris? You're making me more nervous."

"I'm sorry, it's just," Christopher said. "I mean, what if they didn't—"

But they did. The front door opened, and out came Olive in a white dress, music sheets tucked under an arm, bare feet barely touching the grass as she ran. She looked back and laughed. The door banged open again and out came Christopher, the Christopher that belonged to that time and place, hefting Olive's cello. He laughed, too.

They had a nipa hut on the front yard. Olive climbed into the miniature house, reached out her hands for her instrument. Christopher handed it to her with a grunt written all over his face.

He slung his arms over the window and kissed his sister heartily on the cheek.

In the car, Christopher ached for that kiss. After the crash he would sit inside that nipa hut, imagining Olive and that gigantic instrument that he never learned how to play sitting beside him, and stare at the sky until it changed color, until it gave up on him, too.

"White shirt, blue jeans, flip-flops," Ben announced. "He might be painting; there are stains on the shirt."

White shirt, check. Blue jeans, check. Christopher's wearing sneakers, and nothing could be done about the paint stains.

"Maybe you can take off your shoes," Ben said.

"And burn my feet on the pavement?" Christopher said.

Ben shrugged.

"I paint on the second floor."

"I know. *He* does, too."

Christopher didn't comment. Olive's tuning her cello.

"He's not you, Chris."

Suddenly, the Christopher on the front yard looked at their car. Christopher jerked on his seat, ducked his head.

"The windows are tinted, you moron," Ben said.

"It's like he saw us," Christopher said, still refusing to sit up.

The Christopher outside gave Olive another kiss, then ran inside. The front door closed.

"You're being paranoid," said Ben.

Maybe he was. Christopher sat up, removed his seat belt.

"You know what to do," he said.

"You spread plastic on the floor when you paint, right?"

Christopher nodded.

Ben took out his gun, checked the silencer. "That'll make things easier, then."

"You don't shoot him," Christopher said.

"Chris, I'm the one holding the gun anyway. If things get out of hand——"

"I want to shoot him."

Ben shrugged. "Your call. Ready?"

They both got out of the car. Ben walked on ahead—he would enter through the kitchen door at the back of the house. Christopher approached the nipa hut. Olive loved playing there. Even on the most merciless summers the bamboo floor remained cold to the touch.

Christopher slowed down his steps even if the heat's starting to get to his head and his eyes. The music swelled. Olive had her back to the street, her arms rising and falling.

Christopher touched her hair, and it was like that was enough to get him through the days. He itched to call Ben, call the whole thing off. This, he thought, touching his sister's hair, this is enough. Let's go.

The music stopped abruptly. Olive glanced over her left shoulder.

"How did you do that?" she said.

Christopher took a deep breath, smiled.

"What?"

"You just went into the house," she said, "and now you're back here. How'd you do that?"

Christopher looked at his sister's eyes, said nothing.

"*Kuya*, are you all right?"

"You should play facing the street," Christopher said. "Somebody could grab you and—"

"And run away with my cello?" Olive laughed. "*You* can't even *walk* with it."

Olive was speaking to him. They were talking. Ben, Christopher screamed in his head, Ben, this is enough. Let us go.

"Please face the street, Olive."

Olive sighed comically, but eventually complied. Christopher helped her move the instrument. "Why can't you just learn the violin?" Christopher said.

"Shut up." This was an old argument. "You're wearing shoes now, too?"

"The sun's burning my skin."

"Yeah," Olive wiped the sweat from her face. "The summers are getting hotter. Oh, guess what, I've finished reading Hawking!"

"You have?"

Christopher sat beside her. At this point, Ben would be on the second floor, chatting with the other Christopher: Hey Ben how you been, glad to see you, would you like to have dinner with us, Olive's downstairs practicing again, nice to see you. Nice to see you.

He saw the long line of scar tissue on his sister's right arm, where the glass of the shattered bus window cut her. Maybe on one of her legs he'd find the same line of brown stitches, like clay, like pasted-on worms.

She survived the crash. She was in the bus, but she survived it.

Christopher touched the scar on Olive's arm. Should he and Ben find the other Olive, the one who never got on the bus? The one who waited in Baguio for Ben and Belinda, who were in Session Road, just twenty minutes away, ready to bring her home safe and sound? The one who didn't have these scars, these memories?

Christopher put his arms around his sister, touched her cheek, kissed her hair. He burst into tears. Olive looked up at him in alarm.

"*Kuya?*" she said, very quietly.

Christopher sniffed, smiled.

Olive's eyes and eyebrows asked, *What is it?*

"I'm sorry," he said. "I just missed you."

"You gave me a kiss just a minute ago!" Olive said.

Christopher laughed.

"You're," Olive said, giggling, shaking her head. "You're weird."

I'd like to take a picture of this, Christopher said. I'd like to record this moment.

"I'm not going to the next music fest, if that's what's getting you worked up," Olive said.

"Where's it going to be?"

"Chicago," Olive said.

Wow, Christopher mouthed.

"Yes. Wow. But I'm not going," Olive said. "I'm staying here."

Christopher tucked a stray wisp of her hair behind her ear, touched her earlobe affectionately.

"Were you mad at me," Olive said, "for not following your instructions? I mean, I knew *Kuya* Ben was just a ride away but I got tired of waiting."

"You didn't know what's going to happen," Christopher said.

"I should have just waited for them to come get me."

The bus hit another vehicle on its way back to Manila. A truck of vegetables, the reports said. Three students died—two violinists and a cellist—and a young teacher. The rest got imprisoned in broken glass and twisted metal, smelling like cabbages. A promising child pianist broke three of her fingers.

Christopher fell to his knees and clutched one end of Olive's bedspread when he heard the news. The bedspread smelled like lavender powder; he washed away the smell with his tears. There's one way to make this right, Ben said, on the third day he refused to move from that spot, refused to eat, refused to drink, refused to talk to anyone. Belinda went berserk when she heard of their plan, but she never told anyone in the Institute. This is wrong, were her first and last words about it before they left.

And what of the soul, Belinda asked, after the laws were written, after the concept of parallel universes was accepted by the Institute. She was still an undergrad then, Ben's kid sister, Christopher's student, driving him crazy. And what of the afterlife, she said.

*That's* the afterlife, Christopher said to his class. You die in a car crash, but in a parallel universe you survive. In another, you may have not gotten on that car at all. That's your afterlife. *Lives.* It's a multiple-choice heaven.

Or, he added, it can be a chance for redemption. With so many worlds, one world is bound to be perfect. In one world, a god with so many choices is bound to get it right.

Belinda said, "The religious will go ballistic over this."

"Oh, yeah?" Christopher said. "I think it's beautiful. I think it gives you hope."

Olive was studying his face. "What are you thinking?" she said.

"Play something for me, Olive," he said, and brushed her hair with his fingers.

Christopher did not recognize the music. When she was through he smiled and said, "I'll go in for a sec."

"Okay."

"I love you," Christopher said. "You are everything to me."

Ben was on the second floor, feet planted by the doorway. "Is your sister going to be a pain in the ass?" the Christopher inside the room was saying. "If she is, I'm not going to play."

"Just give Belinda some red wine and she'd even play strip poker for you," Ben said.

Laughter. Christopher stood beside Ben. "Let's go," he said.

Ben, who already had his hand inside his pocket, turned his head. "What?"

"Who are you talking to?" the other Christopher said.

*"Kuya?"*

Olive. She was standing downstairs, by the door.

"Yes, bunny?" the other Christopher said from inside the room.

Olive was staring right at Christopher, and her mouth hung open when she heard the other voice.

"Let's go," Christopher said.

They ran down the stairs. Olive had her hands over her mouth. They banged past the door, past the nipa hut, into the car. Ben quickly shifted gears. They shot out of the street.

"I can't," Christopher said, his hands on the dashboard, heaving with sobs. "I can't. I can't. I can't."

"All right," Ben said, touching his shoulder. "All right. I'll take you home, okay? I'll take you home."

Home was a humid April evening in 2028, Christopher staring blankly at the windows in his sister's room, Ben and Belinda arguing downstairs, the argument climbing over the banisters.

"You need to speak to him, damn it!" Belinda was saying. "Call his doctor. He could be in shock, for God's sake."

"He wants to be alone, Belinda."

"But he—"

*"He wants to be alone."*

The argument ended. The front door opened, closed, opened again: "Hey, Chris, pal, we're leaving, okay? You'll call if there's any problem, right?"

Christopher wanted to answer but he had no energy left.

"Okay," Ben said. The door closed. A car started, left the street.

Christopher reached a hand toward the answering machine, pushed a button. "Hello, *kuya*, are you there?" Olive's voice said.

"I'm here, baby," Christopher said, in tears again, clutching her teddy bear to his chest. But Olive didn't hear him. Why didn't he answer the phone that night? Where was he, what was he doing?

"So anyway, I'm already here," she was saying. It was already dark, she was saying. She was talking about lights, fireflies, tiny specks flitting in the distance. Somewhere a piano came to life, a violin,

Olive surrounded with music, and all the while she talked about the lights, *Kuya*, the lights were so beautiful.

# Monsters

They were happy once, that much Paul could say. Not that they weren't happy anymore. They *were* happy. At least, Maya was. That was the aim of all this, wasn't it? It all boiled down to that, all this self-control, coming down to the office every single day, cuddling his daughter whenever the opportunity arose. Such *opportunity* being, as Maya herself had realized with a debilitating sigh one morning, *every minute and every second of every day*. It felt as though there was always a shadow lurking nearby, a shadow with flesh enough to grab her from his arms.

Again. That word, *again*, again, just that one word that shouldn't be there but was always there, stubborn, attaching itself to that incident that Paul never, in his wildest dreams, in the sickest of all the sick dreams that only his past could ever offer, thought would ever involve him. And yet there it was. That word, *again*, in his world, and Maya's, connected to that incident, to the thousand splintered memories of it. He was doing this, all *this*, this stab at humor and normalcy whenever his daughter's within earshot, this clicking away into websites and forums, to compensate. That was what it all boiled down to—for his daughter to be happy.

And she was. This morning she went out to buy five small bottles of hair dye—sky blue, orange, mauve, blonde, and brown—and cheerfully locked herself up in the bathroom. That she could lock herself up in a small space—and *cheerfully*, too—almost filled Paul's eyes with tears of joy. It also filled him with dread. "Self-destructiveness, self-mutilation or self-abuse" was on the checklist of SurvivorsInRecovery.com, and so he took a stool from the kitchen and sat outside the bathroom the whole time Maya was in there, talking to her about whatever came to mind, asking the same question over and over until she gave even the vaguest semblance ("Unh." "Uh-huh." "Right.") of an answer. This annoyed her, of course ("Papa, you're really not making sense."), but he needed to hear her voice, just to reassure his paranoid, shattered self that his daughter was all right, and that the razor blades in his razor were actually still *in* his razor.

"What's taking so long?" Paul asked when he finally ran out of questions. He had covered weather, politics, literature, even advertising ("Did you like the Chocolate Brewery commercial they finally approved? They played it during the morning news."), practically everything they could possibly talk about, and after every other question Maya had barked, "I'm okay, *okay?* Would you like me to hum so you could at least sit at a table and finish your breakfast?"

Paul laughed, just to show her that it was all in fun. He had always known that his daughter was incredibly smart (SaveOurChildren.com stated in an e-journal that a child's intelligence has a considerable effect on their recovery. Smarter victims recuperate faster. Thank God, Paul whispered after reading that), but it still surprised him whenever she came up with remarks like this. He was still like glass, fragile and transparent, despite all his efforts to appear otherwise. She could still see through him.

"Wait," Maya said, laughing, her voice muffled. "I want to make it look perfect."

"Are you sure you don't need help?"

"You've asked that an hour ago. *No.*"

"Did you use up all of the bottles?"

No reply.

"Maya? You used all of the colors?"

From inside the bathroom came the sound of Maya giggling.

"*No,*" Paul said, smiling.

"Just wait and see."

"I can't even begin to imagine how *that* would look like."

More giggling. "Just wait and *see.*"

So wait and see, Paul did, and broke into genuine chuckles when the door opened with a sharp click and Maya burst out of the bathroom with the bottom half of her shoulder-length hair dyed in all the bottled shades she had purchased, the strands closest to her checks a soft sky-blue, the strands following a shocking slash of blonde, then brown, then orange, then finally mauve, the back of her head like an eruption of lilacs, this flower-power, psychedelic rainbow framing her face, making her eyes look brighter, cheerier. Paul liked it.

"You like it?" Maya asked, toweling her hair dry.

He liked it.

Paul opened his arms and Maya entered them, and Paul enveloped her, his daughter, deeply inhaling the peroxide smell of her, the baby-cologne smell of her. He kissed her loudly on the cheek. He didn't know how he could get her past the school gates come Monday, past the scrutiny of the security guards, and those nuns— perhaps in *their* book this was the very definition of *self-destructiveness,* i.e. ruining your God-given hair color chemically—but he had seen destruction first-hand and it was not of the biblical type, not of the four-angels-standing-in-the-four-corners-of-the-earth type, but something relatively smaller, like silences within silences, or a friend's hand withdrawing away.

They were happy. Once. They were happy now. But this happiness felt strained, to Paul, as if it were merely a duplicate of that former happiness, that former life.

Maya gasped and pulled back. "Oh, no!" she said, touching her locks. "How will I get into school?"

"Well, I suppose we'll just have to dye it back," Paul said, but in his head he was saying, Screw them. Screw you, he imagined himself saying to the guards and the nuns. She could shave her head, re-design her uniform, *I don't care.* My daughter could heal however way she wanted.

The Chocolate Brewery commercial came on again while Maya was drying her hair in her bedroom. "Maya! Maya!" Paul called frantically, but by the time she dashed into his room the jumping can had faded and the commercial was over.

"Oh," said Paul. "You missed it again."

Maya flopped down beside him, making the two of them bounce slightly on the mattress. "Why don't you just show me the copy they gave you?"

Maya was trying to tie a headband at the nape of her neck. Paul helped her. "I could, but I'd like you to see it *as* a commercial."

His daughter frowned. "So you mean to say it's *not* a commercial if I just watch it from your personal DVD."

"Yes, because then it won't play between programs." Paul paused. "I'd like you to actually see it play between programs." Another pause. "*As* a commercial."

Maya kept on staring at him. *Riiight,* the look seemed to say.

Then Paul said, "I'm worried about this trip, Maya."

"Don't you want to see *Kuya* Dominic? And *Ate* Cassie?"

Paul sighed as though he were expelling his entire soul and changed channels.

"You didn't even give them our address. Not even a phone number."

Paul looked at the TV as though it were the most depressing object on the planet. Maya stared at the TV as well and couldn't help but copy the look on his face.

Paul sighed again.

"I miss them," Maya said. "I'd like to see them. Don't you?"

"Well, yes—"

"Well, they'd be *angry*, maybe, but—"

"Will it really make you happy, if we go there?" Paul asked. Maya nodded eagerly.

"Just one day," Paul said, even though he had already made this clear the week before. "We can't stay over."

Maya nodded and nodded.

"The drive's going to take hours—"

"We can commute if you don't feel like driving," Maya blurted out.

"You know I'll do anything for you." Also, Paul couldn't even begin to imagine the backlash he'd receive if he e-mailed Cassandra and cancelled.

"So we're going?"

Paul smiled.

Maya squealed and lunged at him and hugged him so hard they almost fell off the bed.

Maya had already powdered herself and jumped into and out of three outfits before finally settling on a plain white blouse with the butterfly embroidery on the front, and a black silk skirt with lace ruffles, yet when she checked on Paul, he was still in his bathroom.

"Papa," she said, rapping on the door. She could hear the water running, and so she at least knew there was a grain of truth in what he'd promised her. "Just how many 'quick showers' are you planning to have?"

Paul was just rinsing, but for some reason couldn't find the strength to turn off the shower, or step back. The urge, the *readiness*, to return to the site of the crime was a good sign of healing, but hopefulmother86 from the Small Voices forum asked for wariness and skepticism. Returning could conclude the healing process (*it is a cycle see and with that particular cycle over and done with your child and yourself can finally move on and start a brighter life together a new cycle if you will*) but it could also open up a can of worms, stir up memories—*turn closure into a catastrophe*—and put you back to square one. But what square are we on, Paul wondered.

"Papa!" Annoyed now. "I'm timing you."

"But that's unfair," Paul said. "I didn't time you while you were coloring your hair downstairs."

"Stop procrastinating."

She said this in English. *Procrastinating.* Who, asked Paul, *who*, within a twenty-mile radius of this god-awful city, had a girl this precious, this smart, this *erudite*, as to know the meaning of *procrastinating*—and possibly also *erudite*, hell why not—and to actually use the word in ordinary conversation before eight a.m. on a Saturday morning? Nobody, nobody but him.

Paul laughed, sending water up his nose and making him cough and retch. "I'm done," he said, turning off the water and toweling himself dry. "I'm done."

Maya, *his* Maya. She deserved all that was good from this god-awful world.

And this god-awful world—more specifically, Maya's guardian, more specifically, *him*—had fallen short, and for years he had been trying to find ways to make it up to her. But he didn't know where to start. He couldn't see the extent of his debts.

Paul frowned when he caught Maya hefting up the bottle of bourbon the office had given him last Christmas. The Christmas before that, they gave him brandy. The bronze-colored bottle was still there, in a kitchen cupboard somewhere, collecting dust and growing scornful of him. He had promised never to touch alcohol again. Or cigarettes. Or drugs. Or.

Or flesh.

Yes.

His colleagues knew that, at least about the alcohol. He didn't know why they bothered.

"We need to bring *Kuya* Dom something," Maya said. She said there was already a box of chocolates wrapped for Cassandra, and Paul felt ashamed. He didn't think of that.

Paul took the bottle from her, weighing it in his hands. Heavy. The bottle of brandy was lighter. He almost told Maya to just bring that. Or something completely different, something not made of glass and could be shattered and turned into a deadly weapon. He was seriously considering the possibility that whatever he might give Dominic as a gift, Dominic would just throw back. Aimed at his head.

Paul checked everything before pulling out of the driveway. And that meant *everything*—the door locks, the windows, the gas tank, the odometer, the fuel pump, the carburetor, his credit cards, his ATM cards, the money in his pocket, and Maya's seatbelt, *especially* Maya's seatbelt—to Maya's dismay. When he finally announced that they were good to go, Paul reached for the ignition and realized that he had left his car keys inside the house.

"Well, will you look—" Paul began to say, chuckling as he did so, but Maya looked ready to strangle him, and so he burst out of the car, unlocked the door, ran up the stairs, took his keys, ran back down, locked the door, and got back into the car and pulled out of the driveway. That took two minutes, on top of the thirty minutes he had used up earlier. There, he seemed to say, looking over at his daughter, but Maya only sighed and shook her head. Even Maya didn't want to use the word *procrastinating* twice in one day.

Maya brought a blue silk ribbon with her and tried the best she could to tie a bow around the bourbon bottle. Whenever traffic slowed he'd glance at her progress. "That looks good enough," he'd say, or, "Why did you have to redo that one?" but Maya wanted it perfect. When they passed the first toll gate Maya said, "There!" and showed him the finished product. Paul smiled at her, but Maya probably saw something flit across his face because a half-second later her own smile disappeared and she leaned closer and turned on the radio. Paul didn't know the song. It was something new. He didn't listen to FM much, but Maya did. She sang along with it, bobbing up and down on the passenger seat, making him laugh. Paul remembered turning on the radio and Carlos insisting on silence, while in the backseat—

He pushed that memory aside. He had to push *all* memories aside or else feel the urge to stop the car in the middle of the expressway. When the worries stole in he needed something to divert them and make them ride down a different path. Maya knew that. Hence: the radio and the singing along. He hadn't driven a long distance in a long time—he did once, towards the opposite direction—but he was all right as long as he kept his mind unoccupied of all things Three Years Ago. As long as his daughter was singing or redoing a bow, as long as the road was straight, redundant, and left him brain-dead and unmindful of the destination.

How do *you* do it? He wanted to ask Maya, this daughter of his now apparently whole. But he was the one who was supposed to know that, wasn't he? He was the one reading up on healing and recovery. But he didn't know.

They entered the town at two. The chief center of activity at this time would be the marketplace, but they were too far away to hear the crowd. The bus station beside it must be busy as well, weekend, more people departing than arriving. Paul couldn't blame them. He remembered hanging out in that place as a grade-schooler, with Dominic and Carlos and Carlos's sister Cassandra. The parking lot was vast and there was a lot of room to ride your bike. The drivers let them play because they came during the dull hours anyway: two, three p.m. Midweek, the sun beating down harshly on the roads, only five people fanned themselves sleepily in the bus bound to Cubao or Divisoria, only one or two people crunched combinations at the Lotto office. He and Dominic would watch the bus conductors sleeping on the green benches, the ennui of siesta hanging oppressive like a thick fog, everyone simply bored out of their minds.

They passed the town chapel. "They've painted it," Maya said, ducking down to see through Paul's arms on the steering wheel. Paul glanced at the structure, made a noncommittal sound. They've painted it white and a striking pink. Before they moved out the priests would request for second collections during Mass, a second Offertory just to get the job done.

Paul knew there was another way to the subdivision, a route he'd heard the neighbors talking about but he himself had never taken. Not exactly a shortcut, just another way.

"You're supposed to turn here," Maya said, her voice cutting through his thoughts. "Papa. You're supposed to turn here."

"Isn't there supposed to be a shortcut?"

Maya looked at him, her index finger still pointing past her window. "I don't know," she said, then glanced out. "Papa! We've gone past it."

There was no other vehicle on the road. Paul reversed with a sigh and took the turn.

"It's all right," Maya said. "We don't need a shortcut."

Paul felt sick. He was the one who's supposed to be doing the comforting.

He kept his eyes on the road when they passed by the wooden house. He didn't have to turn his head to see that they were already at that part of town; he could feel the house as if it were radioactive, as if it had fingers. He almost expected Maya to say, Stop here, stop here, but she didn't. She was just looking at it. He could sense her doing that from the corner of his eyes. She was looking at the house, steadily, as if trying to memorize it, perhaps wondering why it was still standing there. How could anyone in this stupid town let that house remain intact? He would have burned it, if he had the strength. He would have burned that house to the ground.

But she could look at it, even if he couldn't. Maya could stand the sight of it. A good thing. A wonderful thing. What would he do if she asked him to enter that house with her?

"I saw a girl," Maya said suddenly. Paul felt goosebumps rise on his arms.

"What?"

"There was a girl outside the house."

"Really?" Paul instinctively looked past Maya's head although they'd already passed the lot. "What was she doing?"

"Nothing. She was just standing there, looking at it."

Paul didn't believe in ghosts, but he wondered if the house was haunted, if the whole town was being haunted, if there was no closure even in death, if all those children still couldn't find the courage to revisit that house even without their bodies.

They came to Dominic's parents' house. Two stories, spacious front yard, curlicues, varnished wood, a house from another century. Dominic's mother's flower garden was still thriving, which to Paul came as a surprise. He took a deep breath and knocked on the door.

What bothered Paul was the weight loss, but otherwise Dominic looked good. When he opened the door, Dominic flicked a single glance his way, too brief to send a message, and turned his attention to Maya. "My God, what have you done to your hair?"

Dominic bent down and touched the sky-blue strands, rubbing her hair between his fingers. His face changed, like he was going to cry, and he took Maya in his arms and lifted her. *"Kuya!"* Maya said in alarm and laughed. Over her shoulder, Dominic looked at Paul, sadly now, like he was the bearer of bad news. But all he said was: "Hello, Paul."

"Dominic," Paul said, and Dominic lowered Maya to the floor. "We got you something." He handed him the bottle of bourbon.

"I tied the ribbon myself," Maya said. Dominic said the ribbon was very beautiful.

The TV was on inside the house, and in the uneasy silence that followed Paul heard a familiar jingle.

"Maya," Paul said, unable to help himself. "That's my commercial!"

This caused the three of them to move and rush into the living room. Onscreen, a can of chocolate drink mix jumped on someone's kitchen counter. *Here in the Chocolate Brewe-ry,* it sang, *every-one is filled with glee-ee.*

Maya was dancing to the song. Dominic saw her and chuckled. To Paul, he said: "This is what you do now?"

The statement was devoid of judgment: no disgust, no admiration. Paul and Dominic used to edit videos. Dominic sometimes put in an original soundtrack for an additional fee. Cassandra accepted writing assignments from abroad. It was Carlos who didn't shrink from physical contact, working in a PR firm and as a university lecturer, day in and day out surrounded by warm bodies. He was brave, Paul once thought, but now didn't. He wasn't brave; he was reckless. He was selfish.

"Yes." Paul wanted to tell him of how it was still a struggle to work in a room full of people, but Dominic didn't seem eager to hear about any of it.

The commercial ended. "I like it," Maya said, turning to Paul. They shared a smile.

"Dom, are they here?"

Cassandra. The voice came from upstairs. Maya called out to her and ran so fast Paul had to say, "Be careful".

"Cassandra lives here?" Paul asked as they trudged upstairs.

Dominic shrugged.

Paul frowned. "Are you——"

"What? No," Dominic said, smiling, amused. "She said she didn't want to be alone. She just moved in last week." Dominic shrugged again. "She says she'll pay half of the electricity bill." He said this like it explained everything.

Maya burst into the room, and Cassandra shrieked. "Oh, baby," she said, kneeling. "I love this blouse, you look like a fairy! And look at your *hair*."

"Oh," Maya said, remembering something, "your gift's still in the car."

"A gift!" Cassandra said. "I have a gift! That's all right, we can get it later. Come here."

On the walls of Cassandra's room were watercolor paintings, charcoal sketches, collages, some of them framed, some just stuck to the wall with tape. A couple of the collages were already falling apart, the pieces of cloth and the dried flowers falling, a work of art shedding its skin. On the bed was a black clear folder sitting on top of her laptop, the folder bulging with pages.

"What are you doing?" Maya asked.

Cassandra immediately placed a hand on the folder. "Oh, I'm writing a children's book."

Maya's hand darted forward. "Really? Can I—"

"No!" Cassandra hugged the folder tightly to her chest. Paul and Dominic exchanged a quick glance. Cassandra, realizing what she just did, relaxed her hold on the folder, touched Maya's face. She drew her hand back and covered her mouth. She was crying.

"It's not done yet," Cassandra said, her chest heaving. "It's not good enough." She took Maya's hand. "I'm so sorry. I'm sorry, I'm sorry, I'm sorry—"

It seemed as if Cassandra were apologizing for something else, so Dominic said, "Let's go get *Ate* Cassie's gift", and steered Maya out of the room. Paul closed the door and sat on the floor in front of Cassandra.

"Cassie," Paul said. To his surprise, Cassandra placed the folder on her lap and began turning the pages. In red and black and swatches of purple, Cassandra had drawn human faces with long, sharp teeth. Sharks. Giant piranhas. They were running after a little girl. *I'm not scared of you!* the girl was saying.

"I had to draw them, I needed to shut them up," Cassandra said, closing the folder. "I can't show her these."

Paul nodded. "Why did you move in here, Cassie?"

"I'm scared," Cassandra said. "They've begun throwing rocks at the house again. Two weeks ago they destroyed the kitchen door. They could have slipped in." She looked up. "I don't want to kill again, Paul."

"I know," Paul said. He wanted to ask her: "In the end, will the little girl get away?"

After Cassandra had calmed down, they left Maya with her. The sun had hidden behind a cloud, and Dominic wanted to take a walk. Paul didn't know what this entailed. They walked side by side, hands in the pockets of their jeans.

"So," Dominic said. "Had Shirley made contact?"

"God, no."

"She's a monster."

Paul thought that was a strange word choice.

"You know," Dominic said. "There was a time when I thought you'd hook up with Cassie."

"Seriously?" Paul guffawed.

Silence. "It's nice to see you again, Paul."

Dominic asked about work and how Maya was doing in school. Then, he began talking about their shared childhood, the playground now turned into a gasoline station, their high school falling into disrepair, and did Paul see that new building, how ugly it was? Paul smiled faintly at the ground, then stopped walking. "Wait," he said.

They were entering the lot where the wooden house stood. There was a girl standing there, in a white dress, a dress for church, and Paul recoiled at the sight of her. This must be the girl Maya had seen earlier. The girl in white bent down, lifted a rock off the ground, threw her hand back. The crash wasn't deafening, but both Paul and Dominic jumped. The girl had broken one of the last two panes of a window facing them. She threw another rock, aiming for the last pane, but the rock sailed through the jagged hole beside it. The girl clucked her tongue.

"Did your sister die here?" Dominic asked. The girl regarded him for a moment, frowning, but didn't find him interesting enough. She walked away.

Paul and Dominic watched her. "What are we doing here, Dom," Paul said.

"I thought this was what you came here for," Dominic said, but he wasn't looking at him, so Paul couldn't tell if Dominic himself believed what he was saying.

"Why the hell would I want to come back here?" Paul said. "Maya misses you, otherwise—"

Paul realized that he was on the verge of destroying something. "I'm sorry," Paul said. "I should have at least answered your e-mails."

"At first we thought he got to Maya," Dominic said. "There were so many bodies, and there was one girl who looked so much like her—"

"I'm so sorry," Paul said, and by then Dominic was already crying. Not hysterical like Cassandra, but silent, soundless, the tears just filling up his eyes and falling. *Did your sister die here?* He had asked the girl who clearly wanted to squirm out of her church clothes looking for a window to destroy. How much Dominic had wanted her to say yes, Paul thought. If she had said yes, they could've said, I'm sorry. There could've been a chance to be forgiven.

Paul wouldn't think of asking for forgiveness. He didn't believe they deserved to be absolved.


Before Maya was born, they didn't care about anything. They were young, they lived in the city, and they picked up their victims in bars, in student watering holes. They knew how their ancestors attacked. They'd heard all the stories: waiting on rooftops, hiding behind trees, jumping on people passing unlit roads. Teeth, claws, red eyes. But they had a car, they had make-up and drugs, they had the glare of the city to guide them. The night's catch were torn open like bags in the backseat, the leftovers thrown out of the rolled-down windows. The news offered theories of a serial killer, cutting up bodies and scattering them across the expressways. The first time they heard this, Cassandra stuck her head out the window, allowed the wind to whip up her hair. She laughed like the news bulletin was the funniest joke in the world.

It was an addiction, a hunger, it could be controlled. But why? They would ask each other, as the sun set, as another night began. What for?

Then Paul met Shirley, a law student who left for the States after Maya was born and never came back, and he found out what for, all too quickly. His friends adored his daughter: Carlos and Dominic took turns changing her diapers and Cassandra rocked her in her arms at night, humming a song. When Maya turned a year old, Carlos got the university job and moved out of the cramped apartment they shared. He would call from time to time, but he never showed up for the birthdays, the dinners, the various holidays. The rest of them moved back to their hometown, looking after their families' properties. By then they had turned to gutting animals—stray dogs, cats, cows—and, later on, stopped hunting altogether. *What for?* They knew. The reason was now all too tangible.

Maya was ten when a van filled with children was driven away from the school.

The students were really supposed to have a school excursion on that day. When a man climbed into the rented van and said, *Your teachers will meet you there,* they believed him, even though they didn't really know where they were going. Some museum, some boring place. The air was heavy and thick and the sky overcast, not exactly the perfect day for travel. Maya's memory of that day remained fragmented, so nobody knew how the driver managed to get all the children into the wooden house—a thirty-minute ride away from the school—calmly. One of Dominic's cleaners passed by the wooden house, and when she arrived she remarked to him, off-handedly, that there seemed to be "an animal" trapped inside it. "Maybe a large dog." The cleaner could not recall hearing children.

Dominic was unperturbed. That morning, Carlos had given them a call. A feast, he said. The three of them didn't think it was a good idea, but Maya would be at a school trip, and it would be the first time they would see Carlos after so many years, so why not, why not.

The call that would say his daughter and six other students were missing and that the van's real driver and the school security guard posted at the south gate were found dead in the parking lot wouldn't reach Paul until hours later. By then, the information would be worthless. He drove to the wooden house in his car and he only gave the van a cursory glance, thinking how odd that Carlos would drive a car like that.

Carlos had already slit open the sixth child when they arrived there, and the smell of blood, which before filled Paul with pleasure, made him bend over and throw up at the doorway.

Cassandra saw the uniforms of the dead children and screamed.

It was Dominic who attacked Carlos, baring his teeth. Paul walked deeper into the house, away from them, holding onto the wall for support. No, no, he whispered under his breath, trying to recall the color of his daughter's scrunchie. Or did she put barrettes in her hair before he took her to school that morning, and what color were those? Why didn't he pay attention? "No," he moaned, when he came upon a girl's body.

Beyond the dead girl, Maya was lying sideways in one corner of the room, her uniform drenched in her classmates' blood. She was shuddering, facing the wall, her hands over her ears.

They didn't see Paul carry Maya into his car and drive away; they were too absorbed with the blood on the floor, the gray faces of the children. Dominic said Carlos retracted his teeth when Cassandra's words finally sank in ("This is Maya's class, *this is Maya's class!*"), and he stood there, in the middle of a room smelling like a slaughterhouse, and said, "Oh God Oh God." They walked around the room, stepping over the bodies, peering into their faces. Maya? Maya? The smell was arousing something in them, but they were too deranged with grief to respond to it. Some of the children's faces were too destroyed to be recognizable.

"Do it," Carlos said, closing his eyes, accepting his punishment.. Only Dominic and Cassandra would be there at his burial. Paul would be miles away, deleting e-mails, changing his cell phone number. The news would give the public a madman, while Cassandra's neighbors would pelt their parents' house with rocks. *Aswang,* they would say, while Cassandra sat hugging her knees on her bed, trying to smother the voice that was telling her to bare her teeth and attack, attack. "Tell Paul I'm sorry," Carlos said, according to Dominic, but it could have been an embellishment. Carlos might not have said a word, just sat there sobbing as Dominic's killing blow landed.

For months, the psychologists couldn't coax a single word out of Maya. Paul couldn't sit still in support groups, their collective despair distracting him. The computer screen was bloodless and the online forums did not have faces, so he turned to these, these parents with children who were kidnapped, who witnessed a brutal crime, who were raped by relatives, who fell victim to family friends, who did not survive.

(How many relatives of their own victims were here? he would find himself thinking. How many of them had comforted him, not knowing who he was? And what could he say to them, what could he possibly say?)

There was a message that kept being repeated: *No matter what you think, this is not your fault.*

"Would you have spared him," Paul asked, "if you saw that Maya was alive?"

"I ask myself that, too," Dominic said. "I don't know. You don't know what your daughter saw."

Maya still cried in her dreams at night, but Paul couldn't decide if that could push him to murder a friend. Carlos didn't know Maya was there. (So if it were a different group of children, it was acceptable?) A feast, Carlos had said, and they were hesitant at first, but eventually they said, why not, why not. They did not say, No children. They did not say, No. In his head, Paul began collecting the flowers he would lay at Carlos's grave.

The sun reappeared, heating up the afternoon, and Dominic bowed his head as though the sunlight bruised him. He wiped his face, a quick gesture. "Cassie and I wanted to move," Dominic said. But they were anchored to their blood. They knew they would die in that town, like their parents, like so many relatives before them. Even Paul, who had allowed his family's ancestral home to fall to ruin after he ran away three years ago. Even he knew he would come back here, hopefully without Maya. Hopefully by then his daughter would have her own family, a normal life, the hunger undiscovered, buried. Should he thank Shirley then, for escaping? (But Shirley was only running away from married life, a far less destructive hunger.) Should he thank Shirley for giving a portion of herself that allowed Maya to escape?

They walked back home. Maya and Cassandra were sitting on the floor in the living room when they arrived, crayons and charcoal and colored pens and empty chocolate wrappers scattered between them. "We're sketching each other," Maya reported, looking up from her pad.

"Your hair is the death of me, Maya," Cassandra said. "I'm running out of colors."

They laughed. Paul knew that sooner or later someone would ask the question, and he would have to consider staying for the night, give a promise of regular visits, set a future date, open up his home and his life. Cassandra was busy with her pastels and Dominic was rummaging around in the kitchen, so for the meantime the question hung, unasked. Paul helped set the table for *merienda* and watched his daughter draw, waiting for the question to fall. He wondered if he was strong enough now to say yes.

# The Just World of Helena Jimenez

The skies in that small town remain dark from the past wars.

The smoke of gunfire and shattered bones covers the sun like a veil. All that is left for those still living are the tiny shacks of the dead soldiers and the old church, and a night that doesn't seem to end.

But they have ways of telling the passing of the hours: heartbeats, the cry of the lizards, bloody tallies on pale skin. And in the mornings, without fail, the Wardens gather in the old church, weaving around the now useless pews, to their Leader standing by the altar, holding her weapon in her hands.

They, too, hold their weapons, waiting for the signal. The Wardens' hands do not shake when they carry the black metal balls, balanced on their palms like an offering to the altar. The balls, fashioned from the cannon balls of their barbaric forefathers, are attached by an intricate chain to their right wrists, entwined around the fingers of their right hands.

And in the mornings, without fail, their Leader stands in front of them and says in a clear voice, "Today, justice shall be served." The balls are then dropped, but will not be allowed to kiss the ground.

The Wardens have long before destroyed the images of the saints and the gods, and they glance at the empty pedestals each morning as they leave, genuflecting to their triumphs. Only one icon has been replaced.

On the altar, behind the Leader, a marble statue of their one and only accepted Superior: the Lady, blindfolded, resplendent in a flowing gown, one arm akimbo, the other holding a sword raised to the level of her shoulders. Her previous images show her carrying scales, but that is before the certainty of the Wardens, before the need to balance both sides has been rendered obsolete.

Now the statue of the Lady carries a black, metal ball, glistening like an omniscient eye at the end of a chain.

Helena was sitting right outside with her sketchbook when her brother invited the lawyer to the living room for a drink.

Helena knew his brother needed the drink more than the lawyer. An hour ago the two men had a talk in his brother's library, and the lawyer made her brother cry. Helena knew this, because she was standing right outside the door when it happened, trying to make out the words. When her brother started shouting, the words cut clear through the wood.

"So *now* they want to re-open the case?" her brother said.

Then her brother was crying. Helena opened the door slowly at that point and saw the lawyer standing by a bookshelf. "Stephen, please," she heard the lawyer say, but he remained standing where he was, not moving even to give her brother a pat on the shoulder.

Stephen was sitting by his study table. He gave a start when he heard the door open and he turned his face away from her. "Helena," he said then, wiping his face in a way that he probably thought was inconspicuous. "I thought you were outside."

There was a silent pause as the lawyer straightened his tie and his brother tried and tried to dry his face.

Helena walked up to him. "What's wrong now?" she asked him in that numb voice she had carried from the day they moved out of New York, out of that suburb, that house.

Helena would often find herself sitting outside of her brother's house, staring for hours at the road, and her hands on her lap and open as if offering something. She would ask herself, What do I feel? She would be so disturbed by the question that she wouldn't be able to move. What do I feel?

Stephen wouldn't tell her what he and that lawyer were talking about. But she had heard the word, *case*. She had heard the word, *re-open*. And again she sat outside, staring, asking: What do I feel? She could feel dread somewhere, and disgust, but it was as if they were outside of her, like scorned friends, and she couldn't make them come in.


The lawyer's name was Parker. Helena had met him before. Parker was their lawyer's assistant back in the States, and she could still remember the look on his face when he saw her flinch at the sound of his name, and at the sight of him.

Parker was half-Filipino, she was told, right after Stephen saw the panic in her eyes, and she remembered thinking, What's the use of having a Filipino mother if your skin is white and your hair is blond and you speak just like *him* and you sound just like *him* and your cheek is clear enough to contain a scar and there are spaces between your fingers big enough for a trigger—

The words were on the verge of being spoken. It was the look on Parker's face that stopped them, froze them before Helena could even open her mouth.

Helena could still remember that look because she saw it again just last week, this time on the face of one of Stephen's students. Stephen was rattled that day, Helena could tell, because he kept rearranging the objects on his desk, putting his pen here, a folder on one corner, transporting a short stack of books from one side of the tabletop to another so carefully as though the mere act could change his life, and for some reason still couldn't find the examination papers that the student had come to get in his office that morning. The student was tall and thin, freckled, and blond. An American.

"Syriana," the student suddenly said, appraising the movie poster tacked on the office wall behind Helena, who was sitting on a wooden bench perpendicular to Stephen's desk. Stephen stopped moving at the sound of her voice. The student looked at him, at Helena, then smiled sheepishly at the reaction she had caused, perhaps thinking she had just committed a serious Filipino faux pas.

"Yes," Stephen said after several beats, fingers moving again, hauling objects. "You've seen it?"

"Yes," said the student, smiling openly now, proud of herself. "I remember this scene. I remember Matt Damon and his wife by this fountain in Switzerland. My mind has been, like, floating, and I thought they were still in the United States, until Matt Damon or the wife said something like, When are you gonna fly to the United States. And I was like, *Where are they anyway?*"

The student chuckled. "I mean, they're in Geneva, but the place looked like Central Park."

"One day everywhere will look like Central Park," Stephen said. "Try cruising through Manila. Turn off the lights to hide the black hair and the brown skin and you'll see McDonald's and 7-Eleven's and Wendy's in every corner. One day, everywhere will look like where you came from. Just shoot the brown people dead, and you're home. Home means only white people in sight, isn't that right? Isn't that what you guys want, to see home everywhere?"

Stephen's voice was rising, and as he spoke the student looked at him with her mouth slightly parted. Halfway through his tirade, her face collapsed, finally understanding what the outburst was all about.

"I don't know, sir," the student said, because Stephen appeared to be waiting for an answer. "I'm just one person."

Stephen was not able to find her papers, and because she had left the room too quickly, he was also not able to apologize.

"You shouldn't have said that to her," Helena whispered, because she saw Parker's face in that student's face, which could even be Stephen's face, up on that stand five years ago: hurt and wounded, already judged but still pleading to be understood.


The Wardens are everywhere.

With their dark hair and dark clothing, they blend perfectly into the town's crevices. Like a black teardrop falling into a black ocean, they step into corners, into unlit alleys, into homes, on rooftops, on the belfry of the old church, silent, and immobile. The people of the town can pretend they are not there. In their homes, women can make love to their men. In narrow streets, lovers and friends can sit together and exchange secrets. On the vast grounds of the church, on the cold rooftops, children can hoot and feed the birds or play. They can do all this, but they know their freedom is not absolute. They know the Wardens, though seemingly lifeless, are watching them. From the corners, from the windows above, from the darkness, they know the Wardens can see their every move.

The Wardens do not speak, do not blink, and they do not leave a post empty. The Wardens do not miss anything.

Once a woman strangles her man on her bed, once a lover or a friend takes a knife and stabs another in that dark, dark street, once a child pushes a playmate over the edge of a roof, the Wardens will flex the fingers of their right hand and immediately liberate their weapons.

It has been said that wars have brought sounds with them, many sounds—screams, moans, gunfire, blasts and explosions—but after the wars, after the Wardenry was set into place, the people need only be wary of two sounds: the sound of a Warden's cannon ball kissing the ground, and the sound of the chain whistling through the air as the ball is lifted and thrown into the skull of the Trespasser.

"Helena's so big now," Parker was saying.

The sliding glass door was slightly open, something Stephen probably failed to notice due to the curtains, and so Helena could hear them: their footsteps, the soft pop of a bottle being opened, the rustle of pants, clink of ice. "How old is she now?" A pause. Helena pictured Parker taking a sip from his drink. "Fifteen?"

"Yes." There was a gentle *swoosh*—her brother sinking into the sofa.

"School?"

"Online classes, tutors. She tried the regular classes, but—"

"I'm so sorry."

During those early therapy sessions, she was given a sketchbook not unlike the one she now had, and a box of crayons. They used to give her dolls, but she wouldn't touch them, and so they gave up on that, turned to the possibilities in her artwork.

She drew only one image, over and over: two circles, one inside the other, the outer circle red, the inner one black. After coloring her drawing, only the black circle would remain looking like a circle. The red one always ended up looking more like a splash.

What does this mean, sweetheart? They ask her, but Helena wouldn't answer. Wasn't it obvious what that red splotch was, what that black ball was? She would continue to color, using up the black and red crayons, smudging her fingers, filling her nails with the smell of wax.

She knew they'd shown Stephen the drawings. She couldn't understand why they scared them so much, why it didn't worry them that it was a place they couldn't even visit, and couldn't visit them. There were many worlds, and she fell into that world only once, into the body of a girl who was and wasn't her.

She remembered standing in a pool of blood, embracing an older girl in gratitude. Everything was dark, in that world, but her family was alive. She remembered wanting to stay there forever.

When she got back (*Catatonia*, they said. *Recovery. Waking up.*) she made the mistake of mentioning this to the counselors, who smiled sadly and took notes.


During the early days of the Wardenry, an old man enters the church with a young woman and asks for an audience with the Wardens.

"Halt, old man," says the first Warden Leader, sitting at the feet of the Lady, surrounded by the Wardens waiting for their turn to guard the town. When the old man takes another step, they all stand at attention, save for the Leader who lets a smile creep across her lips.

She knows what the old man wants. Both he and the young woman are wearing the red robes of the dissidents, making them stand out garishly against the drabness of the roads, the blackness of the old church's occupants.

"You are very young," says the old man, in a tone both fascinated and appalled. The young woman stands behind him, glaring at the Wardens, wrapping her red robe closer around her body.

The Leader slides to her feet and walks toward him.

"And yet you were able to kill my wife and her friends."

The Leader smiles once again, sadly this time. The old man is talking about the Mass Punishment on the church patio, four women and three men, struck to the head at the count of three.

"We did it at night, while the town slept," says the Leader, the smile gone. "You were not supposed to see that, old man. There is no need to turn a punishment into a spectacle."

"One can hear your weapons swinging for miles and miles," the old man says.

"Your wife" says the Leader, "and her friends almost killed three men, old man. The men's families heard the swinging weapons as well. But not our weapons."

"My wife is avenging her family," says the old man. "Those three men are former landowners. They made a lot of people miserable. They made my wife's father suffer."

"Where were you during the Citizens' Gathering, old man?" the Leader says, arms crossed, the black ball oscillating ominously at the end of the chain. "We've agreed to begin a new age, to start over. We've agreed to put all past crimes behind us."

"We have *murderers* in our midst, rapists, criminals, all roaming around free in this *new age* of yours," the old man says, shaking. "We have *victims*. If you do not want the people to serve justice themselves, you have the responsibility to—"

"Do it for them, yes?" the Leader says. "And how far back will we go, old man? You are suggesting we visit every single house and get a list of the people the citizens want punished. And how about those who will be punished? I'm certain they would have their own list as well. And the people in those lists will have a list as well. In the end we Wardens will carry out, not a Mass Punishment, but a complete wipeout. The list will cull past angers, past relationships, past sins and sinners, and obliterate every single person living in this town today. You think you are *clean*, old man? You think you have lived a straight and decent life? Then wait for the lists, and I wager you'll see your name at least five times, in the lists of five people who for the longest time you've considered your closest friends, who, until now, have made up their minds to simply forgive you. But no, you are respectable and law-abiding, and so now they are forced to recall the Trespasses you've done them, and we have to punish you five times over.

"Revenge is a loop, old man. We have agreed to erase all misdeeds that were done before the Gathering in order to end this loop—"

"And start another one?" the old man says.

The Leader laughs. "Justice is not a loop, old man. Justice is the point at the end of a straight line. Justice is the end, the conclusion, the aim."

The old man stares at her, then begins to sob.

"And would you rather we all kill each other?" the Leader says. "A day—*one* day—after the Gathering and the setting of the New Laws, a massacre almost occurred in the south part of town. We were able to prevent it. We were able to save the life of an entire family. Now you, old man, may consider that obstruction inauthentic, mechanical, but we don't *care*. You may look at us with pity in your eyes, we who follow erroneous edicts, we who naively see the glorious pursuit for freedom as Trespasses, we who perceive what you would consider a truly *free* individual as a criminal, but we don't *care*. The youngest in that family is an eight-year-old child."

The Leader can hear the weeping young woman. We see her struggling with an object hidden within the folds of her red robes.

The old man is not able to speak for a long time. Then: "My youngest son is among you." He walks about, searching their faces, prompting the Wardens closest to him to release their weapons. The unanimous clang does not upset him, or stop him. "Where are you, son? Where were you while your mother is being murdered?"

"How dare you let our mother die!" the young woman shouts, whipping out a gun from inside her robes and pointing it at a Warden standing three rows behind. But the Wardens are quick; she is dead before she can even find the trigger.

The wet sound forces the old man to turn around. He stares at his daughter. "No," he said. He does not move. He does not fall to his knees.

"I advise you to leave immediately, old man," says the Leader. She gestures with her head, and two Wardens quickly step up to him and lead him out of the church.

When the old man is gone, the first Warden Leader calls a Warden by name.

"Were you among those who carried out the Mass Punishment?" the Leader asks.

"No, Leader," replies the Warden.

Pause. "Would you like to bury your sister?"

"I'd be honored," replies the Warden. "But she is not my sister. I don't have a sister. I don't have a family."

The Leader turns to him and smiles. Her Wardens are trained well. The system will last. They will continue on for years and years. "Today," she whispers, "justice has been served."

The two of them weren't the only members of the family who survived the massacre.

But Helena refused to think of what happened to Selena as "surviving". The man with the scar struck her head against the wall, and the blow caused such damage that all Selena could do on her own in her final days was cry and convulse.

When they arrived in the Philippines, Stephen opted to take Selena home with them instead of putting her in a hospital. He placed her in a room on the second floor. The room contained all the right equipment, but the wrong nurse.

The nurse Stephen managed to hire was hotheaded and easily annoyed. Sometimes, she'd neglect Selena and let her shit or piss on her seat. Selena was often on her wheelchair in front of the television, and one day they found her crying haplessly at an episode of *Eat Bulaga!* while her feces trickled down from the hem of her nightgown.

The sound of them barging through the door startled the nurse, who had been flipping through a magazine. Stephen gripped the nurse's neck and banged her against the wall. "You bitch!" Helena heard him shout. The nurse whimpered, and Stephen cursed again, this time using the Filipino word that Helena had yet to learn.

Parker flew frequently to the Philippines to see his mother, and sometimes he would visit them. During one of those visits, two months after Selena's funeral, Helena passed out.

She was standing in her bedroom, listening to the strained, aimless chatter of the two men downstairs as they fixed dinner, when she suddenly felt a piercing pain in her temple and fainted. She woke up to the sound of his brother's voice.

"I feel sick," Helena told him, and stood up from his lap and ran to the bathroom. She heaved air. Then the pain came again, and Stephen and Parker saw her crying on the bathroom floor, clutching her head.

"Sweetheart?" Parker said, kneeling beside her. Helena put her arms around his waist, digging her head into his chest. "My head," Helena said, over and over.

"Here's your brother," Parker said, signaling to Stephen, who was already jabbing at the phone's keypad. "I'm going to call an ambulance."

Migraine was the diagnosis, and Helena was stumped by the simplicity of it. She had assumed it was something more deadly: a brain tumor, a creeping aneurysm. All throughout the gurney ride and the hospital tests, the part of her brain that the pain permitted to think thought it would be something that would leave her weeping at noontime comedy, staining her seat and her dress and her skin with the color of her excrement.

She imagined herself convulsing in her sleep. She imagined herself wishing so much to die but being unable to say it, her tongue dry and useless, stuck perpetually to the roof of her mouth.

And then it hit her. That's what Selena was crying about. She wanted to die, but couldn't convey the message.

Helena thought it would be disastrous if she waited too long before telling her brother. *"Kuya,"* she whispered to the back of his head as Parker drove them back home. She was stretched on the back seat. Both men thought she was sleeping and gave a start when she spoke.

"Does your head still hurt?" Stephen asked.

Helena's head was still fogged up due to the medicine injected into her, but she knew she was thinking clearly. "Are they sure it's just migraine?"

"Don't say 'just', sweetheart," said Parker. "My Mom has it, and it can really hurt."

"Papa had it," Stephen said. "Do you remember?"

"But are they *sure*?" Helena said.

"That's what the doctor said."

"Maybe he missed something," Helena said. "Maybe I have cancer."

"No, you don't," said Stephen. "They checked for that, too."

"But I *can* have it," Helena said, and Stephen replied with a sigh. "Maybe not now, but in the future. It's possible, right? Or I can hit my head pretty bad. Be in an accident."

"What are you talking about, Helena?"

"I want you to promise me something," Helena said. "If whatever happened to *Ate* ever happened to me, promise me that you won't let me live."

"What—"

"I don't want to *be* like that. And I don't think *Ate* did, too."

"Helena," Parker said.

But it was dark. She couldn't see Stephen's face. "I need him to promise me *now*," she told Parker. "If I don't hear his answer *now*, it might be too late and I won't be able to talk and he'll do what he wants. So I need him to promise me *now*."

"Helena," Stephen said, "stop it."

"But when will I speak like this, then?" she asked. "When I'm already pissing on my wheelchair? Parker can write something up. Right, Parker? Something for my brother to sign?"

Parker didn't move a muscle.

"Helena, please," Stephen said.

"You *need* to promise me," Helena said. "*Kuya*, if that happens to me and you still insisted to keep me in a room, I'll—" She groped for a word. "I'll hate you. Okay? I'll hate you."

"I can't" Stephen said, but stopped.

Promise? Listen? Think? What? "Promise me," Helena said. "*Kuya?* Promise me."

"Helena," Parker said gently. "Come on."

Helena ignored him. "I'll take that as a yes," Helena told her brother. Stephen's shoulders were as still as a wall. "All right, *Kuya?* I'll take that as a yes."


"Justice and the Law," the first Warden Leader says, "need not be oppressive. Before the Wardenry was officially formed, we members have studied the follies of past totalitarian regimes. These regimes created New Laws without telling their people, and made their people ignorant of the Law, made them live in fear. They created Laws without logic, and without heart, so their people hated the Law. Their people grew rebellious. They created Laws that do not apply to every single citizen, and so their people doubted the Law, made them scornful of the Law's Enforcers. Why should the people live their lives in terror and uncertainty, not knowing if their next move will bring a bullet through their head? Why should the people be denied Justice?

"In this new age," says the first Warden Leader, "you, Citizens, will know the Law, and any changes that will be made to it, so you will no longer fear it. You, Citizens, will be given a Law with mind and heart, so you will no longer feel the need to rebel against it. You, Citizens, in the eyes of the Law, will be treated equally, so you will no longer doubt it.

"And we, your Wardens, will not love you. But we will not hate you, either. We will not make ties. We will not make friends. We will be taken from our families, and will not create families, so we can answer to no one but the Law. We will watch you and listen to you, so we can catch the Trespass as it happens, obliterating the need for trial, for evidence, for witnesses, for testimonies, for pleas. We will be everywhere. We will not make mistakes.

"Together, we will create a Law that we will understand and know by heart, a Law that we will love and embrace, a Law that will be applicable to every single one of us. With those conditions set, there will be no need to balance the scales, or to listen to a Trespasser's motives or reasons. It will be clear that whosoever breaks the Law in this new age truly knows and understands his or her deed, truly knows and understands the punishment for that deed.

"It will be clear that whosoever breaks the law truly deserves to hear the song of our chains."


"So what pushed them to re-open the case?" Helena heard her brother say behind the sliding glass doors, probably already finished with his first drink, probably already tired with the small talk.

The tiny crack between the door and the wall remained undetected. Helena moved closer to it.

Parker sighed. "New witness?" Stephen said irritably. "New evidence? Or is the mayor just planning to pursue a second term?"

Another sigh from Parker. Helena heard him grunt, heard the lock of his briefcase clicking and snapping. "He," Parker began. "There was—"

"What."

"He struck again, Stephen," Parker said. A swoosh, papers riffling like continuous gunshots.

There was a pause. Helena gripped her sketchbook and drew random lines and squiggles on a sheet.

"When?" Stephen said.

"Two days ago. It's all over the news over there. I was wondering if it's already reached—"

"I don't pay attention to the news anymore."

Parker didn't comment.

"Filipinos?" Stephen asked.

"Are you sure you want to read the police report, Stephen?" Parker asked.

There was a long pause in which Helena felt heavier and heavier, as though she were about to hit the ground.

"Midnight," said Parker. "A guy and his twelve-year-old girl. He's a young father, a consultant. He did pretty well. He had the girl at age eighteen, so that makes him just thirty. The two men came in—"

"Two," Stephen said.

"Yes."

"So there were two."

Pause.

"Did they—" Fingers riffling through pages. "The father's alive," said Stephen.

"Yes," said Parker. "And here's why we want to re-open your case. While the two men were roughing him up, they blabbed to him. They spoke about your family. They gave details that the police never released to *anyone*."

Stephen remained silent.

"The father's already agreed to serve as witness," said Parker, like a salesman dangling a new toy.

"If the jury believed us the first time, that girl would still be alive," Stephen said, to which Parker didn't have an answer.

They knew that what finally killed the case was the mistake they made in the line-up.

The defense latched onto it, more viciously and more hungrily than on the other inconsistencies that had confused the jury and eventually invalidated the two of them in their eyes.

But in their minds, there were no inconsistencies. It was midnight when the two men came and stood on their front porch, the man with the scar even ringing the doorbell like a friend.

The Jimenezes had been flying to and from that house in the past two years. They had never heard anything about racist killing sprees within that neighborhood. They had never received any strange phone calls, any slurs. When their father opened the door for the two men, he did so with a smile on his face.

It was their first week as immigrants. They had fixed all the papers; they were going to live in that suburb for the rest of their lives. That night all six of them—Stephen, Selena, Nick, Regina, Adam, and Helena—were allowed to stay up late.

After dinner, Regina, Nick and Adam sat down with their parents in the living room to watch a movie while Selena locked herself up in her bedroom to read a book. Stephen and Helena were in Selena's bathroom, Stephen finally deciding to spend the night with the baby of the family by messing up her face with Selena's cosmetic collection.

"If I see *one* tube," Selena shouted at them that night from her bed, "just *one* tube misplaced on my sink tomorrow, I'm gonna come into your rooms and strangle both of you." With that, she turned off her bedside lamp, put on her headphones, and fell asleep to the sounds of a jazz album.

What did their father see when he looked through the peephole? The man with the scar was tall and pale, thirtyish, clean-shaven. That night, he was wearing a jacket, jeans. With his gloved hands and his gun with the silencer in his pocket he must have looked normal enough. A yuppie, a father of one.

Their father must have mistaken him for a neighbor with a plumbing problem, out to ask for a small favor. *Do you have a wrench?* What did that man say that made their father trust him so quickly, made him open the door without fear?

It was midnight when their father opened the door and received a bullet to the head, midnight when Stephen stopped wiping Helena's face dry, both of them frozen by the otherworldly sound of their mother screaming.

Stephen wanted to go out, wanted to yank the headphones off Selena's ears and wake her. But seconds before he could actually sort through his thoughts he heard footsteps coming up the stairs. He locked the bathroom door, placed the chair Helena had been standing on under the knob. Turned off the light.

Helena began to cry. He pressed her face into his side to muffle the sound she was making, and just stood there.

The bedroom door was kicked open. Selena must have heard that through the fog of piano and saxophones. "What," they heard her say. She must be sitting up now, wrapping the headphones' cords around her shoulder, squinting at the form by the door.

The man threw her facedown on the floor, near the bathroom door. Stephen and Helena felt her land, and felt the man land on top of her. They fell to their stomachs—first Stephen, then Helena, mimicking him—trying their best to see through the plastic slats at the bottom of the door. They saw Selena, eyes glassy as the man touched her. They saw the man. They saw his scar.

"Clearly?" asked the defense. The image was clear that night. At the line-up they could only see their sister's face.

Stephen picked Helena up and ran to the bathtub. "Why don't you take your clothes off for me, darling?" said the man with the scar.

Selena screamed. "Shut up," the man said. Selena wouldn't. "Shut up, shut up, *shut up!*"

There was only the sound, but they knew what he did, and after that impact Selena fell silent. The man with the scar left the room. They couldn't hear anything at all from downstairs. At one point they heard their mother scream, You animals, you animals.

"Where's your brother?" they heard the man growl. In court, the defense asked: "Which man?" They didn't know, they were not sure. "But there were two men."

Yes, there were two men, said Stephen, on the stand, but later on: I don't know.

"Where's your brother?" the man asked. Stephen thought the men saw their family photos, or else just knew how many people there really were in the house.

Stephen stood up at this point, carrying Helena. He removed the chair from the bathroom door, opened the door, started to slip on Selena's blood, caught himself. Don't look, he told Helena, transporting her to his back, and opened the window.

They crawled out of Selena's bedroom window, climbed down the ladder leaning against the roof, and ran, Stephen sweeping Helena into his arms in one swift motion, not slowing down. He felt something hot whisper against his left cheek, saw it hit the wall of the house he's approaching.

"What the—" A man was standing on the porch, stunned at the sight of them, at the source of the gunshot. "Hey!"

On the stand, the man said he heard the man with the gun say, Shit, and saw him walk back into the house and walk back out, "really quick", and dive into a pickup truck parked out front. It was dark, he couldn't remember if there were two men or only one. He couldn't remember the color of the vehicle. He was too flustered to note the plate number.

Hours later, the police found their parents, Regina, Adam, and Nick in the living room, all dead, and Selena, barely breathing on her bedroom floor upstairs. There was blood everywhere, and the sickening pig-smell filled the street even days after that night.

There was nothing stolen, nothing missing. No hair, no semen, no fingerprints. The investigators took note of the positions of the bodies and dutifully took pictures.

Both Stephen and Helena were "positive" about the man, and the scar on his face, on his right cheek near his chin. The police whipped through the case files and found three ex-cons who had the same profile: white, male, 5'10", with identical scars on one identical location on their faces, all with rap sheets a mile long, covering the ground from assault to murder, all with previous and current connections to the KKK or some similar organization.

Separately Stephen and Helena were made to view a line-up. The sight of so many men with scars rattled them to their bones but both Stephen and Helena pointed at the same man. Next, shouted the investigator. Here, they faltered. At the second line-up, they pointed at two different men: Helena chose a different ex-con while Stephen pointed at a lieutenant wearing prosthesis.

But they pointed at the same man again on the third try, converging, absolving themselves. Or so they thought. The man they chose from the line-ups was arrested only because he didn't have an alibi for that night, and because he drove a pickup truck.

But during the trial the defense was able to cook up something, and the man with the scar cried during cross-examination, touching the jury's hearts, their white, white hearts, Stephen would say. The man with the scar said that he *was* with the Klan before, but not anymore, that he's trying to change, that he's active in church. Parker's research and the prosecution's mind tricks doing nothing to break him.

The State couldn't indict a second man, because Stephen and Helena couldn't make up their minds if there *was* a second man. The verdict was not guilty, and they flew back to the Philippines to bury their dead.


It is considered the first Trespass after the Gathering. It occurred at the edge of the town, in a solitary shack perpetually smashed by the wind.

The old people can still remember the patches where the grass and the flowers used to grow in that abandoned field, but now there is nothing but sand, everything buried in sand, the wind blowing into and around the poor house creating whorls into the silt.

The Warden Leader is on watch that day, wrapped in black cloth in order to thwart the grit threatening to enter her eyes. When she sees the man with the scar and his accomplice forcing themselves through the door, she screams, Halt, but the wind carries her voice away along with the sand. Halt, she screams again, and releases her weapon, which sinks several inches into the ground.

The Leader and the Wardens move as quickly as they can, their feet sinking every now and again, their eyes smarting, and converge at the house, surrounding the two men.

The Warden positioned inside the house has the family backed up into a corner, shielded by his body and his arms.

Warden, says the Leader. And the Warden Leader swings her weapon over her head and strikes the two men with one graceful blow.

Thank you, says the littlest of the family members, a girl, who breaks away from the group and presses her face into the Warden Leader's stomach after the bodies fall. Her feet are soaked completely in the Trespassers' spilt blood, but she doesn't seem to mind.

Thank you, she says, hugging the Leader as well as she can with her tiny, tiny hands. Thank you, thank you, thank you, thank you.


Dusk was falling when Parker pushed the glass door aside and stepped out. He was shocked to see Helena sitting there, but tried to cover it with a smile. If he noticed the slight gap between the door and the wall before he got out, he didn't show it.

"Oh, hi, sweetie," he said, touching the top of her head with his fingertips. "I have to go now."

"Where are you staying?" Helena asked.

"Oh," he said, slapping his briefcase gently against his leg, ruminating, "Some hotel. I don't know if I can pass by my Mom's. I have so much work to do."

Helena nodded. "Maybe we'd see each other again."

Parker gazed at her quietly for a long, long while. "Maybe." He turned to the living room. "Stephen."

"Take care," Stephen said, stepping out, and sat down beside Helena. The two of them watched Parker leave.

Helena sat still beside her brother. What do we do now? she wanted to ask him.

"Helena," Stephen said, after a silence. "We have something very important to talk about."

Every night, together, they would check the locks on all the doors over and over. They would peek into each other's bedrooms at random hours. Be careful, they would say to each other whenever they parted ways, even if it was just to take out the garbage, or to fetch something forgotten upstairs, something left behind.

"All right," Helena said. That night, Stephen didn't get around to telling her what she already knew. Before dinner the phone rang, and Stephen answered it, and his reply led to another phone call, Stephen calling people up and being called, tying himself up in several conversations at once.

Helena went up to her room with her sketchbook, recalling the feel of the wood of the witness stand, cool like her father's old narra bench (her father used to brag that he got it from his own father, but her mother laughed this claim off, saying they actually bought it from an antique store in Ilocos), but not as gentle, or gracious.

Outside Helena, it was night, and inside of her she felt the dark descend. "Oh," she said, pleased. She found herself sitting at the dinner table, her mother handing out the plates, his father busy cutting up the meat. Stephen, Selena, Nick, Regina, and Adam. She looked at their faces and smiled.

"What's with you?" Selena said, and pinched her cheek. In one corner of the room stood a Warden, his clothes ink-black, his weapon in plain sight. Helena looked at him and smiled at him too. She was safe now, she thought, receiving the plate being handed to her. She was home.

# THE STORYTELLER''S CURSE

**M**artin found order and power whenever he wrote his stories, but he did not believe in a higher order, he did not believe in a higher power. During his darkest hours—when his father died, or when his wife and son left him—Martin believed if the universe was indeed governed by a god, he had poor accounting skills, sucked at time management, and had dire need of an assistant. How could someone with such an immense and endless power mess up creation so badly? If there is a god, Martin thought, then he must be flawed. If there is a god, then he must be a man.

And Martin would say to him, *Go fuck yourself.*

Which was exactly what Martin said when a powerful entity (who looked like a nondescript college student with droopy eyes and a tired face, that screamed *Papers!*) slammed into his chest and stepped on his foot at the train station. It was the day marking the month after Regina finally took out her huge, red luggage, packed it with clothes, and left the house with their car and their son. The last time she used that luggage was a decade ago, when they traveled to Tokyo. Martin kept the engagement ring in the small bag he was going to carry inside the plane, and as it was scanned by the airport X-ray it must have appeared right smack in the middle of the screen, bright as day. *It was the deadliest weapon I had ever carried,* Martin joked to their friends year after year during their anniversary. That day at the airport the man manning the X-ray kept a straight face, but mouthed *Good luck* when Martin happened to glance at him. It filled Martin with joy, the fear falling off his shoulders like a wet coat. The world seemed so kind.

When Regina took out her luggage, ten years later, the engagement ring and her wedding band were sitting abandoned on her bedside table, ownerless. The red luggage smelled like mothballs, busy nights, unfulfilled trips. Martin imagined Regina turning to her open closet and yanking out hangers and clothes, wounding herself with stray brooches and lace, but in truth she moved slowly, methodically, a woman going on a vacation, a woman with a checklist, a woman with all the time in the world.

*She'd be back,* was what Martin thought when the door closed and the car left the driveway. Jerome had shot him a confused look as he followed his mother out the door. For one moment, Martin wished he'd break away from his mother's side and run to him.

Jerome, as a baby, liked him enough, bobbing on his lap, tugging at the skin of his cheeks, smiling, toothless, at his bright face. He grew up to be a quiet child, but Martin found comfort in his son's silence, in Jerome's tilted head and pressed lips as Martin read (and sometimes made up) a bedtime story for him at night. Some nights, he imagined Jerome as a sixteen-year-old boy, a high school student sitting with him on the couch to watch the news, or a basketball game, the minutes ticking wordlessly by. He imagined Jerome creating his own stories, within that silence.

Every day after his wife and son walked out the door, Martin would sit at the edge of his bed, on the couch, by the kitchen table, and imagine his son hating him.

Martin continued his day-to-day activities as though nothing was amiss. He still woke up at seven a.m. every morning, still opened all the windows in the living room, still switched on the TV set to watch the news. But the news didn't matter to him anymore, serving only as background noise as he walked around the kitchen like a man lost in the wilderness. He made eggs for himself that first morning, and ordered take-out chicken for dinner when he came home that first night. He refused to cook dinner in their kitchen, because to do so, in his mind, was to accept his family's permanent disappearance from his life.

He still went to work, taking the train and distracting himself with music plugged into his ears. He taught literature and language at the University, and yammered endlessly about Shakespeare and Gregorio Brillantes to prevent himself from thinking too much about departures. Between classes he wrote and un-wrote fiction, creating and discarding one story idea after another. He stayed late at night to watch the academic building empty itself of people, and then he would walk the halls with his bag and his books, savoring the cool and the quiet. This cool and quiet had more life than the cool and quiet waiting for him at home.

Home. After only a week his room looked more like a garbage bin than anything else, his laundry piling up, his study table covered with unrinsed coffee mugs. One Sunday, he rolled up his sleeves and decided to clean up. He hauled his clothes into the machine and polished anything that could be polished. He remembered the time Regina moved in with him, the first time they went furniture shopping. Every time he looked at a couch or a table the first thing he'd ask was, *Is this hard to clean?* How Regina laughed and how easy it seemed to get used to domesticity, to quiet nights, to a certain rhythm. How easy it is to embrace a life together. They brought stuff to the house willy-nilly. Before they got married, he remembered making notes in his head: *She bought that lamp, I bought this chair.* After a few years together, they had accumulated so much stuff that he lost count of the things he owned. He considered doing the list on Excel, but thought it a crude thing to do. Sometimes he lay at night wondering how they would divide the furniture if ever they—

Then he'd stop thinking, because he didn't want to think of this, until he found himself among the many objects Regina found useless enough to leave behind.

The fact was, he had an affair with another woman: a younger woman, an intern who stayed with the department for a month or so and moved on. She smelled like flowers. She excited him. She didn't push him away when he kissed her in his own office. He didn't think he would be one of those men but he became one of them, in the blink of an eye. It was easy. He slept with her once and he slept with her again, and again, and again, and every night he hated Regina for her unkempt hair and for being tired all the time and for giving him a child that did nothing but stare. The fact was, he loved them more than anything, but what use were his words now? What use were his pain, his guilt, his wish to be absolved?

He kept recalling that first night Regina stayed over at his apartment, how her hair smelled, how it curled on her shoulders as she lay beside him, how he held her hands. Her soft voice as she talked about a fantasy novel she was reading, how she giggled as she tried to affect a British accent and failed. How he wished for rain to drown the summer heat and make the night perfect, even though it was perfect. "And what would you give me, good sir?" she said at one point, and he played along, even though what he said was no lie. "The world," he said. "The world, the world, the world."

He was trying to hold onto an image that could comfort him and shield him from the heat and the press of bodies. It had been a month, and all that was left was a moment's snapshot of Regina turning away from him and closing the door, and it wasn't enough to buoy him up in this sea, it wasn't enough to remove him from this day, it wasn't enough.

"Go fuck yourself," he said in anger after a student stepped on his foot, the pain shooting up to his hip. The student didn't say anything, but at that moment Martin was already cursed.

That night, Martin wasn't able to sleep.

The day passed by like any other day: uneventful and empty. He had taken a cup of coffee in the afternoon, but he had always taken coffee in the afternoon, so it wasn't the caffeine that was keeping him up. It wasn't a high brought by the day's peculiar activities, of which there were none. It wasn't the heat, because in fact, it rained right after his last class, cooling the air considerably, and he walked across the hallway thinking of soup, and bed, and sleep.

Lately he had taken to downing a nightcap and hitting the sack before midnight. By three a.m. he was still wide-awake. He began thinking of Regina, of how she warmed her side of the bed. He stood up and read the student essays he planned to read during his free time later that week. By five, he pushed away the pile of papers and turned on the T.V. to catch the early morning news. He began thinking of Jerome, of how he fit in the crook of his arms as he slept, his smell. The news was a rehash of what had been aired the night before, so Martin stood up and entered his son's room for the first time that month. He sat on the edge of the boy's bed and cried as though his son had died. As though he had died. Perhaps he had died. Perhaps he was dead now, to Jerome.

In his room, the alarm went off like a hysterical mourner. It was seven a.m.

All throughout that day he thought he would fall asleep on his feet. Fall with his face flat on the floor during class. None of this happened. He went through his classes not wishing for bed, as though he had a good night's sleep. As though he had the *best* night's sleep, in fact, since normally he'd start yawning around two p.m., and he'd have to grab a cup of coffee. That day: nothing, no longing for siesta. All his senses were alive and working. "Sooner or later I'd start hallucinating," he said out loud as he sat alone in his office. He read up on sleep deprivation online. The longest a human being had stayed awake was 11 days. "I have ten more days before I die," he thought. He read about microsleeping. How many more days before his brain shut down?

It was as if he was being prepared for an interrogation, but what answer could he give under the influence of such torture? *I'm sorry. It was my fault.*

*Please let me sleep tonight.*

He would write a story.

Martin got this idea at four a.m. after what felt like hours upon hours of tossing and turning. He had exhausted his list of all the possible things he could do to while the time away. Read a book, correct more papers, do the laundry. At three, he kicked off his slippers and lay down. He closed his eyes. How could his brain still be functioning after so many hours with no rest, no dreams? If there was a switch, he wanted to flip it. Where was the button he could push? It was the waiting that got to him, the empty hours. He wanted to close his eyes and go away. He wanted to escape.

He would write a story.

But what story?

Martin crawled out of his bed and looked for the tiny notebook on which he had scribble scenes, dialogues, and the occasional opening paragraph that he believed held promise. Most of the words were crossed out, so he flipped through the pages, combing through the pen lines for a story prompt.

He sat in front of his computer at half-past four, opened a blank document, and typed **Day 0**.

*Day 0*

It was Clara who first woke up.

She woke up lying on her back between John and Billy, covered in dew and grass stains and smelling the same smells: earth, foliage, the faint perfume of flowers. Now, here, everything around her had a distinct metallic tang, as though she had just swallowed coins.

She woke up blinking at the sunlight streaming through the red leaves of the tree.

Something felt different.

Clara sat up slowly. John and Billy were sleeping on their sides, both of them facing her. They were all covered in blood: their clothes and especially their hands. There was a brook nearby, but they had fallen asleep before washing up. Or they were made to fall asleep. Clara looked at her hands and idly picked at the dried blood now starting to flake along the cracks of her palms.

She stood up. She felt one of the boys stir but didn't look back to check. She took a step, and then another. A wind blew but not one leaf fell from the tree. Not one leaf. She wanted to ask, Where's Ted?

but remembered, and she also remembered the promise made to her, the promise made to them, and so she took another step and another.

Clara? she heard John say. When she didn't stop she heard the boys say, Clara, wait, and stand up and follow her. Did it work? she heard Billy ask.

Suddenly, Clara stopped.

She had already fallen to her knees when Billy and John got to her.

It was a road. They were sitting on the shoulder of a road.

It worked, John said. Billy had begun to cry. Clara. Clara. It worked. We did it.

Clara took a deep breath and screamed.


*Day 1*

**Grocery Store.** Clara, Billy, John, and Ted walked from one aisle to another, Billy weighed down by his backpack. You should have just left that by the counter, Clara said, picking up a can of tuna. Cat food? Ted said. Come on, Clars, where are the sausages? John pushed the cart ahead of the group, filling it with toilet paper. I have my camera here, Billy said, shrugging. It's not that heavy. Do we have to buy water, or does the place have a faucet? John said. Or a well? Or a river? Ted laughed. I think the bus will carry enough for the class, Billy said, but you can bring your own bottle. It's just the one night, John, Ted said. We'll make it through. God, I hope I don't get my period, Clara said. Jesus, Clara, John said. Come on, Clara, Ted said. What? said Clara, picking up a pack of sanitary napkin and chucking it into the cart with the can of tuna. Ted retaliated by adding a can of meatloaf. Clara sighed. Do you think we'll have to go through stupid hikes like this in college? Clara said. The group laughed. But campfire stories! Ted said. And snuggly sleeping bags! And the night sky! Bet there will be ants, Clara said morosely. John and Billy added several bags of chips, a pack of cookies, a chocolate bar, a bottle of mosquito repellent, sunscreen. I thought they said we're not allowed to take pictures, John said. Only of this particular tree, Billy said.

**Kwento.** They call it the Tree of Mapulon, after the old Tagalog god. The story goes that it used to be surrounded by a village, and that it grew and was regarded like any ordinary tree, until the village was burned to the ground and the tree remained, now with leaves as red as fire. When the smoke cleared it became clear to everyone that it had been marked by the god of seasons, and shouldn't be touched. When the village was rebuilt they called it *Sa Paanan ni Mapulon.* At the feet of Mapulon. The villagers supported themselves through raising livestock and harvesting *palay* and root crops, and food was plenty for several decades, with the village being blessed with good weather. Then a storm came, and after three days of never-ending rains, the people offered a portion of their harvest. Still, it continued to rain, so one of the men of the village offered a chicken and left it bleeding on the exposed roots of the great tree. Then they offered a pig. A cow. A carabao. A little girl. The rains stopped when the child's throat was slit, but every year Mapulon seemed to want more. All of a sudden one child wasn't enough. Pregnant women fled the village, fearing their newborns might be turned into sacrifice. They would turn up dead in a day or two, lost and wounded in the woods.

The village elders said the old god was of the air, the soil, and sunshine. He shouldn't have been given a taste of blood. They decided not to give anything more. It was a decision that came several decades too late. One day a storm came and destroyed the village, but left the tree unscathed, as always. *Sa Paanan ni Mapulon* was never rebuilt.

And now it's a tourist spot, John said.

Every story has a happy ending, Billy said. They laughed.

What the hell are you two yammering about? Clara said.

**Exit.** They liked the feel of the grocery store late at night: the aircon on full blast, the bright fluorescent, the sleepy college guy behind the counter ringing up their items like a robot, the aisles suddenly as wide as the sea with the absence of other customers. This should last us, right? John said as they walked out with their bags, and Ted said, It's just the one night. If I had my period it's going to feel like forever, Clara said, and the boys all said, Ew, as though they had rehearsed it.

*Day 4*

When they finally ran out of food and water they also ran out of things to hope for, and all of a sudden their confinement felt all too real. It was how Clara thought of what was happening to them. *Confinement.* They were sitting on an open field, no walls in sight, only trees (and this tree, fire-red), but every time they tried walking away they would be pulled back by a single thought: *I don't want to leave.* But they do want to leave, every single one of them, and they would sit under the great tree and wonder, confused, alarmed, *Why am I still here?*

Billy had begun pointing fingers. You're menstruating, he said. He smelled your blood.

Who? Clara said, angry now. Who smelled my blood? Who the fuck are you talking about? Billy wouldn't say.

She wasn't menstruating. It should come any day now, and Clara couldn't help but think how uncomfortable it was going to be. Where would she throw away her used pads, what if she stained her pants? She thought of her parents, she wondered what picture they had submitted to the police and the newspapers. I hope they didn't use my Facebook profile pic, she told Ted, who was then lying on his side. I looked stupid in that. Ted laughed, then gasped. My stomach hurts, he said.

The everyday worries kept her sane, but she looked at Ted's contorted face, the red leaves of the tree above them, and she began to cry. I want to go home, she said.


*Day 1*

The big dog had been following them since the moment they stepped off the bus. What are you talking about? John said, and Clara said she had been seeing a dog—a black dog as big as a Doberman, if not bigger—just padding along beside their group as they hiked through the forest. What would a dog be doing around here? John said. Maybe it's a deer. *A deer?* Ted said. What is this, a Disney film? They all laughed at that, but Clara was unsettled. It was a hot day, but she couldn't be that delirious. I'm pretty sure it was a dog, she said.

The tree was just one of the many stops in the trek. Bored and sore, Clara checked her online accounts on her phone as the tour guide said something about a village burned by a god. The tree was breathtaking at first sight—that sudden, unexpected blaze of red— but Clara was hungry and in dire need of a soft place to lie on. No pictures, please, the tour guide said suddenly, and Clara, startled, almost dropped her phone. I—I wasn't—Sorry. Clara looked up and saw the biggest bird she had ever seen perched on one of the tree's branches. The bird was black as a raven, an inkblot on a field of red, with a wingspan that Clara believed could completely envelop her. The tour guide seemed unperturbed. When Clara looked around her, she saw the boys staring at the tree with furrowed brows. You see that thing, too? Clara said, suddenly afraid, and the bird squawked and it was as though the day had imploded.

It was dark, and there were now just the four of them under the tree. What—Clara said, too surprised to scream, or to even finish her question. All their phones were dead. Her wristwatch told her an impossible thing: it was already nine p.m.


## Day 15

Clara shared a meal with a man.

Before that, she was convinced they would die. Clara spent most of the second week sleeping, hoping that by the time she opened her eyes, she'd be back on her bed, surrounded by pillows.

Or dead, even though she could not imagine death.

But she held on, they held on, and it was torture to wake up each morning with parched lips and hollow stomachs and still be alive.

The man came when night fell, when they were all asleep. He leaned over Clara and shook her awake. Come with me, he said. He was wearing a suit with no tie, and left behind a fragrant mist as he walked, barefoot, on the grass. Come, he said. I have set the table for dinner.

Clara followed him even though she could hardly walk, even though, no matter how hard she tried, she could not see his face.

There was a table behind the tree. It was covered with white silk and carried bowls of fruits and bread and mixed vegetables and steamed rice and gravy for the roasted chicken, which sat fat and plump on a silver platter. On smaller crystal containers were butter and fruit jam and mayonnaise and slices of cheese, and cakes and sweet rolls and chocolate squares. The centerpiece was a vase filled with wild flowers. Clara pulled back a cushioned chair and sat, and gaped. Everything smelled like comfort, like a fresh morning bath, like a hot drink on a rainy night.

Please, said the man, cutting up the chicken for her, and Clara threw away the stories about enchanted offers and unknowing imprisonment. For several minutes she ate whatever she could grab, shunning the cutlery and endlessly filling her plate with food.

She was already halfway through her second slice of chocolate cake when she realized something. You're not going to let us go, are you? She told her faceless host, who added a sugar cube to his coffee and said, Oh, you poor child. You poor, poor child.

Clara cried as he sipped. Are you punishing us? she said.

The man sounded aghast. Why would I punish you, child? Did you do something wrong?

Then why? Clara said. She was already shouting, but the boys remained asleep on the other side of the tree. Why us? Why are you keeping us here?

The man placed his cup back on the saucer. Clara imagined he was smiling. Because you amuse me, he said.

When she woke up, they discovered that they could no longer feel hunger. I don't feel alive, Clara said.


## Day 2

Someone will find us, Clara told the boys, and broke the chocolate bar into four pieces.


## Day 836

There should be something we could do, Clara said.

Once again she was sitting at the white table with the roasted chicken and the jam and the cakes and the sugar cubes and the cheese and the crystal and the man whose face she still could not see. Once every week the man—always fragrant, always soothing—would lean over her and shake her awake and say Come to dinner, and every time she would say no. Let us go, and we will join you at your table, she whispered once, but the man only laughed and touched a finger lightly to her nose. Now, now child, he said. Where's the fun in that?

His finger felt like the sun.

Tonight Clara felt the weight of the days on her shoulders, and so she said yes. She wanted to negotiate with the man, and if that failed she thought the table had enough knives to stick in her throat. *Clara,* she whispered to herself as she followed him to the table, as she pulled back a cushioned chair and sat *(Clara)*, as she took a loaf of bread and a piece of cheese and bit *(Clara)*. *My name is Clara.* She could barely recall how they came to be imprisoned in that place, she'd lost count of the days (Billy kept a tally once on the blank page of his book, but when he reached 100 he tossed the book away, horrified; That can't be right, he said), and she couldn't remember her parents. *What were their names?* But at least she knew hers, at least she knew she was an entity separate from the trees and the water and the grass. How do you feel? the man had asked before they sat down, and Clara had said, Old.

And now Clara waited for the man to respond to her.

Well, the man said, drinking wine from a glass that sparkled in the moonlight, how glad I am that you brought it up. The wine was the color of the leaves of the tree, and it seemed to grow darker the longer Clara looked.

There is a way? Clara said.

I can make a way, the man said, his elbows resting on the table, his fingers forming a steeple in front of his mouth. Pardon my frankness, but I *am* beginning to get bored with the lot of you. The way out could prove to be a good show, though.

Clara could hear the smile in his voice.

Please, Clara said, crying now. Please let this be real. Please let us go. Please.

Now, now, child, the man said. No tears at the table. Here, have some wine.

Clara received the glass. To freedom! the man said, and clinked his glass against hers.

But what am I supposed to do? Clara asked, confused.

Oh, an easy task, child, the man said. You'll just have to kill one of your own. Now down your wine, eat a pear, cut yourself a slice of cake. Has there ever been a night finer than this? To freedom!

## Day 900

It was already dark when they finished.

None of them spoke. They set aside the rocks now covered with blood, brain, and bone and busied themselves with the task of arranging the body. Ted fell on the roots of the tree and bled there, so they didn't have to exert too much effort in dragging him to position. John rolled him over so he lay on his back, and Clara and Billy straightened his clothes and retied his shoes. A side of Ted's skull had caved in, but Clara focused on his eyes. He looked peaceful. He's free now. She followed his empty gaze and looked up at the tree's branches. The leaves looked redder than before.

Then they slept.

## Day 0

Martin slept. He woke up refreshed, made eggs for breakfast, tidied his room, and went to work. He hoped to try calling his wife again, even though the last time he tried he couldn't connect. But he had slept, and he was feeling he could accomplish something.

The story he saved on his desktop and forgot until that evening.

It was raining hard that night, but the knocks still cut through the noise of rainfall. Three sharp knocks. Martin stood up, his heart hammering against his rib cage, thinking of Regina, thinking of his son.

But what he found on the porch were three teenagers, two boys and a girl. One of the boys was wearing glasses and was bent over the girl, who was sitting on the step with her arms crossed, facing the street. They were all wearing jackets, zippered with the hoods up. At their feet lay their backpacks, spattered with mud and grass stains.

The boy gasped in relief when Martin opened the door. "Oh, thank God somebody's home," he said. Then he burst into tears, which surprised the other boy as much as it surprised Martin. "John," the other boy said, hurting.

"Can we come in, please?" said John. "We just need a place to stay while it's raining."

*John.* All three of them looked disturbingly familiar. Martin tasted bile at the back of his throat.

A gust of wind blew, and out of reflex Martin said, "Get inside."

John, euphoric, did not wait for him to change his mind. He gathered up the bags with both of his hands and stepped across the threshold. "Come on," he said. The girl glanced over her shoulder. She was crying softly, her eyes bloodshot. "We can come in?" she said to the other boy.

"Yes," Martin said. "Hurry, the rain's entering the house."

The other boy helped the girl stand up. Martin closed the door behind them. John was going to the living room, seeing the couch and the bright light, but Martin led them farther on to the kitchen and sat them at the table. It was warmer there. John and the other boy unzipped their jackets to take them off. The girl fumbled with the zipper, and took off her jacket slowly, as though she was still learning the intricacies of clothing. *Their shirts were clean,* and Martin thought, *They changed their clothes, they washed off the blood in the rain.*

"My name is Martin," he said. "You are John?"

"Yes, and this is Billy, and that's Clara."

*I'm dreaming,* Martin thought. "What happened to you?"

For a moment nobody answered. Then Clara said, "We got lost."

There was nothing but eggs and stale bread in the fridge, so Martin called the nearby 24-hour pizza joint and ordered food for his guests. The pizza joint was a small place run by widowed sisters. It was Jerome's favorite place. It had wood paneling, checkered tablecloths, and the smell of simmering tomatoes and cheese perpetually hanging in the air. There were only three waiters and two riders for the deliveries and Martin knew each one of them.

The one who answered the phone and took his name and address sounded like a new guy. "Have you been sleeping well, sir?" the guy said, suddenly, after Martin rattled off his orders.

"Excuse me?"

"Have you been sleeping well?"

The new guy sounded concerned. Martin felt a weight in his chest. Not fear, just a very faint realization.

"And god said, Let there be light, and there was light," said the guy at the pizza joint.

Martin said nothing.

"And god said, Let the earth bring forth grass, the herb yielding seed, and the fruit tree yielding fruit after his kind, whose seed is in itself, upon the earth: and it was so. And god said, Let the earth bring forth the living creature after his kind, cattle, and creeping thing, and beast of the earth after his kind: and it was so," the guy said. "Whatever this god says, it appears, and it is so. Such a god must have no flaws, or the universe will die after a single utterance."

*What?* Martin thought.

"I could have killed you, you know. Turned you to ash. And for what? For screaming at me after I stepped on your foot? Every day I pray that whoever created us is not like me, so rash and hateful, and such a poor judge. I pray that whoever created us is still alive, whatever that may mean for such a being, and did not just delegate the powers to me as a cruel joke."

Martin wanted to refuse what he was hearing, but there was the story on his desk, there were the three teenagers in his kitchen. And this voice, so pained and soft, that he knew, for some reason, to be telling the truth. "Can you take it back?" he asked.

"Your pizza will be delivered within 15 to 20 minutes after this call," the guy said, and hung up.

Martin went back to the kitchen. They were still there. *Maybe I'm still awake, and all of this is nothing but an elaborate hallucination.*

They almost jumped out of their skin when he came back, their faces terrified and open.

"Pizza should be on the way," he said, and puttered around the kitchen making hot cocoa so he didn't have to look at their faces.

He placed the mugs in front of them, but drank his cocoa with his hip against the sink, his arms crossed. The silence must have been so overwhelming that John blurted out, "You live here alone?"

Martin was surprised by the question. He looked at the three of them, these three whose origin frightened him. But there had always been the need to confess. "I have a wife and a son. They left me. I cheated on my wife with this young intern that I thought I loved. But I realized I meant nothing to her, and that she meant nothing to me at all."

John and Billy were so shocked by the sudden barrage of information that the kitchen fell silent again. It was Clara who spoke up. "You cheated on your wife?" she said softly.

Martin felt a loneliness so heavy he almost dropped his mug. He nodded.

Clara's eyes were red-rimmed and tired, but they softened when she asked, "Did the other girl know? If she knew, then that lessens your guilt a little bit."

"It's not as if guilt can be shared," John said. "It's not *pizza*."

She continued to speak to Martin, looking as though she had just woken up from a long and restless sleep. "I killed a friend," she said.

Billy was visibly aghast, but John managed to contain himself. "She's really tired," he told Martin.

"He said I had to kill one of my friends, but he didn't give me a name," Clara said, her tears now falling in thick streams, "so one day I picked up three sticks from the foot of the tree and marked them. I pulled the stick marked with his name."

Martin didn't write that scene, but he had thought of it. Was that how it worked? Creation begetting creation, ideas made flesh that he could not control? It scared him more than anything. Somewhere stood a tree with leaves of blood. Somewhere, a boy lay dead and buried. Somewhere, a god sat at a white table, sipping his coffee, oblivious to pain, laughing with amusement.

*I am Mapulon,* Martin thought with sadness and revulsion. *And I said, Let there be a tree with red leaves, and there was a tree.*

John and Billy were staring at Clara, looking like they had just been punched.

"You said he chose Ted," Billy said. "You said he gave you a name."

Billy began to cry as well, but Martin didn't like the look on John's face. All of a sudden Martin saw flashes of murder, his own kitchen smelling like a slaughterhouse.

Martin heard the doorbell, and hurried out of the kitchen to answer it. Waiting outside the front door was a young man wearing a black cap and a black raincoat, dripping with rainwater and carrying three boxes of pizza. The front porch smelled like pepperoni, ketchup, bacon. Martin knew it was the same young man from the train station, the one he thought was a college student.

"You need to help me," Martin said.

"What you name, becomes," the young man said.

Martin considered this. "It is only a story. It does not exist."

A sound like a universe changing its course.

"And it was so," the young man said.

They went back to the kitchen, now empty. On the center of the table are three cups of hot cocoa, untouched. The young man shed his raincoat and cap and, without a word, opened one of the pizza boxes. They sat down and ate in silence, like old friends.

"You could rewrite stories, you know," the young man said. "You didn't have to destroy."

"I don't trust myself anymore," Martin said.

Martin turned toward the windows above the sink. It was still dark outside, but it had gone quiet. The rain had stopped. "Can you take it back now?" he said.

"You only have to say it," the young man said.

"It's yours," Martin said.

The young man nodded, finishing another slice and his cup of cocoa. Martin didn't feel any heavier or lighter. It was as though nothing at all was taken from him, nothing at all was given away. After a few moments, the young man stood up and rinsed his mug in the sink. All the while Martin worked up the courage to ask his name, where he came from, if he had always had this power, but Martin was too scared to hear the answers.

"How much for the pizza?"

"Don't worry about it." The young man wiped his hands on his pants, put his raincoat back on, and held his cap in his hands. He turned to Martin and smiled before leaving the kitchen. "It's on the house."

Martin remained at the kitchen table. He heard the front door close. It would be morning soon. He wished his wife and son were here. He could have easily wished them back to this kitchen, this house, he could have turned back time, but what kind of a reality would he conjure, flawed as he was? *What would you give me, good sir?* he imagined his wife asking him, as she had asked him eons ago.

"The world," Martin said to the air smelling of turned earth, the stillness the rain had left in its wake. It was true. He could have made it true just minutes ago but now he wondered what such a gift, coming from him, would mean to her, if it would mean anything at all. "The world, the world, the world."

## REUNION

He was finally able to speak with his older brother in 2008, in a room at the end of a hospital corridor in Manila, by the wall with the window, as the final light of the day came slanting in, as dusk settled and colored the sky. They were both staring through it, thinking of the words to say. Meanwhile, yellow light faded with each passing minute, the glow so much like sunset in their early days, descending upon their shoulders as they walked side by side on the field. He remembered that: the walk, the wait, and the plan in his brother's head so clear it was almost palpable. Their fear: they *were* afraid, both of them. *Both* of them. He remembered that clearly. It was a memory that glimmered more brilliantly than all the others.

He had seen him before, of course. In Marbach, for example, during the madness of the Children's Crusade, marching toward Italy where they would later disintegrate, some of them (including his brother) disappearing forever. He saw his brother dart away from the boy from Cologne, the one who supposedly received the Message, as he himself moved in and gripped the boy's arm, whispering urgently: *umkehren, umkehren.* Turn back, turn back. The boy didn't listen, of course. The Holy Land needed their aid. *What Holy Land?* He had wanted to scream; he was weary and furious. *What aid?* He had followed the boy, who spoke to him while the group was in Mainz, out of curiosity and mild amusement. Then, he saw his brother among the boy's followers. As the boy gently pried his hand away he tried to push through the knot of marching children. He wanted to come to his brother and say, *Listen.*

He had lost count of the many times he had attempted to approach him. In China, during the famine, he saw him shoving pulverized stones into his mouth in a silent backyard. Walking several paces ahead of him in the shadow of the Tower of London, and he was waiting for the queen to be imprisoned. Standing, morose and alone, in the Hall of Mirrors, reflected in one of the looking-glasses as the dancers of the ball rose and fell all around him like a wave of fabric. He knew his brother was among the crowd escaping from the soil that wouldn't yield; the land that betrayed them. He knew he was there when the factories rose, when soot and sound fell across the cities.

But he knew, also, that his brother could sense his presence, and did his best to avoid him. Once, in Cambridge, in 1850, they ended up in the same dormitory, students at the dawn of a new age. (There was always a "dawn" and a "new age"; he wondered what this particular one—mechanized and ruthless—would bring.) For days he would look for his brother in the faces of his classmates and professors, but would fail to find him. He knew his floor, his room number, so one night he finally summoned the courage to climb up the staircase and stand outside his doorway. A light was flickering inside the room, and from the shadows seeping through the gap between the bottom of the door and the floor he saw with a jolt that his brother was standing on the other side.

He touched the door, his fingers resting lightly on the wood. He was getting ready to say his brother's name.

"Don't," a voice on the other side suddenly said.

He jumped back as if the door were on fire.

"I know you're there," his brother said. "Just go."

And he did, because he was a coward, because he was heartbroken, because the very act of forming his brother's name in his mouth after so many lifetimes had drained him, and now he wanted to just go back to his bed. Years and years ago his brother had said to him, "Let's go out into the field", and he followed. He knew he shouldn't be surprised to feel himself pulling away from that corridor, as he watched his feet walk down the stairs. Back in his classes, he kept imagining that someone was calling his name. His real name, not the name he was given in that particular life. That was impossible, of course. Nobody knew his name.

He had one other close encounter with him before 2008, and this time, he was able to see his brother face-to-face. It was 1902, in the Philippines, the country they will choose to live in for several decades. (It was a country filled with the usual maladies: a history of invasion, more than one declaration of independence, corruption, discontent, diaspora—things that didn't surprise him, having seen them in other shores, other times. Later, he would see this country give birth to a generation with members who would find beauty still in a country so much less that it once was, but would feel in their bones that something was amiss, something had been taken from them. Their forefathers would try to talk to them about a lost greatness, but would do so spitefully, as if the loss were their fault. They would go through life with a pensive expression on their faces, trying to remember.)

In 1902, Manila fell to cholera. The boats and the trains traveling to the provinces were temporarily stopped, and more than 200 special police swooped into the city to guard its exits. In that life his name was Niño, and when the plague came he was twelve years old. He knew nothing of what had caused it; being a child, he was never spoken to seriously, and even if the adults did speak, Niño was quick to realize that they also did not have a clue. Later, lives later, he would read in a book the theory that the disease was brought into the metropolis from Canton, which was suffering from it, through a shipment of cabbages. Cabbages. It was almost hilarious. In 1902, all Niño's parents could think of was judgment and darkness. All at once, their neighbors were waking up sick and vomiting over the side of their beds. They became fearful of the disinfectant carts: the sick driven away in an ambulance, their relatives forced into isolation, the food inside their homes destroyed, everything else submerged in acid. They were horrified, but not surprised, when stories about fathers who kept their sick children locked in secret rooms traveled the paralyzed streets. Who could blame the young man who carried his dead sister in his arms, and placed her on a slab of stone several meters away from their mother's house, in a place where her origin would not be traced? Who could blame the mother with two healthy sons, who pushed her sick youngest out onto a dark street and told him, *Stay here I will come back for you,* and did not come back? Who could blame the daughter who said *Not mine, not mine* when confronted with the dead body of her own mother? Dead bodies were found in fields and rivers, discarded and nameless. Every night, the people would dream of a man with the feet of a rooster knocking on their doors, and wake up covered in sweat, dreaming they had answered.

One of their neighbors, a kind young woman named Luisita, lost her husband to the plague. She accepted the fumigation and quarantine with a calm that astonished even the health inspectors, but one night they heard her screaming from inside her house: "This town should be burned! This town should be burned to the ground, so we could start anew!" Sometimes she called her dead husband's name.

Niño's father, who was a businessman, began talking to his mother about bribing one of the special police so they could slip out of the district. "And how do you suppose are we going to travel from there?" she said with alarm. "Are we going to *walk* to Cavite? Is that what you are proposing?" They had money, but they were not rich enough to own a car.

While this apparently futile plan was being hatched, Niño slipped out of the house. He always left the house whenever his parents fought, but this time he went further and opened the wrought-iron gate and walked out onto the sidewalk. He turned around the corner and listened to the soles of his shoes slapping on the pavement. Behind the houses was an empty field of grass and weeds and trees, unlit. Every now and then the clouds shifted, and a moonbeam would hit a leaf here, a wild flower there, making them glimmer. It was an empty lot that had been bought by one of the Americans, and for weeks after the purchase his mother wondered, not without a hint of envy, how his house would look like. The speculations ended when the plague came; she became positive the American would just sell the title to the government.

Niño stopped walking when he came upon a dead body in the middle of the field.

He waited for the clouds to shift again, but he knew from the smell alone that it was another victim of the plague. After a few seconds the moon shone through, and he saw that it was a little child, a little boy, maybe three or four years old. Well-dressed, probably came from a family just like his. Well-fed but now gaunt and shriveled up by his illness. Judging by the positions of the blades of grass around the body, Niño could tell that the body had just recently fallen, or had just recently been lain there.

All of a sudden, he became aware of someone panting. "I can't—" someone said. A boy Niño's age was on the other side of the body, the top of his head facing Niño. The boy was bent over, hands on his knees, breathing hard. "I can't go any further," the boy said. "I was—I was supposed to take him to the edge of town, by the river, but the health inspectors seemed to be *everywhere* and I just—I can't—"

The moon had disappeared again. Niño recognized the boy almost at once. He asked, "Is he your brother?"

Apparently the boy didn't know he was standing there; he had been talking to himself. He straightened up with a jolt and stepped back in alarm. Then, perhaps seeing Niño's size, calmed down long enough to say, "My cousin. He's my cousin, I don't have any bro—"

The boy stopped talking. The moon remained hidden, but of course by then the boy already knew who he was talking to even without seeing him. Niño saw the boy's shoulders slump, saw him take another step back.

Niño felt frantic. "Please," he said. He imagined his brother carrying the little boy on his back across the field, and was suddenly assailed by a familiar sadness. "Please," he said helplessly, desperately, knowing his brother wouldn't stay. He burst into tears.

Even through his grief, Niño still perceived the look of surprise on his brother's face. At the sound of him crying he saw his brother take a step forward and reach out a hand, perhaps responding instinctively, not thinking.

Beyond the edge of the field came the sound of a scream, an explosion like glass breaking, and the pale glow of a distant fire.

Niño glanced back. He couldn't see it completely because of the other houses and the trees, but he knew Luisita had done what she had wanted to do and had torched her own house. He heard his mother screaming: *Niño! Niño!*

He turned back to face his brother again, but there was only the dead boy, left there on the grass. He knelt beside the small body and looked at it in silence, his brother's name sitting inside his mouth, waiting to be shouted. All around him the blades of grass reflected the yellow glow of the escalating fire.

Since then, he saw his brother only in the periphery, if he saw his brother at all, like a shadow at the edge of his vision. Standing in a crowded bus, walking aimlessly in a marketplace, once even passing by outside a restaurant where he was eating dinner with his wife of that lifetime. That night he and his wife were arguing about migration. She wanted to move to the States 'out of this wretched country'; he wanted to stay, because 'anyway, everywhere is wretched, everywhere is beautiful'. His wife wondered aloud why he kept treating everything she said as a joke, and something else that he didn't quite catch because that was when he saw his brother walking outside the window.

"I wish for at least a *second* you'd pay attention to me," his wife said.

He sighed. He had always wondered why he even bothered to preserve friendships in a universe where his memory never crumbled, in a world where, in effect, he lived forever. But he knew time offered no mercy; it ran just as slowly in a single lifetime. Every action would be made to count. Every relationship. Every birth. Every death.

*Every death,* he thought, watching his brother disappear from view again.

In 2008, his name was Jonathan, and his brother (he would learn later) was named Brian. They were both sixteen years old. It had been a hundred and six years since their encounter during the plague. The country was no longer under American occupation. Christmas was near, and they were stuck in traffic behind a red light. Jonathan was sitting in a car with his father, the backseat covered with groceries and boxes of decorations for the new tree. At the head of the long line of vehicles, Brian and two of his friends were sitting impatiently inside a jeepney. The three boys, fresh from a soccer game, now showered and dressed on the way to the mall and maybe the cinema. They talked animatedly about the opposing team's horrible pass that ended the game, but Brian soon tired of the repetitive put-downs and pulled away from the conversation, choosing instead to stare blankly at the windshield and at the cars passing on the perpendicular lane. Their left-to-right motion almost lulling him to sleep. Inside the car carrying Jonathan and his father, the radio blared news about another fuel price rollback, an update on the global financial crisis, a brief debate about Charter change, Britney Spears' comeback tour, this year's top ten rock songs. Jonathan changed the station again and caught the tail-end of a woman caller's rant: "I mean, it was worse, it made me feel worse. I asked him, 'Who was it?' and he told me, 'She doesn't know it yet.' Probably heard it from a movie, the bastard. *He was ready to give me up for something he wasn't even sure yet.* Like his present job was so bad he'd rather leave it and be unemployed for who knows how many *months* than continue working. Am I that bad?"

Jonathan's father gave a brief laugh and shook his head. "Oh, I love Christmas," he said, making Jonathan wonder if he was laughing at the caller or at the red light that seemed to take forever to change.

Jonathan and Brian knew where each other were, but dismissed this awareness.

Minutes before this moment, a man sat in a bank two streets away, talking his head off at a younger man waiting to cash his check. "It changes when you become a father," the man said. "You want to stop your children from getting tired all the time. Tired of commuting, tired of waiting in line, tired of not having enough. My children go to public school and after the last storm they said they had to have their classes under a tree. Can you imagine that? And in this heat, too. But, you know, you think it's beyond your power. And *then* you realize, it's not beyond your power. You can work abroad, or take another job, you can earn money, you can put them in private school, buy an air conditioned car. You can shield them from these things. But you commute, too. You also wait in line. You also don't have enough. You can only do so much."

The younger man said in his interview with the police that after saying all these, the man suddenly looked unsure of where he was, getting ready to panic. Moments later, he nodded to himself, pleased, as though hearing a signal, as though he had just finished an oration and was satisfied with the reaction of his audience. He declared a hold-up.

After that instant, the younger man's memory became foggy. But he was sure there were other armed men, and that the security guards had miraculously disappeared. He knew a teller and two bank customers were shot, he knew the robbers were able to leave the bank quickly in what he assumed to be their getaway vehicle, idling outside the glass doors, waiting.

And yet, watching the news reports later in the hospital, Jonathan still couldn't get some things straight: did somebody call the police, or did they just happen to be nearby? And was that robber (and which of the robbers?) just deranged, or was he really aiming at the police car behind them and the gun just got yanked out of position by one of his companions? Or maybe there was more than one gun. Maybe there were two, three weapons dislodging bullets out of the van's window.

Brian saw the dark-blue van emerge from the vehicles cruising from left to right on the perpendicular lane, saw it like an object suddenly coming into focus, frozen against a background of movement. It swerved away from the motion like a hand parting a curtain and plowed down the empty lane, on the other side of which Brian and his friends sat dumbstruck in the jeepney and Jonathan and his father, still several vehicles away from the chase, listened to a woman ask, *Am I that bad?* Following the van was a police car, enveloped in its lights and the sound of its siren. Brian didn't know what was happening until it happened, until the bullets came and his friends fell, he was sitting near the entrance of the jeepney and he could have gotten it in the head or in the chest as well but the gun moved or was yanked and so the bullet drilled into the side of his left knee instead. Down the length of the lane the van went, the gun or guns firing wildly, hitting another passenger or two. A bullet hit the windshield of Jonathan's father's car and buried itself in Jonathan's right shoulder; another shattered the side mirror on the driver's side but left his father unharmed. For several seconds Jonathan didn't even know he had been hit.

Before he passed out, Jonathan heard the screaming. He thought it was the plague again, the Children's Crusade coming to its doom in broad daylight. He thought his brother was calling his name.

And so it happened that they were brought to the same hospital. Three days after the shootout, Jonathan knew his brother was in the same wing, the realization coming to him as a faint humming beneath his skin. He knew where he was, his room number, it would be like when they were students in that dormitory. Except that this time, Jonathan promised himself, he wouldn't walk away. His mother had been urging his father to have him moved to a "better" hospital within the week, so might as well go now, might as well walk through that doorway before the years eroded and the lifetimes buried him again.

On the afternoon of that second day his father fell asleep watching him sleep. Jonathan wasn't really sleeping; he was just waiting for his father, guilt-stricken and exhausted, to smoke a cigarette outside or buy something. But what he did was better. Jonathan insisted on wearing his own clothes; after pulling out the needle of the IV drip, affixing his sling, and slipping into his rubber shoes (he liked them big so he could slip his feet in even when the shoelaces were tied), he looked like he just came from the hospital's outpatient clinic. Many parts of him throbbed and hurt, his clothes were wrinkled, and the laces of his right shoe needed to be re-tied and tightened, but otherwise he could walk through the corridors without panicking any of the nurses.

The corridor he ended up in was silent and deserted, but he knew it was the right corridor. Walking past the numbered doors, Jonathan realized that the silence was an illusion. Whispers sailed past hinges and cracks, worried murmurs, sometimes strains of music from the radio or a portable player or a TV. *The TV!* Jonathan froze, wondering if he had turned off the set. He didn't, he didn't, and he relaxed. His father liked to sleep with the television on, it would take a while before he realized his son was not in his bed.

Jonathan walked on, his left hand cupping his right elbow. Brian's room was at the end of the corridor and the door leading to it was slightly open. Jonathan was getting ready to barge in when he heard voices. Brian was talking to his father, or his uncle. Someone male, older. Tired.

Suddenly there was the sound of weeping. Jonathan, aghast, managed to remain silent.

Something unintelligible from the older male. Probably, *What is it?*

"You keep saying they're asleep," Brian said.

"They are asleep, Brian. They're in a coma."

"You *keep* saying that," Brian said. "But they're dead, aren't they?"

"What? *No.*" The older male surprised, hurt. "No, no."

"They're *dead.*"

The voices were lowered, the older male offering something. Food? The promise of food. Brian sighed. "All right," he said. The door was opened and Jonathan pressed himself flat against the wall.

The man facing him looked to be in his forties, but could have been younger. Jonathan looked at the man's eyes and saw that the man recognized him, but couldn't seem to place him. "You should be in bed," the man said distractedly. He didn't make a move to steer him away. After a moment, the man seemed to have forgotten him altogether and staggered out of the corridor.

Jonathan watched the man leave, waited for him to disappear around the corner. Then he took three quick strides and stepped into the room.

Brian was sitting on a wheelchair positioned near the window, a pillow placed under his injured leg, his right elbow resting on the windowsill, his right hand covering half his face. Someone had wheeled over his IV drip and put a black sweater over Brian's hospital gown. Brian must have wanted to be near the window, out of his bed.

Brian was looking at his reflection or at the world beyond his reflection. When Jonathan stepped into the room, he saw the eyes of Brian's reflected face shift and stare at him. Brian was still calming the hiccups left over from his sobs, the skin around his eyes still pink and raw, still wet with tears.

He looked defeated. Why, *why,* Jonathan thought. This wasn't a game, this wasn't a chase. He's not the police, and his brother wasn't the robber. Jonathan closed the door behind him, and Brian looked away.

"Cain," Jonathan said, and it was as if a door long pinned against a storm were suddenly thrown wide open, the wind rushing in. Brian sighed.

"Abel," Brian said.

Jonathan nodded. There was a couch pushed against the wall, facing the foot of the bed. Jonathan sat on it, gently elbowing away a paper bag filled with books and other knickknacks. Taking up the rest of the space on the couch was a dirty-looking jacket and a large throw pillow still covered in plastic, probably a gift. The only source of light was the sunlight coming from the window, the light now waning, much of it blocked by Brian. Jonathan glanced at the sky outside and thought it looked like rain.

Brian had let his arms drop to his lap but still wouldn't look at him.

"Who was that?" Jonathan asked, throwing the question like a blacksmith throwing a strange new metal to the fire, wondering what would happen next.

Nothing. Brian looked out of the window, looking tortured.

"Your father?"

To his own ears, Jonathan sounded as if he were pleading. Brian must have heard it, too, because he threw him a quick look before averting his gaze again. Brian nodded, and Jonathan sighed with relief.

"I heard they've caught the guys who did this," Jonathan said. "Does your father say anything?"

Silence.

"I just wanted to talk, that's all," Jonathan said.

"I have been exiled," Brian said, speaking to the window, "not just from the soil where we came from, but from you. We shouldn't be talking to each other."

Jonathan was filled with horror and anger. A memory from an old life came to him, and he heard a child saying, *The Holy Land needs our aid,* and Jonathan felt a growing desire to scream at the child *(What Holy Land? What aid?)* and shut him up. And yet, now, sitting in this room with his brother, all he could do was repeat what he had already said: "I just wanted to talk."

They fell silent. Jonathan stared at his left shoelace as though hypnotized by it. He was still thinking of what he was going to say next when he looked up and caught Brian staring at his sling.

"I had it in the shoulder," Jonathan said

Brian stared at him for a long, long while, as though mourning him and the sight of his sling, and Jonathan, for a reason he couldn't articulate, suddenly felt a swelling in his chest. "It doesn't hurt that bad," he added in a soft voice, and Brian reared back and looked away, surprised that he could be read so easily, that he had allowed himself to be so naked.

"How's your leg?" Jonathan said. He wanted to get up and sit closer to his brother.

"At times like these, I wish we were still in the Garden."

The remark startled Jonathan into inaction. Again with the story of the Garden. He sighed. "That's just something our parents told us."

"Really," Brian said. "Then how do you explain the fact that we die and survive and remember everything? Our parents were given something in the Garden, and later lost it. What we have is a remnant, a poor substitute."

*A remnant,* Jonathan thought: *Something inside a plastic container. Leftover food shoved into a visitor's hands before he is pushed out of the house.*

"And everyone else," Brian said, "Everyone else. They experience one life, one death. That's it. And then nothing. Our parents died, and we never saw them again, same with the many parents we've had. The friends we've made, lovers, our own *children.* They died, and we never saw them again. The Garden has been closed."

"Maybe everyone survives," Jonathan said. "Maybe everyone's memory is intact."

Brian looked at him then, his eyes sad.

"Maybe they're just pretending."

The truth was, he couldn't tell. He had met people who believed in survival and remembering after the last day, in many variations, shades, and ferocity, but he would look around him and not see a familiar face, a spark of recognition, a welcoming smile. Just fleeting memories, consciousness where the old stories could not find their grip, where they wither and disappear like dust. Among them, how could he find a home, how could he find a place where he belonged to and which he could say belonged to him? One day, he believed, he would find himself standing in the center of a ruined place, gathering up the fragments of a forgotten story as he would the hands of a friend, or the scraps of metal from a building just bombed. And he would be alone, he knew.

*I have been exiled,* his brother had said, and Jonathan wanted to say that he already knew what the words meant, had known it for as long as his brother did.

"It was a gift," Brian said, "having the life that we have, being able to close our eyes without fear, knowing with certainty that sooner or later we will open them again. It was given, it could be taken away. We shouldn't be talking to each other."

"Nothing's happened so far," Jonathan said.

Brian turned his head; again that sad, sad look.

"Your friends aren't dead," Jonathan said.

Brian didn't comment. Jonathan thought he would know if someone from the same crime scene had died; news among the survivors' families traveled fast, and his mother traveled with it. When one of the wounded died yesterday he heard about it from his mother. He was a driver, she had said as she combed his hair. Single, no wife and kids. *No wife and kids,* his mother nodding, repeating the detail, latching onto anything she could be grateful for.

*And then nothing.* Jonathan thought: what if everyone else goes to a place inaccessible to him and his brother, a Garden closed only to them? Gone were their parents, the members of the Children's Crusade and the many other crusades, the victims of various famines and plagues, the little child in the field, the people shot in the bank and inside their vehicles—all gone to a place where time and repetitive histories could not touch them.

*And then nothing.* But perhaps, there is rest. He's not sure of this. He wondered how he could be sure, how he could possibly find out.

"Have you visited them yet?" Jonathan said. "They're not dead."

"They will be," Brian said, looking at his own hands.

Jonathan took a deep breath. He felt transported back to Mainz, its dark skies, the bodies of desperate children blocking him, the innumerable moments of almost-words and closed doors.

He wanted to say, *Listen.*

He wanted to say, *This is not the Judgment.*

*There is no Judgment.*

*Out in that field, who were there? Just you and me, your plan and your anger.*

*You put the Mark on yourself as punishment, knowing how easier it would have been to be killed than to walk desolate for years and years. Your brother is dead, you didn't want things to be easy. You told everyone another story, which, after several lifetimes, you learned to believe.*

*I was still alive when you carried me on your back for days, not knowing what to do. I shouldn't have done it, you said.*

*You asked for my forgiveness before the sun set and the bird came, that bird that showed you how to bury a body, and I gave it. Tell me, who else should you ask forgiveness from? Who else must forgive you?*

*Please, I don't want to stand alone in the center of a ruined place.*

The thoughts came to him, composed and arranged and neat, the images sharp enough for him to taste, but the words flooded his brain in a meaningless torrent, crashing into each other, dissolving his certainty. *This is not the Judgment. But what if it is?* he thought. He imagined his father waking up in his room, he imagined Brian's father coming around the corner, his arms filled with food for his grieving son. Jonathan felt a sharp pain shoot down his upper arm from his wound, and he hissed and touched his right elbow, feeling helpless, feeling the minutes pass by.

"Do you want to lie down?"

Jonathan looked up and saw Brian looking at him in alarm. They both saw that there wasn't enough room on the couch, and Brian indicated his own bed with a jerk of his head.

Jonathan was too surprised to speak. They regarded each other for a moment.

"I haven't visited them yet," Brian said miserably, answering the question Jonathan had already forgotten he had asked.

"Maybe we could go see them then," Jonathan said. "Later. Tonight."

"Okay," Brian said, jolted upright by the sound of his own answer. Jonathan could almost hear his brother debating with himself, turning the word over and over in his head. A blast surprised them, together they turned to look out the window. The rain had come: hard and without warning. Brian stared at the sunlit sheet of water, enthralled by it. The room cooled instantly. *Okay,* his brother had said, and Jonathan felt a great weight being lifted from him and realized that he could stand up, realized that he could sit on the edge of the hospital bed and watch the rain with his brother.

SIREN SONG

# Siren Song

**I.** Magic fled from the small town of Maharlika on the night a woman's bloodied torso was found near the river. Gerardo Nagtahan, one-third of Maharlika's entire police force, stood in paralyzed horror when he chanced upon the half-body during his nightly rounds. Gerardo knew everyone in the town, and the woman, celestially beautiful with cream-colored skin and hair the color of coal, wasn't anyone he knew. A stranger. His thoughts, scattered and manic, at once focused and went to that other stranger, Roland Leviste, who lived in a rented house at the edge of town. Roland remained a stranger in Maharlika despite the fact that he had lived there for more than a year. Now, Gerardo felt a sad vindication: they shouldn't have accepted that man, they should have driven him away, they should have banished him the moment they laid eyes on him and saw his past, saw what he did to those poor girls. They should have listened to me, Gerardo thought.

That was when Gerardo realized he couldn't *listen*. The town awoke early and went to bed early, and at night, when everything was silent save for the sound of frogs and river songs, he could sometimes hear the residents in their sleep, hear snatches of a dream, a whispered prayer.

And most of all, the river—*the river!*—was eerily silent. Devoid of song.

Gerardo looked past the torso and saw, several feet away, the woman's bottom half, gleaming in the blue moonlight, buoyed by the river. Gerardo could have screamed, but instead, he fell to his knees.

It was a severed mermaid's tail.

II. Many believed the word 'maharlika' referred to the nobility, but in fact it referred to the nobility's warriors. The nobility were called the *maginoo*, and the *maharlika* were bound to serve them in battle.

In 1569, however, in a small, coastal town in Central Luzon, the *maharlika* sheathed their swords and the *maginoo* did not cry for war. Instead, they waited for the Spaniards to reach their land and embraced them and dined with them as though they were their long-lost kin.

In the next two years, Salcedo and De Goiti repaid their hospitality by fighting Rajah Sulaiman and eventually conquering the Kingdom of Maynila. When Salcedo went back with his forces to the small town to claim it for Spain, the *maharlika* were already waiting for him, swords now unsheathed. The Spaniards won but it was a near-slaughter. It was the bloodiest battle the young *conquistador* had ever fought. It was widely believed that the wounds Salcedo suffered in that small town contributed to his early death at the age of 27.

He named the town Villa Isabella, after the Spanish queen. Only two or three *peninsulares* stayed behind to live in that small town, and all of them left after a couple of weeks. They said night after night they heard strange sounds coming from the river, and the sounds— like angry songs, like cries of rebuke—wouldn't let them sleep. They believed the town was a cursed place.

III. On June 1, 1863, Doña Klara de Luna, a young mestiza married to the *cabeza de barangay*, woke up with the insides of her head vibrating like a taut wire.

It was a Monday. The day before, the new *fraile*, bless his heart, talked at length about the 'lost and ignorant' citizens of Villa Isabella, and the town's 'evil air'. Villa Isabella changed town priests as often as twice a month. The *frailes* couldn't stay too long. Most of them got sick as soon as they arrived. Constant change in church leadership caused anxiety among the churchgoers, including Doña Klara, who dutifully sat beside her husband on the front pew every Sunday, fanning herself in the oppressive heat, wishing the current priest would stay longer than his predecessor. Her anxiety increased tenfold when the new priest suddenly paused in the middle of his sermon, paced around the pulpit, stopped, and said, *Tila cayo'y nacaligtaan na ng Dios.*

It appears that you have been forgotten by God.

How horrible a thought! Doña Klara went to sleep that night and had a frightening dream about an earthquake, a church reduced to rubble, the faithful trapped beneath the ruins. *This is that* fraile's *fault,* she thought upon waking, and immediately recited a *Padre Nuestro* to wash away this sinful reflection.

But the entire day the images in her dream burned themselves deeper in her mind. Her constant worrying gave her a fever and confined her to her room. The house of the *cabeza de barangay* overlooked the river, but even the sight of the sparkling current through the window and the cool air did nothing to calm her nerves. When her husband asked her how she was, she wanted to say, *I am waiting for the earth to start shaking.*

On Tuesday, she sat alone in the dining room and tried to enjoy her breakfast. She nibbled on the bread and had a bit of the egg yolk, but her stomach recoiled, refusing them. Doña Klara raised her hand to pick up her glass of milk, but before she could do so, the glass of milk, like an obedient child, slid across the gleaming tabletop and rested against her open palm.

Doña Klara screamed and dropped the glass in horror. Warm milk splashed against her legs, and she jumped up and stepped away from the cursed object.

One of the maids rushed into the room. "Señora?" she said.

*The glass moved!* Doña Klara wanted to say. *The glass moved and reached my hand on its own!*

But she couldn't say a word.

On June 3, 1863, a strong earthquake hit Manila and destroyed several buildings, including the Manila Cathedral. Buried beneath the destroyed church were three singers, four choirboys, nine members of the Cathedral Chapter, and an undetermined number of people who attended the rites for the celebration of Corpus Christi. Doña Klara heard the news from her husband, and listened to the story that came to her in a dream two days before. A story she already knew.

When no one was looking, she would will an object to move—for a door to close, for a pillow to turn itself—and it would move.

In July, she began to have dreams of a Villa Isabella with no *peninsulares*, no forced labor, no extraordinary taxes. In the air was that intense sense of liberation. She dreamt of the river, of a kind woman submerged in the water. She dreamt of a single word: *Maharlika*.

But she also dreamt of three priests killed via the *garrote*, soldiers marching to their deaths, women getting raped and brutally killed by strange men with white skin. Her dreams scared Doña Klara, because she knew they were beyond her time, way beyond her time. They were scenes that would happen after her death.

*Tila aco'y nacaligtaan na ng Dios,* she thought, because she couldn't understand this power, and she believed this power didn't come from God, but from his dark adversary.

There were times, however, when she would wonder why any hint of power and control was always attributed to the *Diablo*, while silence and weakness was considered a godly trait. Was that how she was supposed to live? To suffer and suffer and suffer and suffer.

One night she dreamt of the river again and the kind woman. This time the woman, black-haired and beautiful, emerged from the water and crawled to the shore. Crawled, because instead of legs, the woman had the tail of a fish. The woman's breasts were bare. Doña Klara was afraid the *(mermaid?)* woman would die if she stayed out of the water for too long, so she ran to her before the woman could crawl any further.

The mermaid looked up, grateful. She sat up, and kept the lower half of her body in the river. Doña Klara knelt in front of her, felt the wet soak through her skirt. The mermaid touched Doña Klara's face, neck, breasts. The mermaid's hands were as cool as the river's current, and Doña Klara gasped in surprise, and then pleasure. The mermaid lowered her hands, and Doña Klara began to cry. *This is not a dream,* she thought, *This is not a dream, is it?*

The mermaid smiled and shook her head. Behind her, around her, the river came alive with tiny waves, arms and hair and flapping tails.

*Klara.* The mermaid's voice echoed in her mind, soft and soothing. *Wake up.*

The residents of Villa Isabella stirred from sleep. Some of them, like Klara, would have the gift of foresight, and the ability to move things from afar. Some of them would be able to spontaneously start fire. Some of them would be able to manipulate water. And some of them—the new *fraile*, the *peninsulares*, those who did not have roots in the land—would flee the town the next day, having awakened from a most disturbing dream.

Throughout her life, Doña Klara would write her predictions and observations in a leather-bound book that once served as her diary. That diary would remain in the De Luna mansion, but would be available for the perusal of the entire town after her death.

One of the last entries in the book was entitled, *Ang Kasagraduhan ng Sirena sa Bayan ng Maharlika*. The Sacredness of Mermaids in the Town of Maharlika. Unfortunately, only the cover page of the entry remained. The rest of the pages had been torn out. Her relatives theorized that she might have kept the pages somewhere in her room, or in the library, but they were never found.

IV. Roland Leviste had been plagued with nightmares from the moment he arrived in Maharlika with his small bag of clothes and a battered pair of rubber shoes, but then he had always been plagued with nightmares. Never in his life had he had a good night's sleep—except, perhaps, during the nights he killed. The last girl who died in his hands was a college student who kept screaming, "Don't rape me! Don't rape me!" as a joke. She treated everything as a joke. Her laughter grated against his eardrums. They were in some seedy motel room with a cut-up sofa and stained sheets and a cracked mirror; it was possible that the girl could scream rape all she wanted and no one would have come. Roland panicked and hit her in the stomach. She fell doubled-up on the floor, and he hit her on the side of the head. Roland was unnerved. He should have drugged the girl before bringing her to the motel. He drugged all of his victims before cutting them up. It was the cutting that he wanted, the elegant sawing through skin and muscle and fat and bone, the blood squirting on his face and pooling around his legs as his muse slept—not this, not this direct contact, not this violence. But the girl had seen his face, and so he had to go through with it.

He had to stop before he could finish doing it. He threw down his tools and ran to the roach-infested bathroom to throw up, peel off his blood-spattered clothes, and bathe. For the next several months Roland traveled from one city to another, jumping from one job to the next, and not be able to kill. At various times during a single day he would stop what he was doing—cleaning a car, tending a counter, wiping a table—and cry into his hands. His bosses and colleagues pitied him. In their heads they created a story for Roland's life: orphan, widower, abandoned father.

Finally, one morning, Roland got up and jumped on a bus that would take him away from the city. On the side of a dirt road, he approached a *pila* of tricycles, and asked to be taken deeper into the town. They refused. *"Taga-labas ka, ano?"* a cigarette-puffing old man said. *"Wala hong sasakyang pumapasok sa karsadang iyan."*

Roland asked why, but none of them answered.

He decided to walk.

After an hour of walking, Roland saw the startling blue of the river, and the deep green of the trees, and knew, at once, in his heart, that he would never kill again.

When Roland knocked on the first door he saw to ask for shelter and food, a murmur passed across the minds of the residents of Maharlika. *Turn him away,* the horrified voice of Gerardo Nagtahan said. They saw Roland's victims as they were hacked to death, the scenes passing and convulsing like a dying eel in a current.

It was Catalino Reyes, the town's oldest resident and Maharlika's *barangay* captain, who calmed down Gerardo, and tried to quell the fear and indignation rising in Maharlika. He felt Roland's despair, his need for forgiveness, his want of a new beginning.

He opened the door.

Roland couldn't understand why everyone in the small town seemed unapproachable. In the market, where he found work as a fish vendor in Catalino's son's stall, he couldn't make buyers stop to chat with him, no matter how cheerful he sounded. Catalino's son almost always seemed to have a headache whenever he spoke with him. "Do not mind them," Catalino said. "This town is not used to outsiders."

Other than Catalino, only Anton de Luna, a descendant of Doña Klara, and roughly Roland's own age, took the time to make Roland feel at home. Anton was the town teacher and librarian. He held regular classes in one of the rooms in the De Luna mansion and helped people track books in the family library. Some of the books were donated by the oldest families in town and dated back to the 1600's. Roland was invited to take a look, but the older books were off-limits to him, for some reason. In the beginning Roland kept inviting him to his rented apartment for a drink, but Anton always refused, citing his stomachache. Anton had stomachaches every night, it appeared, and Roland eventually stopped his invitations. The man was nice to him, but Roland got the point.

"They don't want outsiders," Anton said once, "because they don't want to put up a show in their own town. This is their home, not a stage. They don't want to become performers and play pretend in their own home."

"I don't understand," Roland said. "Why do they have to pretend?"

"Everyone lapses into a performance at some point," Anton said, "in one way or another."

And Roland felt frightened. It felt as though Anton had looked into his mind and saw everything that he was trying to hide.

The week before the mermaid was found, Roland had a recurring dream. The dream came to him every day for seven days. In the dream, he was sitting by the river, and a beautiful woman with dark hair was talking to him.

*What do you want?*

*I want to cleanse myself.*

*Come join me in the water.*

Always, Roland would refuse, because he knew that if he joined her, he would cut her in half.

Immediately after Gerardo found the dead mermaid, the residents of Maharlika rushed to Roland's rented house and descended upon him like a tidal wave. There were some residents of Maharlika who could turn a man's bones to powder with a single glance, but that power was gone now. It did not stop them. Blind with fury, lost without their gifts, they dragged him out of his bed and out the doorway, not caring if his head hit the ground or the steps. They hit him with fists and sticks and rocks, they tore out his hair and scratched his face and peeled off his skin. By the time they had strung him up a tree with a rope, he was no longer recognizable, with his swollen tongue and his gouged-out eyes. They left him there, to be fed to the birds.

It was Anton de Luna who cut him down the next morning and buried him in the soil beneath the tree.

V. While Roland was being ravaged to death by his crazed neighbors, Amanda de Luna was walking around the university oval, papers in hand, trying to memorize a poem for one of her classes. Around her were students and alumni glistening with sweat, running in the near-dark. Somewhere among them was Clarissa, who for days had complained about her waist and her thighs and leg muscles and her speed. "I look like a sack of rice," Clarissa said. Amanda imagined Clarissa would run until she was depleted, shrunken, no more.

After their parents died, she left her older brother in Maharlika and went to the university. Though her brother mailed her checks every month or so, she paid her own fees by providing proofreading services to a group of Koreans. She used the checks only during emergencies, or when she was too saddled with schoolwork to proofread for money. She wanted to cut her ties from the stifling small town that nobody has heard of, where she had lived like a stone for sixteen years. There were things that she missed: the Sunday breakfasts in the big Spanish house with her brother's students (their house was the only school in Maharlika, and her brother its only teacher), the wet market jutting like a lip over the river, the various species of fish being sold in the stalls, the river itself with its perfect sapphire hue, the mermaids who swam to shore and gave her shells and rough pearls as gifts, and her brother. Her soft-spoken *Kuya* Anton could hardly contain his thunderstorm of a sister. Amanda knew she had to leave, while she could still think of Maharlika with nostalgia. Before she could hate it.

The mermaids' gifts followed her out of town. While her brother settled comfortably with precognition and psychometry ("My brother can read people pretty well," she'd tell her city friends) from a very early age, Amanda herself had to go through a whole slew of abilities for several years before she could settle. At the age of two, she discovered that she was able to bilocate: a boon for hide-and-seek, but a bane for her playmates and her parents. She dropped that quickly after only a few months, and gained remote viewing, then pyrokinesis, then transvection. There was a year in her life where she could see into another room without leaving hers, create fire from thin air, and fly. However, she dropped all three at the age of fourteen, and gained precognition, retrocognition, remote influencing, and frighteningly strong telekinesis.

She thought she would never settle; there were residents, barely spoken of, who would demonstrate one ability in the morning and lose it in the afternoon. She was worried she would be one of them. But she turned sixteen, grew moodier, and settled with all four gifts.

She was happy with them. Sometimes, she would see horrible things that she couldn't immediately understand, but she was happy to be able to protect herself without depending on anyone for help. Once, she was walking in the city and a man groped her breast; she broke his arm bone in three places with a single glance. Once she sensed a robbery occurring in the building across the street while she was in a bookstore, and she influenced the men to put down their weapons and face the wall until the police arrived. It was her habit to walk home in the dead of night and commute while carrying considerable amounts of cash, and she did so without fear. She would answer leers from strange men with an unblinking stare. She had been stopped by men with ice picks or guns, and every time she would smile and feel pleasure in her invulnerability, and the men's false belief in theirs: they simply did not know what they had gotten themselves into.

In the past, whenever she dropped an ability, she would feel incomplete, unsafe, as though she had been left naked in a sea of strangers.

Amanda stopped dead in her tracks.

Clarissa, who was just about to make her turn, saw her and stopped as well.

"Amanda?" she said, wiping sweat off her face. "Are you okay?"

It took Amanda a long time to reply. "I need to go home," she said.


VI. She would have left right then and there, but Amanda believed she had lost her shield. There was no electricity and no phone lines in Maharlika, so she couldn't contact her brother. The question burned within her. But she had no choice; she had to wait for daybreak. She curled on her side of the bed that night, wide-awake, wondering.

She left early the next day. She decided not to wake Clarissa. After a moment's hesitation, she swiped Clarissa's pepper spray off the bedside table and placed it in her bag. In the darkness of the bus she sat anxious and angry and frustrated, her knee jackknifing, her arms embracing her bag tightly, her wet palms leaving prints on the fabric.

The line of tricycles on the side of the dirt road was conspicuously absent. The walk home felt longer than usual. The path was deserted. As Amanda walked toward Maharlika, she saw farmlands filled with stalks of *palay* turned brown by the sun. The trees had shed their leaves and appeared to be dying. In place of the loud chorus of crickets and frogs and birds, she could only hear the howling wind and the eerie buzzing of flies. It wasn't long before she found a dead cow on the side of the road.

Maharlika looked like a ghost town. Every window and door on every house was closed, and the market, which usually roared with activity, was silent. *"Tao po?"* she said, but there was no answer. Amanda walked toward the river and became very conscious of the sound of gravel crunching beneath her feet. The water was the color of charcoal, gray and dead beneath the gray sky. Again, buzzing flies. On the shore was a small, square space covered with coconut leaves. On the leaves were fruits and raw meat arranged on a large *bilao*, but the mangoes and guavas and papayas were already decaying, the pieces of chicken and cow already bled dry by the sun and covered by flies and maggots.

What were the offerings for? Amanda knelt by the water and dipped her hand into the river.

"Amanda!"

What—

"Amanda!"


The sound came from behind her. Before Amanda could turn, something broke through the surface of the water and lunged at her hand. Amanda recoiled, screaming. The creature emitted a high-pitch sound that hurt her ears, but Amanda still couldn't stop screaming. Her heels displaced gravel as she pushed herself back in a frantic attempt to escape. She was still screaming when Anton came to her side and covered her eyes.

The thing beneath the water had sharp fangs and red eyes and claws—and a mermaid's tail.

VII. The metamorphosis occurred immediately. The mutilated mermaid was moved to the church for the burial. During transit, she transformed into a mound of fine, white dust, like a starfish removed from the ocean. Not long after, a boat capsized while passing through the river, and three fishermen were reduced to blood and bones. Maharlika soon discovered that the mermaids had lost their human features and had developed a taste for human flesh. The mermaids, in their present monstrous incarnation, could no longer sing. The river had been emptied of fish, as though the fish had disappeared along with the mermaids' song.

The following day, the mermaids started mating, emitting howls like a gathering storm. Maharlika covered its ears. When the mermaids were done, the offspring they produced were a far cry from the mermaid broods that once swam the shallow waters of the river with their scaly backs and tiny fins. Amanda used to watch them, she remembered, those tiny mermaids swimming in a single group, a rainbow-colored band traversing the river. Now the water was filled with blobs of transparent eggs, inside of which were fish red in color and the shape and size of piranhas. Their mouths wouldn't stop opening and closing, and the sound they emitted sounded like the cries of human babies. They drove the town mad.

The residents' powers were gone forever, but not the memories of what they had seen—glimpses of the future, a person's true nature. In the final town meeting before the residents locked themselves up in their homes (and before he killed himself by throwing himself into the river), Catalino Reyes asked the once-clairvoyant if they had seen this coming.

Nobody did.

"Nobody," Amanda echoed, sitting at the same table where, more than a hundred years ago, Doña Klara summoned a glass of milk.

"I made some tea for you," Anton said, and placed the cup in front of her, along with a plate of fruits and bread. He was wearing a crisp white buttoned-up shirt, the sleeves rolled up neatly to his elbows, and gray slacks. He was always dressed like a teacher, even without students. After closing all the windows, Anton turned on the gas lamp. With the dining room filled with a soft yellow light, Amanda could make-believe it was evening, and her parents were just in the kitchen, supervising dinner.

"I still have fish in stock," Anton said, "but I don't think you'd be in the mood to eat fish right now. Do you want me to fry some eggs?"

Amanda shook her head.

"The househelp had left. *Manang* Gloring said she has a sister in Batangas who could take her in."

"This town is going to be abandoned," Amanda said.

Anton patted her hand. "We'll be all right," he said, and smiled. "Maybe I can go live with you now."

Amanda's hand trembled beneath his brother's. "I need to tell you something."

"You're living with a girl."

That gave Amanda pause.

"What?"

"I had a vision," Anton said, "before you left for the city? It was all symbols, but the overwhelming message I got was: you are with a girl. I knew her name had a hard 'k' sound but I could only sense softness in her."

"Clarissa," Amanda said, and suddenly felt sad.

"That's her name?" Anton said. "That sounds right."

For a moment, Amanda couldn't think of anything to say.

"You're happy with her?" Anton said.

Amanda couldn't reply. She was thinking of her parents again. That cloudless morning, when their father, an empath, left town for the city 'to meet a friend', Anton was confined to his bed, writhing from a searing pain in his stomach.

They would learn the next day that their father had been found dead in a hotel room. 'Rat poison', they said. He died alone, miles away from his wife and children, surrounded by strangers. "Why did he do it, Mother?" Amanda asked once, and her mother said, "Because he was born into this world to suffer and suffer and suffer, and he didn't want to suffer anymore." Their mother chose to suffer in his stead, and died in a fall after deciding that she, too, had had enough.

"Do you still get the stomach pains?" Amanda asked.

Anton closed his eyes, as though suddenly blinded. "Every night," he said.

"And now?"

Anton shook his head.

"I knew you were an empath," Amanda said. "I knew it that night, even if you didn't list that in the town register."

Anton said nothing.

"Is that why you did it?" Amanda said.

Anton reached for her hand once again, but she drew back. Anton looked hurt. "Amanda," he said.

"I had a vision of you, years before Father died," Amanda said. "I couldn't decipher it then. You were older. You were in a kitchen, with another man who looked really scared, and he was watching you cut a large fish in half."

"I didn't know," Anton began.

Amanda was already shaking in anger.

"Amanda," Anton began again. "I didn't know the rest of the mermaids would become that way, after a mermaid death. I didn't know the river would die."

"And if you did?" Amanda said, trying to sniff back her tears. "If you did, would you have done it differently?"

Anton didn't answer.

"That man the town hanged was innocent," she said.

"He was a murderer," Anton said. "He killed girls your age."

"So that makes it all right to throw him to the angry mob? Did you know that they peeled off his skin?"

"Amanda—"

"Don't touch me!" Amanda jumped to her feet, away from her brother, as though Anton had turned into that creature in the river that almost bit off her hand. "How dare you do this to us? How will I ever feel safe again?"

"I'm sorry," Anton said, now crying. "I was hurting—"

"The hell with you!" Amanda said. She lifted a plate from the table and threw it on the floor. It crashed upon impact and created a loud sound inside the room. "Father hurt. Mother hurt. But they never—"

"Would you rather I have killed myself?"

Amanda couldn't hold back any longer. She burst into tears.

"But I couldn't," Anton said. "I was hurting but I couldn't kill myself, Amanda."

Amanda couldn't speak through her tears.

"I'm a coward, Amanda," Anton said. "I'm sorry."


VIII. There was no rule about the murder of mermaids because no one in town would even think of doing them harm. And why would anyone do so? The mermaids were kind and peaceful, and kept the river teeming with fish. Harming the mermaids was so unfathomable that no one even bothered to ask what the punishment could be for such a crime.

Unknown to the residents, Doña Klara wrote about this forbidden topic in her missing entry, which Anton found by accident in the library after Amanda's departure from Maharlika. The pages, folded and hidden in an old town register that was in turn buried in an avalanche of books, had become yellow and fragile with age, but the ink was preserved enough for Anton to decipher the words.

Harming (but not killing) a mermaid, it said, would mean retaliation. The perpetrator would be pulled to the depths of the river by the merfolk, and punished so severely that even his bones would not be found. His family, up to the seventh generation, would no longer receive powers.

Since the mermaid's arrival to Maharlika, there had been three cases of this foul crime, which, to Doña Klara's opinion, was three cases too many. The perpetrators indeed disappeared, and their families lost their powers, but there was no proof that everyone down to the seventh generation lost theirs as well. *Old Testament sensibility,* Anton thought as he read. Klara simply couldn't rid herself of the Catholic in her.

Killing a mermaid, on the other hand, the piece continued, would affect not only the perpetrator and his family, but the entire town as well. Upon the murder of a mermaid, every single resident of Maharlika would lose their powers, and would not regain them until the end of their days, and until the end of their line. They would be as they were before the mermaids came with their gifts.

*Ang pagpatay sa sirena ay pagpatay na rin sa sarili.*

To kill a mermaid is to kill the self.

In the depths of his despair, Anton begged to differ.

Anton saw Roland's murderous nature even before Roland saw it himself. Anton, 13, was cutting up potatoes with his sister in the kitchen, when the vision came to him like a punch in the gut. He was just cutting up potatoes, when all of a sudden he saw the kitchen through the eyes of a man in his early twenties, a stranger to him, and the potatoes turned into a young woman. The sink was filled to the brim with blood.

Anton never forgot this vision.

If you wanted to lose your power, Anton thought, night after night after he lost his father, then it would be better to kill a mermaid than to harm one. To harm a mermaid meant disappearance, and that would be like putting a mark on yourself.

To kill one would mean remaining with the crowd. But how to stay away from the wrath of the town?

Anton needed an alibi. When he finally met Roland, he shook his hand as though he were a long-lost friend.

Roland was two people, and Anton mourned one of them. The kind, innocent man he cut down from the tree and buried with tears in his eyes.

The murderer he removed from his mind and threw to the bottom of the river.

IX. Anton opened the door for one neighbor who asked for a cup of sugar, and before long there were six people in the spacious living room, drinking coffee and sharing bread. Amanda sat in one corner, silent, and smiled only when a neighbor acknowledged her presence.

"It's kind of you to come see your brother after what happened," they said, and Anton smiled, and Amanda smiled, and both of them said nothing.

An old man named Rafael said, "There are rumors going around saying that the mermaids would form feet, and we'd have to hack them to pieces as they left the water."

Rafael's wife genuflected, looking horrified.

"We can't allow ourselves to worry about things we're not sure of," Anne replied. Anne was one of Anton's students.

"But what if it happens?"

"Perhaps we can look for Doña Klara's diary."

Amanda saw her brother look at her. *If you want to tell the truth,* he seemed to say, *do it now.*

Amanda looked at her feet.

"I've tried looking for it for years," Anton said. "It's not here."

Anton walked with the group to the front door. Before she stepped out of the house, *Aling* Marya, Anne's mother, touched his arm and whispered, "Your stomach isn't bothering you?" She was not used to seeing Anton up and about at night.

"No," Anton said.

"Me too," Aling Marya said, and smiled. "We are of the same mold as your parents, bless their hearts. I feel nothing now but my own pain."

"Let's *go,* Mother," Anne said, her hand on her hip.

They left. Amanda stood by the doorway repeating the words in her head. *I feel nothing now but my own pain.*

Anton and Amanda parted ways after that, and in a house so big, it was not a difficult thing to do. After an hour, however, Amanda got spooked by the high ceiling and the inhuman sounds coming from behind the window, and went to go look for her brother.

Anton was in the kitchen, making dinner. At the moment he was cutting up potatoes. On the stove, something fragrant was simmering.

Her brother didn't notice her watching. When Amanda approached the kitchen island, Anton jumped a little. Without a word, Amanda took a knife and a chopping board and chopped up the garlic. She felt her brother begin to relax beside her. They prepared dinner, side by side, in silence. They had done this many times before.

"Maybe you can stay with us," Amanda said. "I'll tell Clarissa. You can work as a teacher there. You'll earn more. They won't pay you in chickens."

Amanda saw Anton smile as he stirred the soup.


X. Magic. Amanda thought of flying across the market, her father's frightened face, the sound of applause. A broom moving on its own as she rearranged her books at the foot of her bed. The heat in her palms as she held on a stick, the sudden bloom of fire.

Magic. Amanda thought of clear skies and stars, steamed rice and fish, bagoong soaked in vinegar. A cup of coffee in the early morning, the feel of grass, the city lights. Clarissa. Her brother carrying her on his back, her parents dancing on the cool patio as it rained. The ground pounding with life. A poem humming in her head.

# Once, in a Small Town

All the dead came back. The townspeople, young, old, diminished and burdened, woke up to the sound of dogs barking and opened their doors to a vision they had dreamt of from the very day of their abandonment: their loved ones, clean and unscathed, standing on their porches and smiling. Sons, daughters, mothers, fathers, cousins: they all came back, perfect, as though they had never been dead, as though they had never gone through the events that had killed them. Those who died in a fire came back with smooth skin. There were no bullet holes in the bodies of those that had been shot. There were a few who died in various accidents—a fall from the top of a staircase, a car crash on a dark road, an electrocution—but they carried no wounds to even suggest that such horrors had occurred. Even the children, who died from beatings, neglect, or games that have gone awry, looked unharmed. None of them carried a smell, or had traces of cemetery soil under their fingernails. Hello, father. Hello, mother. Hello. What took you so long? What's for dinner? they asked, as though they had just been away on an errand. They had no memory of their deaths.

Most of the women who opened the doors fainted. Those who managed to stay on their feet looked out of their gates and saw their neighbors with at least one resurrected loved one standing puzzled on their yard. What's going on? Each of the loved one said, Why won't you let me in? and the townspeople at once realized that they were not dreaming. A group of men banded together and marched to the town memorial park to see if the graves had been disturbed, thinking that their dead had broken through their coffins, but when they arrived at the cemetery, they found that there were no graves. The men came to the town priest to seek his advice, but the priest was serving dinner to his sister who had died of a fever five years before. Why think of the Devil on such a blessed night? The priest told them, scooping rice into a china bowl. Heartened, the men came back to their wives and families to bring the news. Much cheering was heard in all the streets, and the dead—puzzled, and puzzled further by the merriment—were allowed to step into their homes.

The next day had to be the happiest day in that town's history. The townspeople had agreed to not confuse the resurrected ones further by acting unnaturally, but some of them were not able to help it. They cooked big breakfasts and watched their loved ones eat with a ferocity that could have scared themselves. They brought out the best utensils, their china, and tuned the television to their loved ones' favorite program. Mother's acting strange today, one resurrected child would say to another, and the mothers would burst into tears because their children were alive, alive, alive.

However, as the day wore on, the townspeople noticed that it was becoming harder and harder for them to look at their resurrected loved ones in the eye. For even though their dead had no memory of the fire, the crash, the hate that killed them, the townspeople remembered. They remembered the long wait and the news, the arrival of the candles and the flowers, the smell of coffee, the nights when they couldn't hear even their own voice. The town priest, for instance, remembered wiping blood-colored vomit off the strands of his sister's hair, and this memory, vivid and persistent, kept him from enjoying fully the sound of her laughter. Somehow this memory felt realer than his sister's presence.

The townspeople soon realized that since the memories of their dark days were still intact, their loved ones' resurrection made no difference. Their loved ones might be alive, but they died over and over in their heads. That afternoon, the townspeople decided to just let their loved ones die once again. They stirred pesticide into their food, held their heads under water, and smothered their faces with pillows. They carried their bodies to the town memorial park and, crying, buried them in shallow graves.

When they got home, the townspeople washed their hands and took out the pictures of their dead. They lulled themselves with memories of what their loved ones did when they were still living. Night fell, eventually, and they slept with smiles on their faces.

The following stories have previously appeared, at times in slightly different versions, in the following publications:

"Once, in a small town", *Very Short Stories for Harried Readers*, edited by Vicente Garcia Groyon, Milflores Publishing, April 26, 2007.

"An Abduction by Mermaids", *Philippines Free Press*, April 26, 2008.

"Parallel", *Philippine Speculative Fiction IV*, edited by Dean Francis Alfar and Nikki Alfar, Kestrel, February 28, 2009.

"Night Out", *Expanded Horizons* (http://www.expandedhorizons.net), May 31, 2009.

"Earthset", *Philippines Graphic*, June 15, 2009.

"Reunion", *Philippines Free Press*, September 12, 2009.

"The Just World of Helena Jimenez", *The Farthest Shore: Fantasy from the Philippines* (http://farthestshore.kom.ph), edited by Joseph Nacino and Dean Francis Alfar, Estranghero Press, October 2, 2009.

"The Man on the Train" (originally "I Am the City"), *Expanded Horizons*, November 3, 2009.

"Sand, Crushed Shells, Chicken Feathers", *Philippines Free Press*, March 22, 2010.

"Salot", *Demons of the New Year* (http://newyeardemons.kom.ph), edited by Joseph Nacino and Karl de Mesa, Estranghero Press, March 24, 2010.

"Monsters", *Philippine Speculative Fiction V*, edited by Nikki Alfar and Vincent Michael Simbulan, Kestrel, April 24, 2010.

"Intersections", *Expanded Horizons*, Feb. 2, 2011.

"The Storyteller's Curse", *Philippine Speculative Fiction VI*, edited by Kate Aton-Osias and Nikki Alfar, Kestrel, May 28. 2011.

"Ana's Little Pawnshop on Makiling St.", *Alternative Alamat*, edited by Paolo Chikiamko, Rocket Kapre Books and Flipside Digital Content, December 14, 2011.

/ ## Acknowledgments

My heartfelt thanks to:

Nida Ramirez and Visprint for the invaluable help;

Dean Francis Alfar and the rest of the spec fic gang for the undying support and encouragement;

the editors of the various publications who first gave my stories a home;

my friends (online and offline) for reading and promoting my work and for their kind words;

my family—my parents Belen and Rodolfo and siblings Jasmin, Robie Jay, and Allan—for keeping me in their thoughts despite (or because of?) my propensity to kill off characters in my stories (as my mother once dutifully observed);

the Lazarte family for making me feel welcome in Parañaque;

and Jaykie, for the love (and for letting me use his laptop and wi-fi connection whenever I needed to "edit something quick").

Eliza Victoria *is the author of several books including the Philippine National Book Award-winning* Dwellers, *the novel* Wounded Little Gods, *the graphic novel* After Lambana *(a collaboration with Mervin Malonzo), and the science fiction novel-in-stories,* Nightfall. *She has won prizes in the Philippines' top literary awards, including the Carlos Palanca Memorial Awards for Literature. Her one-act plays, written in Filipino, have been staged at the Virgin LabFest at the Cultural Center of the Philippines.* Dwellers, Wounded Little Gods, *and* After Lambana *were released worldwide by Tuttle Publishing in 2022.*

*Visit her at elizavictoria.com*